SHAT

REFLECTIONS

Behind The Smile

Nova Justice™

For permission requests, contact Inner Light Media LLC at InnerLightMediaCo@gmail.com.

Book cover and illustrations by Nova Justice™

ISBN: 979-8-9944805-0-2 First Edition: 2025

To my husband and children:
Thank you for loving me through the long nights
and the hours I was "away," even when
I was sitting right next to you.
This story demanded more of me than I ever expected—
but your belief in me kept me moving forward.
I love you more than you could ever know.

And to the story itself:
"Why did you haunt me?" I asked. "Why every hour, every day,
until I finally put you on paper?"
"Because," you whispered back,
"I am too heavy to carry alone.
The truths of too many are tucked inside this fiction,
and they need a way out. They need to be heard—
seen—reclaimed. But first, they need you to listen."
"Listen to what?" I asked. "What can I possibly do?"
"Tell my story," you said.
"But I'm afraid," I confessed. "I'm scared
I won't do you justice, and that you won't reach
the ones who need you most."
You said,
"Give me your hands, and I will give you my strength.
Together, we will give it to them."
So I listened.
It's done.
You're free.

Beyond the Page

Optional ways to experience the story more deeply

This page includes two optional QR codes for readers who would like to engage more deeply with the story.

The first QR code links to a character gallery on NovaJusticeOfficial.com, where you can put faces to the names of the characters and get to know them as the story unfolds.

Character gallery

Reader only music access

The second QR code links to a private, readers-only page where the official soundtrack created for Shattered Reflections is available at a discounted rate.

The music follows the emotional arc of the story, deepening the connection to the characters—while standing on its own as a soundtrack I'm deeply proud of and meant to be replayed, felt, and lived with.

Scan either code with your phone's camera at any time.

Contents

Reader Discretion Advised

Shattered Reflections: Behind the Smile explores themes of control, abuse, and trauma. The story contains a brief scene depicting sexual violence, included to authentically convey the severity and emotional impact of the character's experience rather than for shock value or sensationalism.

One

A Clear View

Alex adjusted the weight of the twins in her arms, breathing in the soft, powdery scent of their skin. Corbin let out a sleepy sigh, while Liam—never one to settle—nuzzled deeper into the crook of her neck. Their small hands clung to her shirt, their warmth pressed into her like a heartbeat, grounding her in the uncertainty of now.

The space around them was tight. Cramped. A patchwork of love, necessity, and last-minute problem-solving. Sheldon's shed-turned-apartment had never been meant for a family of five, but here they were—wedged into corners, balanced on top of each other like a human game of Tetris. Not ideal, not comfortable, but it was holding. For now.

It had been a hell of a farewell to their old home, the one she'd poured her heart into—every inch carefully crafted to feel warm, safe, and entirely theirs. She adored that little house—the cheerful yellow door that made her smile each morning, the hand-picked kitchen tile she had insisted on, even when it went over budget. The way the afternoon sun kissed the hardwood floors, and transformed the quietest moments into something luminous and full of life. Letting go had been harder than she expected. But with twins now filling their world, two bedrooms just weren't enough. As much as it hurt to leave, they had outgrown the life they built there.

And the next one? Seventeen acres. No neighbors in sight. A sprawling property where her kids could run wild, build treehouses, race ATVs, and chase after the chickens she'd already named before they'd even moved in—Tootle, Noodle, Snickerdoodle, Clucktastic Thunder, Chick Norris, and, of course, Sir Pecks-A-Lot. The dream was so vivid in her mind that she could almost taste the crisp mountain air and hear the rustling of wind through the trees.

But that wasn't today. Today was a window AC unit buzzing in the background, a picnic table doubling as a dining room, and a couch sagging so deep it nearly swallowed you whole. It was cluttered, loud, claustrophobic—and built with love. Her brother's kind of love.

Across the room, six-year-old Harper let out a high-pitched giggle as she tried to yank a frayed rope toy from their husky, Muttonhead. The dog, of course, was winning. Walker stood nearby, arms folded, a faint smile tugging at the corners of his mouth. In the soft light, he almost looked at ease—but Alex noticed the tightness in his shoulders, the weight he was still carrying. He didn't complain much, not out loud, but the tension was there—in the way he rubbed the back of his neck, the heavy way he exhaled when he thought no one was watching. This transition had scraped against both of them, but Walker, ever the soldier, bore it like armor.

Alex shifted Liam against her hip, her gaze drifting around the room. As chaotic as it all was, she felt a spark of excitement. This was only going to be a couple of months. No big deal, really. She could handle this. Because she could feel it—like a breeze slipping through a cracked door. Change was coming. Something new. Something exciting. And she couldn't wait to see what was waiting for them on the other side.

In the days leading up to Alex and her family's arrival, Sheldon had thrown himself into transforming his shed into something livable. It wasn't much—just a temporary stopgap between the sale of his sister's old house and the delayed closing on their dream home—but he wanted it to feel like more than four walls and a roof. He hauled up an old couch from the garage, rigged together a makeshift kitchen using spare cabinets and a camp stove, and even carved out a little playroom nook for Harper with mismatched toys, a swing, a basketball hoop, and an oversized beanbag chair nestled beside a window that overlooked the woods, perfect for watching deer wander through at dusk.

It was endearingly thoughtful and wildly impractical—which pretty much summed up Alex's brother. But in his whirlwind of hammering and hauling, he'd overlooked one rather glaring human necessity.

"Wait."

Melena, his wife, had stopped mid-step as she peered into the shed the night before Alex and her family were due to arrive. Her hands flew to her hips, eyes narrowing in suspicion.

"Shelly, where are they going to pee?"

Sheldon blinked, confused. "Uh... outside?"

Melena froze. "Outside? You expect your sister—and your six-year-old niece—to stumble out here in the dark and squat behind the shed?"

He gave a casual shrug, like it was no big deal. "I mean... if it's bad, they can run into the house."

Melena's eyes widened, her jaw slack with disbelief. "You mean hike through the dark, across a hundred yards of weeds and gravel, to go in the house? Are you crazy?!"

Sheldon opened his mouth to respond, but it was too late.

The Spanish came fast and furious—sharp, expressive, and completely unfiltered. Her hands flew as she paced, muttering and gesturing like she was physically batting his stupidity out of the air.

Sheldon stood there blinking, trying to decipher what he could, scratching his head like he might find a clue under his ball cap. *I think she just called me stupid,* he muttered to himself as she stormed off toward the house. *Damn, I love that woman.*

With one final string of Spanish that included something suspiciously close to "moron," Sheldon heard Melena shout she'd be back first thing in the morning with a solution.

And she was.

The next day, she showed up with a portable toilet, a privacy screen, and a few mismatched two-by-fours, bossing Sheldon around until he helped her wall off a corner of the shed. By noon, they had a makeshift bathroom complete with a curtain, a lantern, and a can of lavender air freshener.

"It's not fancy," she said, hands on her hips, "but nobody's squatting in the dirt on my watch."

Sheldon looked at the setup, then at her, a grin spreading across his face. "You're amazing."

Melena shot him a look. "Damn right I am."

Now, standing in the doorway of the shed, Alex looked out into the quiet night—the soft glow of the moon, the gentle breeze, the single overhead light casting a pale circle around her. Harper and the boys had just fallen asleep, their first night tucked into this makeshift space. In that stillness, Alex couldn't help but reflect.

She and Walker had been through so much to get here.

His voice broke through her thoughts. "You good?"

Alex met his gaze, searching for the version of him that had once been a little less weighed down, the version with softer edges and a lighter heart. Stress had a way of dragging out the worst in Walker. He wasn't cruel, never violent—but his temper had always been sharp, quick to cut, quick to lash out in frustration. She had once absorbed his storms in silence, letting him unload while she shrank into herself and let it pass.

Not anymore.

Years ago, before they had kids, Alex and Walker weren't in a good place. Walker was a perfectionist—hardwired for control, rigid in his expectations. His classic line? "If you want something done right, do it yourself."

He'd come home tense and frustrated, the pressure of everything he carried boiling beneath the surface. And Alex, ever the peacemaker, always wanted to help. To ease the load. To keep the calm.

But somehow, whatever had gone wrong—at work, with the finances, the car, the mood, the marriage—always seemed to trace back to her. The house wasn't clean enough. The money was too tight. He wasn't getting enough sleep. Or sex. If she so much as tripped over her own feet, his first reaction wasn't concern; it was irritation. Not *"Are you okay?"* but *"What the hell were you doing?"*

And she took it. She absorbed it. Over and over again.

Alex had spent most of her life trying to be likable—not out of vanity, but out of survival. She'd grown up in a loving family, but they were poor. Her mother, though kind and nurturing, was disabled and could only work a few hours a week. Medical bills piled up. Her father, a sweet and hardworking man, had never learned to read. His job prospects had been limited to physical labor—grueling, thankless work that wore down his body and chipped away at his already fragile sense of worth.

With her intuitive nature, Alex internalized it all. She felt the weight of their struggles as if they were her own. She noticed the way others looked at them, or didn't. The subtle dismissals, the condescension. She learned early that being seen could mean being judged, and being judged often meant being hurt.

So she adapted. She learned to make herself easy—accommodating, agreeable, invisible. Anything to avoid the sting of rejection or the pain of being seen as too much.

As she got older, her looks didn't help. People saw the pretty face and drew conclusions—stuck-up, fake, unrelatable—before she ever said a word. Women kept their distance. Real friendships—the kind that dug deep and stayed? They always felt unattainable. It hurt in ways she rarely admitted, even to herself. She never felt like she was enough.

But buried beneath all that self-doubt was someone who ached to bring joy to others. The decision her parents made to adopt her brother when she was too young to remember the details left an imprint on her soul. That act of compassion inspired something deep within her. She wanted to be a source of that same light—a steady reminder that people mattered, that they were seen.

This became both her gift and her curse—the instinctive desire to lift others up and remind them of their worth, even while she quietly questioned her own. More than anything, Alex longed to be the reason someone smiled. In those moments, she felt like she had a place in the world.

However, over time, the constant feeling of never fitting in—and the steady stream of criticism at home from Walker—chipped away at her. It made her feel like no matter how hard she tried—no matter how much she gave—she would never be enough.

And so she coped the only way she knew how. She'd disappear. Not physically, but emotionally. She'd let her mind detach, allowing her thoughts to drift into that quiet, numb space where nothing could touch her. No sound. No feeling. Just a blank page where she didn't have to exist. She perfected the art of letting Walker's words fall against her like static against a closed window. But the truth was... it wasn't working anymore.

One night, without warning, something changed.

Walker was in the living room, half-watching some nonsense on TV while simultaneously ranting about God-knows-what—dishes, maybe, or laundry, or the toothpaste cap not being on right. His voice rose and fell like background noise.

She stood in the kitchen, her hands submerged in warm, soapy water, scrubbing a glass as if it had personally offended her. Her chest felt tight, her shoulders burning from the weight of everything she had never said.

And then it happened.

It didn't build gradually. It exploded.

One second she was washing that stupid glass, and the next—it was airborne. It left her hand like a missile, spinning through the air with perfect, righteous velocity, and smashed into the dining room wall with a crash that seemed to freeze time itself.

Tiny shards glittered in the air like sparks, the sound echoing into an impossible silence.

Walker whipped around, stunned. She turned toward him, her chest heaving, water dripping from her hands to the floor, her eyes blazing. And from somewhere raw and unfiltered, the words tore from her throat:

"Shut the fuck up and leave me alone!"

For a heartbeat, maybe two, they stood there. The silence between them was thick enough to suffocate. Her heart slammed against her ribs, a wild, thunderous rhythm she could barely hear over the roar of adrenaline in her ears.

Walker looked at her—really looked at her—for what felt like the first time in years. The woman who'd once shrunk under his storms was gone. In her place stood a goddamn bull in human form, vibrating with fury and power and grief, smoke practically rolling from her flaring nostrils.

So, naturally, he reacted as anyone might in that scenario, and started laughing hysterically. Not mockingly. Not cruelly. More like a man who had just discovered something new and deeply fascinating.

"What the hell was that?" he asked, grinning, his brows lifted in amusement. He spread his arms wide to the side, waving an imaginary red cape like a matador taunting a charging bull. "That was kinda hot."

Alex stood there, stunned. The adrenaline coursing through her veins was overwhelming. Her heart still pounded as her mind tried to catch up with what she had just done. She had never reacted like that before—never let herself. But something in her had snapped, something long-simmering that refused to be swallowed down any longer.

Walker, still standing in the living room, let out a low chuckle, shaking his head as he watched her. "Damn, babe. If I knew you had that in you, I might've pissed you off sooner."

His voice was half-teasing, half-awestruck, as if he didn't know whether to be impressed or terrified. There was something in his eyes—shock, yes, but also a strange flicker of admiration, like he was seeing her for the first time and didn't quite know what to do with it.

And then there was that smirk—his irritating, charming grin that always seemed to disarm tension before it had the chance to settle.

Alex's lip twitched involuntarily, the ghost of a smile threatening to surface. But she swallowed it down hard.

No, she thought fiercely. *Dammit. Stay pissed. This isn't funny. This is wrong, and he needs to understand that!*

That night, something shifted. For the first time in a long time, they actually talked. Not surface-level small talk or tired arguments disguised as conversation—but genuine dialogue. Honest. Unfiltered. Raw.

Alex kept echoing a quote in the back of her mind: *For things to change, you have to change.* She finally understood what that meant. Staying quiet, letting things pass, keeping the peace at the cost of herself—it hadn't helped anything. It only made things worse.

She was done with that. She stepped out of her so-called comfort zone and said what needed to be said. All of it. It had been terrifying, but it also felt... powerful. Necessary.

She walked into that conversation knowing it might end one of two ways—and she had made peace with either outcome.

We're going to talk this through and figure it out together... or we're done. Simple. Non-negotiable.

What followed wasn't some magical fix. There was no overnight transformation. But the truth had cracked something open in both of them.

Over time, the fog began to lift. Alex started to see things she'd been avoiding for years—about herself, about the life they'd built, and the way she'd been disappearing inside it.

She was learning that standing up for herself and asserting her needs wasn't a bad thing. It didn't mean she was selfish. It didn't make her unlikable—at least not to the people who truly mattered.

And Walker? He wasn't a monster—just a man carrying far more than he knew how to express. He wasn't broken. He was afraid. Afraid of failure. Afraid of being misunderstood. Afraid of not being enough.

He didn't want a servant or a scapegoat. He wanted a partner. But to reach him, she had to speak his language. He didn't pick up on subtle hints or half-hearted suggestions. He was a military man. His world had trained him to respond to strength—directness. Not silence.

So, when Alex shut down, he took it as rejection. As blame. And that only intensified the pressure he already felt to hold it all together—to be the provider, the protector, the man who never cracked.

But beneath that armor was someone aching for reassurance, someone who didn't know how to ask without sounding angry.

When Alex told him how his words had cut into her without him realizing it, he was devastated. He hadn't seen it before, but once he did, he couldn't unsee it. He wanted to do better, to be better.

Slowly and painfully, they began the work.

It wasn't always graceful. They stumbled, fell back into old patterns, caught themselves, and tried again. They were learning—to communicate, to listen, to unlearn the habits that had been wired into them long before they ever met.

Alex knew she had her own baggage to unpack and her own patterns to break. But they had made a choice—to face it all together. And that, at least, was something.

Walker ran a hand through his hair, exhaling as he stared into the quiet darkness.

"I know this is... a lot."

Alex leaned against the doorframe of the shed, arms folded, her eyes tracing the outline of the trees in the fading light. Crickets chirped in the distance.

"It's temporary," she said softly.

His mouth curved into a tired smirk. "Still wouldn't mind having a real door to close at night."

Before she could reply, footsteps crunched lightly on the gravel, and Sheldon emerged from the shadows, hands tucked into his hoodie pocket.

"Hey," he said. "Got a favor to ask."

Alex straightened a little, eyebrows raised. "You always lead with that. You ever notice?"

He shrugged. "Saves time."

She chuckled under her breath. "What is it?"

Sheldon stopped a few feet away, his face dimly lit by the porch light overhead.

"I ordered a part for my camper. Need you to swing by The Outpost tomorrow and pick it up."

"The Outpost?" she asked.

"Yeah—Roth's Open Road Outpost. The camper dealership in town." He scratched the back of his neck. "Would've gone myself, but I've got three jobs stacked tomorrow and no time to get there before they close. Figured you might have a bit more flexibility."

Alex nodded. "Yeah... sure. I can do that."

The thought of leaving the shed the next day—even for a quick errand—felt oddly refreshing. It was a chance to explore Helena a bit, get her bearings in the new town, and maybe even show off her babies while she was at it. A flicker of warmth stirred in her chest.

Then, almost immediately, the familiar feeling of dread washed over her—car seats, diaper bags, public meltdowns. All the unpredictable beauty that came with juggling two babies in the wild.

But she agreed anyway, completely unaware that what seemed like a simple favor would become the first ripple in a storm she never saw coming.

Two

Mirrored Reflections

Alex secured the twins into their car seats in the back of her SUV, the routine so familiar now that she didn't even have to think about it. Eight-month-old Corbin fussed, his chubby hands batting at the straps as she buckled him in.

"I know, baby," she murmured, offering him a teething ring. "You hate being strapped in, but rules are rules, little man."

Liam, in contrast, sucked contently on his pacifier, his big, sleepy eyes watching her every move. Once they were settled, Alex slung the diaper bag over the front seat, climbed behind the wheel, and exhaled. Another errand. Another day.

Before pulling out of the driveway, she turned in her seat and gave her boys a playful, conspiratorial grin. "Alright, fellas.

Here's the deal: Mama expects good behavior today. That means no big crying fits, no puke parties, and absolutely no shit-nanigans. Got it?" She paused.

Corbin blew a spit bubble in response, while Liam stared at her, utterly unamused.

"Perfect. Glad we're all on the same page," she said, shaking her head with a grin as she typed the address for Roth's Open Road Outpost into the GPS.

The dealership was only fifteen minutes away, but the roads were still unfamiliar. As she drove, she glanced at the scenery—the rolling hills and the quaint little businesses nestled between stretches of open land. It was different from the busy suburban world she was used to, but there was a certain charm to it.

She perked up when she spotted a massive natural foods market nestled between a bait shop and an antique store.

“Score,” she said to herself, already planning a stop on the way back. A good health food store could turn a decent town into a great one.

Alex pulled into the lot of Roth's Open Road Outpost, easing her vehicle into a parking space near the entrance. The dealership looked older, a little worn around the edges, like it had seen better days but still stood strong and functional. The front showroom windows were clean enough, but the building itself bore the wear and tear of years in business. Faded paint and a few missing letters on the signage gave it charm but also a sense of neglect.

She sighed, glancing at the twins in the back seat, both wide awake now and kicking their little legs. "Alright, boys," she murmured. "Let's try to make this as painless as possible."

With practiced efficiency, she lifted them from their car seats and settled them into the double stroller. Corbin immediately reached for Liam's pacifier, and a squabble ensued, but Alex was too preoccupied with adjusting the diaper bag to intervene. "You two sort it out," she said with a smirk before locking the car and heading inside.

The dealership's glass doors slid open with a soft whoosh, and the scent of leather and new plastic filled the air. A bright, inviting voice greeted her almost immediately.

"Welcome to Roth's Open Road Outpost! How can I help you today?"

Alex glanced up to find a stunning blonde woman behind the counter. Her warm smile instantly put her at ease. There was a softness to her—something gentle yet poised. Elegant without being intimidating, her stylish outfit was perfectly tailored, with her blouse tucked effortlessly into a pair of fitted slacks that flattered her slender frame. Her hair cascaded in loose waves over her shoulders, looking as if it had been professionally styled that morning. Even the way she moved—graceful and deliberate—exuded confidence.

Alex, in contrast, felt acutely aware of her own appearance in that moment: paint-stained yoga pants, an old sweatshirt, and her favorite baseball cap, boldly labeling her as 'Shit Show Supervisor.' She resisted the urge to smooth a hand over her messy ponytail, feeling frumpy and underdressed in comparison. She sighed internally. *Fantastic first impression.*

"Hi," Alex said, adjusting the stroller. "I'm Alexandra Halloway. My brother, Sheldon McKay, sent me to pick up a part he ordered."

Recognition flashed in the woman's blue eyes. "Oh, yes! He called earlier to let me know you'd be coming by." She turned toward the parts area but paused, a sheepish expression crossing her face. "Oops—forgot my flashlight. I'll be right back with that part for you."

Alex frowned slightly. "A flashlight?"

"Yeah, the storage room lights have been flickering for, well, a while. We should really get them fixed one of these days. It's like a horror movie back there." The woman chuckled before disappearing into the back, leaving Alex to take in more of the dealership. It was busy, but something about it felt off—like a surface polished for presentation, hiding scratches beneath.

A moment later, the woman reappeared, holding a small cardboard box. “Here it is—one water pump for a Rockwood Signature Ultra Lite 8289WS,” she announced with a grin.

Alex nodded and reached for it. “Perfect, thank you. My brother’s gonna be relieved.”

The woman rested her elbows lightly on the counter, her smile lingering. “I don’t think I’ve seen you in here before. You said your brother sent you—are you new to the area?”

“Kind of,” Alex replied, adjusting the diaper bag on her shoulder. “We just sold our place in Billings. Right now, we’re staying at my brother’s while we wait to close on our new home.”

The woman's eyebrows lifted in interest. “That’s a big move. Where’s the new place?”

Alex’s face brightened. “About twenty minutes outside of town. Seventeen acres, no neighbors for miles. It’s quiet, private... exactly what I’ve always wanted.”

The woman's expression flickered—just for a second. Something passed through her eyes, a shadow of something unspoken, but it vanished before Alex could place it.

"That sounds amazing," the woman said, her voice light again. "I'd love that kind of space." With a smile, she turned toward the babies, her fingers gently brushing against Liam's as he reached out. "These little guys are adorable. How old are they?"

Alex's guarded demeanor continued to soften. "Eight months. And a handful."

"I bet. I have a daughter—Meryl. She's sixteen now, but it feels like yesterday she was this small."

Something in her voice—nostalgic yet subdued—sparked Alex's curiosity. There was a hesitation, as if the words carried a weight she didn't want to reveal.

"I'm Andria, by the way," the woman added. "But you can call me Andi. Most people do."

Alex grinned. "Andi it is, then."

They fell into an easy conversation, swapping stories about parenthood, sleep deprivation, and the art of balancing life and work. Alex found herself relaxing in Andi's presence—something that didn't happen often.

She'd always had a hard time connecting with new people. It wasn't that she didn't want to; it just never came easily. Alex was her own worst critic. She'd come a long way with Walker, learning to quiet some of that inner noise, but around others, that old feeling crept back in—that she wasn't enough.

But with Andi, the conversation flowed. No second-guessing. No overthinking. Just...easy.

It wasn't just that Andi was beautiful—with her sunlit waves of blonde hair and striking blue eyes—it was that she was kind. Genuinely kind. The kind of woman who carried herself with effortless grace while still possessing a softness, a subtle hesitation, that made her feel real. Relatable.

It was rare, and Alex hadn't realized how much she'd missed that kind of connection until now.

Alex's eyes caught the small "Help Wanted" sign taped near the counter. A job. Something to break up the monotony of diapers and dishes. A way to bring in a little income—and maybe feel like herself again, even a little.

She hesitated only a moment before asking, "So...are you hiring?"

Andi's face lit up. "We are! Our last sales girl left kind of suddenly, so we've been scrambling a bit. Do you have any sales experience?"

Alex nodded. "Furniture sales—for years. I actually loved it."

Andi's smile widened. "That's perfect. If you're interested, I can set up an interview. My husband, Damon, handles the hiring—but honestly, I think you'd be a great fit."

Alex took the business card Andi offered, feeling a small jolt of something she hadn't felt in a while. Hope. A job. A new connection. Maybe even the beginning of something bigger.

A fresh start.

That weekend, Alex left the twins with Walker, grateful he had the day off to watch them. His new role as a Consultant Project Engineer for the Montana Department of Transportation was going well—though it was a far cry from his Air Force days working in base safety and accident investigations. Swapping the uniform for spreadsheets had been an adjustment, but that investigative streak in him never faded. He still noticed everything—patterns, inconsistencies, the little details most people missed. Alex had learned from that too, picking up on things she might've ignored before.

As she stepped outside, she spotted Harper gleefully jumping onto the side-by-side with Melena, her laughter echoing through the crisp morning air. Alex smiled, reassured that her daughter was in for a fun-filled adventure. With one last look at her little crew, she climbed into her SUV, dressed sharply, her hair and nerves smoothed into place, determined to make a good impression.

By the time Alex pulled into the dealership lot for her interview, her stomach was a knot of tension. She'd spent the entire drive rehearsing how to introduce herself, what to say if Damon asked about her resume, and how to explain the gap in her work history without sounding like she was apologizing for being a mom.

But the moment she stepped through the door, some of that anxiety began to ease.

Andria looked up and smiled, her voice brightening with a cheerful, "Yay, you're here!" It was the kind of greeting that made Alex feel seen, maybe even wanted—not just as another applicant or customer, but as *her*.

Their conversation picked up easily, falling into the same lovely rhythm they had found the first time. Nothing forced. Nothing awkward.

Then Andi glanced at the clock.

Her smile wavered. Her tone dipped. That light, easy energy she had carried moments ago began to recede like a tide pulling back from shore.

"Well," Andi said, clearing her throat, "let's head back. I'm sure Damon's looking forward to meeting with you."

The words were casual, but her body told another story.

As they made their way toward the back offices, Andi seemed to shrink by degrees. Her posture tightened, her steps grew more hesitant, and the smile she offered now felt hollow and rehearsed—something worn for appearance's sake, not offered from the heart.

And just like that, Alex's anxiety surged back, curling tightly in her chest. Whatever ease she had found in those first few moments vanished, replaced by a warning in her gut she couldn't yet articulate.

The office was unexpectedly cluttered and dimly lit, with papers stacked in haphazard piles. Messy. Impersonal. A space that didn't quite fit the polished showroom.

Then she saw him.

Damon Roth.

Seated behind a large metal desk, the man stood out instantly—confident, polished, in control. His salt-and-pepper hair was neatly styled, and his dark eyes scanned Alex with a sharpness that felt more evaluative than welcoming. The smile he wore was rehearsed—polite, but edged with something more.

"Alexandra Halloway," he said, rising from his chair. "Pleasure to meet you."

Alex stepped forward and shook his hand. His grip was firm, his posture self-assured—everything about him projected confidence. Yet there was something in the way he looked at her... something she couldn't quite pinpoint. Not unkind. Not inappropriate. Just... measured.

Damon launched into the interview with the polished ease of a man accustomed to being listened to. He spoke confidently about the dealership's origins and successes, yet the story he told was unmistakably centered around himself. Every expansion, every glowing review, every satisfied customer—he credited to his vision. His work ethic. His reputation. Not in an overtly boastful way, but with a subtle certainty that suggested the Outpost would crumble without him. As he shifted to asking questions about Alex's experience and availability, the tone didn't change. It wasn't a conversation—it was a performance with occasional intermissions for her to speak. She sensed that her responses really didn't matter; her words felt like mere parts of a script he'd written in advance.

Beside him, Andi sat quietly—too quietly. The bright, warm energy she'd displayed earlier was noticeably dimmed. She nodded in agreement here and there and smiled occasionally but didn't contribute much. Her posture was more reserved now, hands folded neatly in her lap as if she were trying to take up less space.

Still, the job was offered quickly and without hesitation.

Alex blinked. "Wow—thank you. I'll need to confirm childcare, but I should be able to start Monday. Does that work?"

"Perfect," Damon replied, already rising from his seat. "Andria will handle the paperwork. Welcome aboard." His tone left little room for discussion, as if everything had already been decided the moment she walked in.

As Alex left the office, business card in hand, she couldn't shake the feeling that she had just stepped into something she didn't quite understand. Feeling both strangely nervous and excited, she made her way to her car. As she drove back toward the shed, Alex wrestled with a conflicting desire for the interview to have gone poorly. The job was part-time, but the thought of leaving her kids in daycare weighed heavily on her, pressing down with a guilt she couldn't shake. Logically, she knew it was a necessary step—contributing to the family's income wasn't optional right now—but understanding that didn't make it any easier.

Harper, at six, was already becoming comfortable with school, and the idea of her spending a little time in after-school care come fall didn't worry Alex much. But Corbin and Liam? They were still babies. Still breastfeeding. Still so dependent on her. "I can pump. They'll be fine. We can do this," she murmured, as much to herself as to the empty car. She let out a breath and loosened her grip on the steering wheel. Melena had offered to help with the kids, and Alex knew she'd figure out the logistics of daycare soon enough. There was still time.

For now, this was a step—maybe even the beginning of something that looked a little like balance. When she pictured the proud look on Walker's face, her nerves faded just enough to let a flicker of excitement take hold.

Three

Cracked Facade

The days at Roth's Open Road Outpost didn't so much pass as settle—like dust after a summer storm. By the end of the first week, Alex's hands moved with a confidence that surprised her; by the end of the second, customers were asking for her by name. She learned model numbers and option packages like a new language and discovered she was fluent in it—reading people, reading needs, turning a maze of inventory into a line that led families to the door of the camper they didn't know they'd been dreaming about.

But the deals weren't what made her feel so comfortable here. It was the people.

The crew at the Outpost felt like one of those rare campfires you could sit beside and just breathe easy—a steady, comforting warmth that asked for nothing in return.

Jason—aka Bouncer—moved through the service bay like a gentle giant—brilliant, trustworthy, and effortlessly likable. He could figure out anything—mechanical, electrical, or otherwise—and everyone knew it. Frank, affectionately called Tiny due to his smaller stature, had a magnetic charm and quick wit that drew people in. Loyal and hardworking, he was the guy who'd drop everything to help anyone with anything—and have you laughing your ass off while doing it. Edith, known as Eddy, was the dealership's unofficial grandma—quiet, sweet, steady, but also a bit of a gossip. The crew loved getting a rise out of her; if you could make her laugh, her goofy, sudden cackle accompanied by a few cuss words could light up the whole room. Even the new hires blended in as if they had always been part of the crew—a rare harmony of personalities that just worked. And everyone seemed to like Alex, which still surprised her. She felt it in the genuine smiles and easy camaraderie that met her wherever she went.

Here, her ideas didn't vanish into the air—they landed. People actually liked them. She started a one-page "feature spotlight" sheet for each unit—clean, visual, easy to hand a family who was still deciding. It caught on fast. She noticed Jason began printing a version of them to stick on job jackets, so service had a simple snapshot of each job. Customers lingered longer. The crew started asking her, almost casually, "What would you do about the showroom flow?" or "Hey, how would you pitch this floorplan to a retired couple?" She never pretended to be an expert—just offered what she saw with clear eyes. The respect that came back felt... grounding. Like, Oh. I belong.

And then there was Andi.

From the first morning, Andi trained with a kind of effortless precision that made Alex both grateful and a little awestruck. She was warm without fawning, professional without the stiffness. Somehow, she made every person feel like the only person, and she did it without performing. Her phrasing was elegant and simple, never salesy—more like a friend who knew the right questions to ask and how to give you enough space to decide. Alex found herself soaking up the Andi-isms: "Let's build this around how you *actually* camp," "Let me do the math while you daydream out loud," "We're going to make this make sense." People laughed with her, trusted her, signed with her. Employees sought her out like a compass.

Alex took notes—literal notes in a little notebook she kept in her back pocket—of how Andi handled tension, how she effortlessly moved a conversation back when a customer wandered, how she softened a no into a yes that still honored boundaries. It wasn't just talent; it was care, and Alex felt a tug of envy in her chest that embarrassed her. She wished she had Andi's effortless wit, the quicksilver humor that turned awkward into easy. She wished she could be that weightless sometimes.

She was trying, though. She was learning.

What Alex didn't see—what she only felt in glancing moments—was how deliberately Andi kept a seam stitched closed inside herself. The admiration between them glowed like a small light, and Andi clearly felt it too. She liked Alex. A lot. She liked working with her. She liked the way Alex's presence settled the room, even on busier days. But Andi held herself back from the easy slide into friendship. Whenever the two of them were laughing and the conversation started to tilt more personal, Andi would pull up—smile, redirect, offer to grab a file. It wasn't coldness. It was restraint, precise and deliberate.

Part of it, Alex learned, had less to do with her and more to do with the invisible gravity that shaped the building. She saw it on the rare days when Damon drifted in: the way he praised "Alexandra" for her "fresh energy," the way his eyes warmed with approval only when they landed on the new hire. The way, in the same breath, he scolded Andi for not moving fast enough, not arranging something properly, not anticipating what he never actually said aloud. It wasn't just unfair; it was insulting. And while Andi never showed it—never gave it oxygen—Alex could feel the bruise forming under the skin of that dynamic. Admiration and annoyance braided together. A woman who needed a friend and a woman who refused to become a weapon in someone else's hands.

So, they worked. They found a rhythm—something steady and wordless that made the long days feel lighter, like they were building more than sales together.

A few months in, the shine of newness dulled enough for Alex to see what had been there all along: a dealership that could have been a postcard... if someone would just stop and wash the glass.

From the highway, the Outpost looked inviting enough—rows of shiny campers catching the sun. But up close, it told a different story. The campers gleamed, but the building and parking lot looked tired and unkept. Cracked pavement, weeds everywhere, peeling paint, sun-bleached banners flapping half-torn—none of it was catastrophic, but together it made the place feel forgotten.

The first time she'd driven up to interview, she'd wondered if they were on their way down. More than once now, she'd heard customers mention that same first impression in the gentlest way: "Y'all open today?" or "We almost kept driving—thought you were closed." Alex found herself smiling and smoothing and making excuses she didn't believe. "We've been slammed with summer deliveries," she'd say, "We're catching up." People nodded. Most stayed. But she hated that first swallow of doubt in their eyes.

Inside, the showroom carried its own contradictions. On warm days, heat pooled heavy in the air, trapped beneath the wide panes of glass. The thermostat was off-limits—an unspoken rule everyone knew. Alex learned to keep a spare shirt in her bag and a hair tie on her wrist. In winter, she was told, the cold would be just as brutal. Someone joked about the "Outpost winter uniform"—battery-heated shirts under flannels, thin gloves for typing, plug-in heater by your desk—and everyone laughed, but the sound rang hollow. Alex already dreaded it. She hated being cold.

From the horrible lighting with half the bulbs out—especially in the parts and service areas—to the cracked, grossly stained floors and the sagging ceiling, it didn't seem like this was a place that expressed pride in its business or respect for its employees.

But Alex didn't complain. Not to Andi. She'd already learned how that conversation would go. Andi had a way of smoothing things until even Alex questioned whether the problem mattered. "We've been meaning to get to that," Andi would say with gentle certainty. "It's on the list. Promise." And maybe it was. Maybe there was always something more urgent, more visible, more... acceptable to spend money on. Or maybe Andi was doing what she did best: keeping the ship steady with the tools she had, even if those tools were only her voice and some well-chosen words.

So Alex did what she'd told herself she would do when she took this job: she focused on the part she loved. The people. The stories. The way a retired couple held hands in the kitchen of a travel trailer and looked at each other like they were twenty-three and fearless. The way a dad kneeled to show his son the bunk ladder and the boy's eyes went huge like he'd found the secret door to summer. The way Frank would lean against a unit and narrate the first fishing trip in this thing like he'd already been on it, and everyone would grin because for a split second, it felt real.

"No job is perfect," she reminded herself, rinsing coffee mugs in a bathroom sink with a trickle of water because the breakroom sink had been "temporarily" out of order since the week she started. "Pick the part you can love and do that part like it matters."

Most days, it worked.

For Alex, the Outpost was becoming home. The people were becoming family. She could hear the rhythm of the place even from the parking lot—the air compressor kicking on in service, Eddy's perfected clack at the keyboard, Frank humming some old tune under his breath. Yes, the showroom still had dark corners and the AC still pretended to be shy, but Alex had stopped flinching at every rough edge. She was good at this. She was helping. People came to find her with little things and big things, and she delivered. It felt meant to be.

That Friday morning, Andi called her into the cramped nook by the sales counter. The noise from the showroom filtered in: a door latch clinked, a laugh, the squeak of rubber on tile. This corner always felt like the smallest kind of sanctuary.

Andi leaned one hip against the desk, a folder in her hand. "You got a second?"

"Always," Alex said. She half expected a trick question about interest rates. Instead, Andi gave a small smile that didn't quite hide its nerves.

"Damon asked me to let you know..." She paused, reconsidered her phrasing, then went with plain. "He wants to promote you to Assistant Manager."

It took a heartbeat for the words to make sense, and when they did, they lit Alex from the inside. Not flashy. Not performative. Just a clean, solid flare of pride that settled in her chest like a new foundation. "You're kidding."

Andi shook her head. "Nope. He said you're doing great work. That the team's better with you here." Her smile turned real then, warm and bright. "He's not wrong."

Alex laughed, a little breathless. "I—wow. I don't know what to say."

"Say yes," Andi teased, and the moment softened.

"Then yes," Alex said. "Absolutely yes."

Andi slid a small ring of keys across the desk—the kind of handoff that felt ceremonial even in a cramped corner. The metal clicked against wood, the sound crisp and final. "These are yours now. Front door. File room. Parts cage." She hesitated, then added, "It comes with a lot of trust. You've earned it."

The keys were heavier than they looked. Alex turned them in her palm, the cold edges pressing into her skin and pulling a rush of memories—the late-night inventory counts, the early lot checks, all the quiet moments she'd taken initiative without being asked. She'd been trying to build something here, not just for herself but with them. This felt like proof that it existed. That she existed inside it.

She looked up. "Thank you. For everything you've taught me." Her voice thickened before she could stop it. "I'm only this good because you've been... incredible."

Andi's mouth tipped, honesty flickering in her eyes. "You were always this good. I just got to watch."

Emotion tightened Alex's throat, and she tried to deflect it with a grin. "Careful. I might cry and ruin my tough reputation."

"Oh, your *very* tough reputation," Andi deadpanned. "I'm terrified of you daily."

They laughed, the sound soft and private in the narrow space—two women caught in a moment that felt bigger than the room. Their friendship was taking shape naturally, unassumingly, the kind that crept in without fanfare and changed everything. Around each other, they could just *be*—no masks, no pretending, no holding their breath to fit in. It was rare and real, and though neither said it out loud, they both knew they'd found something they didn't even realize they'd been missing.

Then Andi's smile faded a little. "I should probably be honest about something," she said softly. "My health's been kind of a mess lately. Doctors have no clue—one day I'm fine, the next I feel like I've been hit by a truck. It's exhausting." She tried to laugh it off, but her fingers worried at the hem of her sleeve. "The pills, the appointments... it's so much to deal with. Damon helps a lot, pays for it, picks up and tracks my meds, and I'm grateful for that. But still—it's hard not knowing what's going on in my own body. Makes me feel totally powerless."

Alex's chest tightened. "Oh wow, I didn't realize. So the other day, when you had to go out to your car because you thought you ate something that didn't agree with you—was that part of it too?"

Andi gave a small smile. "Yeah. I've gotten good at downplaying it. Sometimes I can work through it, sometimes it knocks me flat. I don't want people tiptoeing around me."

Alex shook her head, sympathy in her eyes. "Still, you shouldn't have to carry all that alone."

Andi's voice dropped. "That's why this means so much—having you here. I can actually take a breath, step back when I need to. You're holding up so much, Alex. It's taken a lot of pressure off."

Alex's eyes softened. "You've got me, okay? Always. Whatever you need—at work, outside of it—say the word."

Andi smiled, the tension easing from her shoulders. "You don't know how much that means." Her voice carried both exhaustion and relief, a soft honesty that needed no polish. She met Alex's eyes for a beat before stepping forward and pulling her into a hug—full and real, the kind that said more than words ever could. In that moment, the professional veneer slipped away, and two women just held on, grateful for the rare comfort of being seen and understood.

Their laughter returned, quieter now, threaded with something deeper. The subtle recognition that somehow, without even meaning to, they'd become vital to each other's worlds.

Just then, Jason let out a sharp whistle as he hustled through the showroom, a sound everyone instantly recognized. Conversations stopped mid-word, bodies stiffened, and the atmosphere shifted like someone had cut the music at a party.

Damon had arrived.

He wasn't supposed to be there that day, which made the warning even more welcome. Alex had already picked up on the pattern—whenever Damon showed up, which thankfully wasn't often, the energy in the building shifted instantly. Laughter died. People busied themselves with exaggerated focus. It wasn't fear exactly—it was strategy. Stay small, stay useful, stay out of his line of fire.

Andi, though? Andi never seemed to get that option.

The moment Damon walked through the doors, it was like a switch flipped. His eyes would cut through the room, scanning for something—*someone*—to tear down. And more often than not, it landed on Andi. It didn't matter if she'd done everything perfectly. He'd still dig for flaws, twist yesterday's approval into today's criticism, just to corner her in front of everyone.

Alex had tried to rationalize it in the beginning. They were married. Maybe that was just... how they were. Some couples had weird dynamics. Maybe he didn't know how to talk to his wife without sounding like a raging asshole. But that theory got harder to swallow the more she saw. This was more than tension. This was control.

What really made Alex's stomach twist was how little Damon cared about who was watching. He had no problem tearing Andi down right there in the middle of the showroom, his voice loud enough for employees and customers alike to hear. It was like he *wanted* an audience—like her humiliation somehow made him feel bigger. And worst yet? He wrapped it in jokes. Laughing at her expense, glancing around to make sure everyone else was in on it too.

But now, knowing what Alex knew—that Andi was privately fighting through a maze of unexplained health problems—it made every one of his little digs feel ten times crueler. The stress alone had to be hell on her body, and he piled more on like it was his morning workout.

Andi never pushed back. She never snapped. She kept her eyes down, moved through the motions, like disappearing might soften the blow.

To Damon, acting like a relentless jerk wasn't just business as usual, it was his undeniable right. It was his way of reminding Andi—and the world for that matter—who was in charge.

So today, when Jason gave the signal that Damon had pulled up—Alex felt it like a gut punch. She stood up straighter, smoothed her blouse, while the whole place changed in an instant. Conversations died. People stiffened. It was like watching a room full of warm bodies turn to mannequins. The energy she loved about the place—gone. Just like that. She saw Andi out of the corner of her eye, hunched over her desk, her posture tightening like she was bracing for impact. The change in her was immediate—and hard to watch.

Then Damon strode in, all fake confidence and poorly-contained contempt.

One glance at Jason's expression—stone-faced, jaw clenched—and the silent tension rippling through the room told Alex all she needed. This visit was going to be an inescapable train wreck.

"Damon, I wasn't expecting you yet," Andi said, trying to avoid eye contact while picking up the phone to make an unnecessary call. "Sorry, I have to call this customer back right away, so—"

His smile fell into a frown as he took the phone from her and shoved some paperwork in her face. "You see this shit?" he asked, pointing at the page. "These numbers are wrong. I know they are fucking wrong because I don't run my business this way, do I?"

Andi opened her mouth to protest, knowing that the paperwork he was referring to was an order that he specifically had approved and asked her to submit the week prior, but Damon cut her off. "Don't even try to fucking explain it! We both know you're completely incompetent."

As if determined to prove his point further, Damon's eyes darted around the showroom until they landed on a nearby display—one he had explicitly instructed Frank to set up in a very particular way just a few days prior. His lips curled in disgust. "And what the hell is this? This looks like absolute garbage!"

Frank—had been silently watching from across the room. At Damon's outburst, he stiffened, jaw tight, but didn't say a word. Alex, having overheard the setup instructions earlier in the week, knew for a fact that Frank had followed them to the letter.

Damon wasn't done. His eyes suddenly locked onto something near one of the campers—a bucket of water sitting on the floor. His expression darkened as he followed the trail of moisture streaking down the side of the unit, his anger bubbling over. "Are you fucking kidding me?" he barked, stomping over to the bucket and kicking it slightly with the toe of his shoe. "What the hell is this doing here? And why is there fucking water running down the side of my damn camper?"

The room was silent. No one wanted to be the poor soul who had to state the obvious.

"Is nobody listening? Hello? Someone better explain to me right the fuck now why there's a fucking bucket of water on my showroom!" Damon shouted, his voice echoing off the walls. He spun on his heel, his glare scanning the room for a scapegoat. "So nobody has a goddamn answer? Fucking idiots! This is unacceptable!"

Alex's jaw clenched as she exchanged a knowing look with Jason. The reaction brewing in the room was almost tangible. This was the same roof leak the employees had been complaining about for years. Every time it rained, they scrambled to find buckets, trying to keep the water from soaking into the showroom carpet. Every single time, they told Damon about it. And every single time, he ignored it—until, of course, it inconvenienced him directly.

But the showroom? That was nothing compared to the back of the dealership. Back there, the leaks weren't just annoying—they were dangerous. The ceiling over the loading dock sagged under the weight of years of neglect, its blackened insulation poking through, an ominous sign of the mold lurking within. The smell back there was enough to make a person gag if they weren't used to it, the musty dampness clinging to the air like a warning.

And the ridiculous thing? Damon knew. He absolutely knew—and he just didn't care. He refused to put a dime into fixing the roof, blaming everyone else for the shape the building was in, as if it had somehow fallen apart behind his back. He wouldn't even pay to properly light the back warehouse—which, hell, might've been intentional. Probably easier to ignore the moldy ceilings and rotting insulation when everything's hidden in shadows. Employees had to use their phone flashlights just to find parts or do basic repairs. And now he had the gall to act outraged? Like this was new? Like they had failed him?

The tension in the room was suffocating.

His fury returned to Andi.

"What the fuck was I thinking?" he spat, shaking his head before his voice snapped louder. "Why the hell did I ever let my wife have any part of this?"

He took a step closer, his face twisted with disgust. "Who's the principal here, huh?" He leaned in so close, he was practically spitting in her face. "Who's the fucking principal?"

His eyes were wild now, veins standing out in his neck.

"I'm the fucking principal! This isn't The Andria Show! This is mine! You got that? Mine!"

The words hung in the air like a slap. Still seething, Damon spun toward a cluttered corner near the sales desk. His eyes landed on a stack of old printer boxes and office junk—stuff the employees weren't allowed to toss, no matter how useless. It had been stacked as neatly as possible, a sad attempt to keep the space functional.

With a twisted grin, he sneered, "And what, pray tell, is this little fucked-up mess over here?"

He didn't bother waiting for an answer before shoving a pile of outdated brochures aside, sending them flying across the counter. With a sickening laugh, he threw up his hands. "This is a disaster! Why do I have to do everything myself? How the hell is this place supposed to look professional when you all can't even keep it clean?"

Alex bit the inside of her cheek to keep from snapping. The curse words were flying in her head at this point. How dare he? This ungrateful ASSHOLE. How were they supposed to keep things spotless when they weren't allowed to throw anything away? It was a losing battle. They didn't even have proper cleaning supplies. More than once, Alex and others had brought their own—wipes, sprays, even a vacuum and carpet cleaner from home—just to make the place halfway presentable. They did the best they could with what little they had. But no amount of effort could compete with years' worth of crap Damon refused to part with. It was like trying to keep a hoarder's house in showroom condition. Impossible. And insulting.

Damon let out a heavy, exaggerated sigh, shaking his head like he was surrounded by incompetence. "This place is a goddamn embarrassment, and guess whose fault it is!" he growled before locking his glare back on Andi like a target. "You did this! Fix it!"

Alex was disgusted. The sheer arrogance—the cruelty—of Damon's words made her stomach turn. This wasn't a bad mood. It wasn't stress. It was deliberate. Calculated.

He wanted to humiliate Andi. Hell, he wanted to humiliate everyone. To knock them down a peg, keep them second-guessing themselves. That was how he kept control—by stirring chaos and watching everyone scramble.

Somehow, this douchebag of a man couldn't—or wouldn't—see that he had the world by the balls. He had everything most people could only dream of. A gorgeous, loyal-as-hell wife who bent over backward for him. Worked herself to the bone. Stood by him, even when he didn't deserve it. And employees? Damn near impossible to find these days. Yet somehow, he had a whole crew of them. Every single one knew their shit. They worked around his chaos, kept things running, handled the day-to-day like pros. They kept customers happy, closed deals, solved problems—all within the narrow, ridiculous limits of what Damon allowed.

When he wasn't there, The Outpost thrived. The showroom had life. Energy. Momentum. There was laughter, teamwork, confidence. Customers noticed. And they came back—not for Damon, but for the people that worked there.

And for Andi.

She was the heart of it all. The one everyone respected. The one who held it together without asking for credit. The unspoken leader who took on more than anyone realized and still showed up with grace. It couldn't be clearer: The only reason this place was still standing—still successful—was because of her.

The mood in the room had shifted from unease to outright hostility. Jason's massive fists clenched at his sides, his jaw ticking. Frank stood stiff and unreadable, arms crossed—his usual humor nowhere in sight. Around them, employees avoided eye contact, absolute anger radiating in every stiff movement.

Alex wanted to speak up, to defend Andi, to defend all of them—but she didn't. Damon fed on confrontation. Speaking now would only make it worse. Still, the injustice burned in her chest.

Then, as suddenly as he'd arrived, Damon turned on his heel and stormed out the front door. The tension he left behind was crushing.

The room broke into murmurs. Disgusted glances followed his exit. Andi quickly disappeared into the bathroom. Alex watched her go, a gnawing sense of sadness twisting inside her. She didn't know everything Andi was dealing with, but one thing was painfully clear:

She deserved better.

Alex stood there, completely still, unsure what to do—how to move, how to even process the tension Damon had left hanging in the air. Since starting at the Outpost, she'd seen glimpses of his behavior that unsettled her. Sharp comments to customers. Dismissive jabs at employees. Andi taking the brunt of it, always shrinking just a little more under his glare. Each time it happened, it felt wrong. It *was* wrong.

Dammit, this sucked. Because honestly? Other than Damon, she really liked this job. The people were great. The pace kept her on her toes. The customers were fun, and the campers? Some of them were so luxurious, she felt rich just stepping inside.

So she'd swallowed the bad moments like pills—choking them down with excuses. "He's just intense." "He's not here much anyway." "No job's perfect." And if putting up with a little bullshit meant being part of something that felt fun most days—well, maybe it was worth it.

But now? Now, she wasn't so sure. Today was something else entirely.

Now, Alex understood.

The locals hadn't been exaggerating when they warned her about working for Damon Roth. If anything, they might've undersold it. Damon wasn't just difficult. He was a wrecking ball, tearing through people's confidence and pride like it was nothing. And somehow, everyone just kept picking up the pieces and showing up anyway.

Just then, Andi came back to the counter—each step stiff, deliberate, as if her body had gone on autopilot to protect whatever was left of her spirit. Her face was blank, expressionless, like she'd stuffed all her feelings into a box and slammed the lid shut.

"Are you alright?" Alex asked gently, laying a hand on her shoulder.

Andi shook her head, fingers pressing to her temple like she was trying to push the whole scene out of her skull. "I'm just... I—" Her voice caught, then she forced herself upright and cleared her throat.

"I'm fine." The words were quick. Practiced. She offered a small, hollow smile that didn't come close to reaching her eyes.

"Could you call Frank to reset the display?" she asked, her voice now composed but flat. "Then go through the units and mark the ones that need cleaning. I'll have Meryl hit those after school."

Without waiting for a response, she handed some invoices to Eddy and walked back to her desk like nothing had happened. Like Damon hadn't just ripped her apart in front of everyone.

Alex stood there for a second, watching her go, feeling that awful, helpless ache you get when someone is clearly breaking in front of you—but pretending they're not. She did as Andi asked, but each step felt heavy. Around her, the others reluctantly returned to their tasks, the usual chatter gone.

Still, there was a kind of silent understanding moving between them—exchanged glances, nods, small gestures that said *we've got each other.*

Alex watched as Frank focused on the display Damon had shredded with his words. Jason moved with forced concentration. Eddy tapped quietly at her keyboard. Everyone was doing what they could, trying to patch the atmosphere back together. It was comforting and heartbreaking all at once.

As Alex settled back into her chair, a half-finished estimate open in front of her, her mind drifted. It was becoming painfully clear that Andi's home life wasn't just stressful—it was probably unbearable. Damon didn't just criticize. He broke her down, piece by piece, and he did it unapologetically.

And yet... Andi still showed up. Still smiled. Still kept everything afloat. There was something so deeply painful and *so* deeply admirable about that.

Alex felt a lump rise in her throat. She thought about some of the things she and Walker had been through, the messiness of relationships, the power struggles, the silent pain. It wasn't the same—not even close—but it made her feel connected to Andi in a way she hadn't expected.

She wished she could do more. Say something that would matter. But the truth was, they weren't *quite* there yet. Not close enough for deep truths.

And with Damon looming like a storm cloud in Andi's life, it felt nearly impossible to find the right time, the right words to reach her.

As the day wore on, Alex kept catching herself glancing over at Andi. She saw the act: the way Andi straightened papers that didn't need straightening. The way she smiled just enough to seem okay but not enough to mean it. Alex recognized that rhythm— that quiet choreography people perfect when the walls are caving in but there's no space to fall apart. You show up, you smile, you keep moving—because if you stop, the whole damn thing might collapse.

She didn't know Andi's full story, but she could feel the shape of it. Heavy. Hidden. Hurting. And God, she wished she could do something—anything—to make her feel a little less alone in it.

During a lull between customers, Alex wandered over to Andi's desk. Her voice was soft when she spoke. "Hey, do you have a minute?"

Andi looked up from her computer, eyes a little tired, a little worn. But she nodded. "Sure. What's up?"

Alex leaned against the edge of the desk, folding her arms. "I was just thinking... my husband Walker can be a real turd sometimes too." She gave a small, crooked grin. "Mind if I tell you a story? It's dumb, but it might give you a laugh."

Andi raised a brow, interest flickering in her expression. "I could use a laugh today. Hit me."

Alex smirked. "So, Walker is one of those super handy, fix-anything kind of guys. Total man's man, right? We were getting our old house ready to sell—cleaning, fixing little things. He said he'd take care of this broken cabinet door above our smooth-top range. No big deal. I didn't think twice—of course he could handle it."

She rolled her eyes, chuckling. "Well... turns out I gave him a little too much credit that day. I mean, most people would think, 'Hey, if you're gonna work on something *above* the range, maybe move the range and grab a step stool,' right?"

Andi tilted her head, playing along. "Yeah, that seems like basic logic."

"Right?" Alex laughed. "But nope—not Walker. That man actually decided to *use the range.* Like, full-on climbed up and used it as his ladder. I swear his brain must've been on vacation that day."

Andi's mouth dropped open with a smile of shocked amusement. "No, he didn't!"

"Oh yeah," Alex said, nodding with wide eyes. "He put his knee right on the smooth cooktop of my range and hoisted his whole frickin' body weight up there to reach the cabinet. And then—*crunch!* Cracked the whole thing like a damn tortilla chip. His knee went straight through it."

Andi slapped a hand over her mouth, eyes lighting up. "Holy shit! I would be so pissed! What did you do? Was he okay?"

Hearing Andi cuss made Alex grin on the inside. They'd kept things pretty buttoned-up and professional until now, so the unfiltered reaction felt like a little breakthrough—like Andi was letting her guard down, even if just a little.

"Yeah, *he* was fine. Just a couple of scratches and a bruised ego. But get this—he gets down and starts acting all pissy— *toward me!* Like *I* made him do it."

Andi let out a laugh. "Oh my God, of course he did. Classic man!"

"Right? I'm standing there like, 'Excuse me, *I* wasn't the one who used a glass cooktop as a step ladder.' But nope, somehow it was my fault for not telling him *not* to do it." Alex shook her head, laughing. "Oh, and the best part: he asked if I'd go find the warranty info so we could call in a claim! I was like, uhm... the warranty doesn't cover stupid, babe!" Alex said with a confident tone. "I swear, sometimes it's like living with a toddler in a grown man's body."

Andi giggled again, and Alex could see the tension in her shoulders ease just a little.

"He was actually mad at *me* for like two days after that!" Alex said, throwing her hands up. "I couldn't believe it. We had to rush out and buy a replacement, which totally delayed listing the house. And to make things worse, we couldn't even find a color match in our price range. Ended up with this ugly coil-top range instead of a smooth-top, and it completely messed up the look of the kitchen."

She shook her head, still amused by the memory. "I swear, I honestly think that stove was part of the reason we didn't get asking price for the house."

Andi laughed, shaking her head. "Men can be so stubborn sometimes. But I guess we love them anyway, huh?"

"Most of the time," Alex said with a small smile, her tone softening.

After a long moment, Alex reached across the desk and gently took Andi's hand in hers, anchoring the silence between them. "I don't know everything you're carrying," she said, voice soft, steady, "but I can feel it. And I just want you to know... I'm here. No pressure. No expectations. Just here. Whether you need to vent, laugh, cry, or say absolutely nothing—I've got you."

Andi blinked rapidly, eyes glassy with unshed tears. For a split second, Alex worried she'd overstepped. But then, Andi's lips lifted in the softest, most genuine smile she'd seen from her yet.

"Thank you," Andi whispered, her voice thin but heartfelt. "You have no idea how much that means to me. I... may have to take you up on that."

Alex gave her hand one more reassuring squeeze, lingering just long enough to make it count. "Anytime," she said. And she meant it.

As she headed back to the sales floor, Alex felt something shift—not dramatic, not loud. Just a feeling of certainty pressing against her chest. This wasn't just office banter or temporary camaraderie. It was something deeper: a once-in-a-lifetime friendship taking root.

This connection with Andi— it felt fated, like the universe had nudged them together with a soft, urgent whisper: *You're going to need her.* A connection that doesn't just offer comfort—it resurrects. It reaches past the walls you didn't know you'd built, breathes air into the parts of you that forgot how to breathe. It stitches you together when you've come undone, piece by broken piece.

It's the kind of friendship that catches your soul right before it slips into the dark and refuses to let go. And maybe, just maybe, it's the kind of friendship that saves your life.

FOUR

THE CHARMING ILLUSION

AFTER THE TENSION AND chaos of the previous week, Alex wasn't sure what to expect when she walked into work Monday morning. She half-expected half the employees to have just quit—vanished without a word, too fed up to show their faces again. Or, at the very least, for the air to still feel heavy, like leftover fog after a storm. But instead, The Outpost felt—different. Brighter, somehow. Lighter. The usual Monday morning groans had been replaced with chatter and energy. Even Jason—who usually ran the shop side of things and handled most of the service scheduling—shuffled in, clutching his coffee like a lifeline, but was cracking jokes as he and Frank, scribbled out the day's service game plan.

Jason and Frank had been there longer than anyone else—seen the worst Damon had to offer. Jason, in particular, had hit a breaking point a couple of years back. He'd quit without notice, leaving the whole dealership scrambling. It had been devastating, especially for Andi, who had to bear the brunt of angry customers and Damon's tantrums over service delays. She never said it outright, but the stress nearly broke her. Damon, of course, blamed her entirely.

Frank had tried to step up during that time, doing what he could to keep things afloat, but the truth was, Jason's technical knowledge was unmatched. Frank could handle basics, but he wasn't equipped to manage the entire service department—and Damon didn't lift a finger to help. No extra training. No pay raise. No backup. Just demands and criticism. Frank still held resentment over that.

Eventually, Damon had to suck up his pride and beg Jason to come back—offering more money and perks to convince him. Jason returned, mostly for his family's financial needs, but also because deep down, he liked the work and liked his coworkers. Even if it meant putting up with Damon and the ever-crumbling walls of The Outpost.

Today, though, you wouldn't know any of that. The guys were all smiles, trading smart-ass remarks and knocking out their morning tasks with surprising energy. For now, everything felt... almost normal.

Alex didn't understand why things seemed so good. Everyone was so upbeat, almost buzzing. She kept waiting for the other shoe to drop—until just before lunch, when the reason made itself known.

"Big announcement," Andi said, practically bouncing as she leaned over Alex's desk. Her grin was wide, her eyes sparkling with a rare kind of excitement. "Damon's throwing an employee party this weekend. He gave me the okay to rent out this gorgeous VRBO just outside of town. He's having it catered and everything."

Alex blinked. "Wait—Damon wants to do this?"

Andi laughed. "I know. Shocking, right? But he can be... generous when the mood strikes." There was something else behind her smile. A flicker of something harder to define, tucked beneath the surface. But Alex didn't poke at it. Not today.

"Well," Alex said with a crooked smile, "I can't say no to a party! I'll get a sitter!"

Andi looked genuinely thrilled. She seemed lighter than Alex had ever seen her—unburdened, at least for a moment. "It's going to be amazing. You'll love this house—it's got a massive rec room with all these old-school arcade games, a Skee-Ball machine, a huge wraparound bar, pool tables, dart boards, and bunk rooms for anyone who has too much fun to drive home. Damon said he wanted to go all out."

From that moment on, the vibe inside The Outpost shifted completely. The tension from last week seemed to dissolve into thin air. It wasn't just excitement—it was relief. Like everyone had been holding their breath, and now they could finally exhale.

Tasks got done faster. Customers were greeted with extra enthusiasm. Even the warehouse crew, usually heads-down and grumbling, were smiling and cracking jokes. The showroom had a bounce to it, like someone had pumped fresh oxygen into the building. It was more than a party—it was something to look forward to. A reset.

The week flew by with everyone amped for the upcoming party. Jason and Frank were acting like teenagers on the last day of school—louder than usual, cracking up at their own inside jokes, and drinking sodas like they were spiked with weekend mischief. Their banter bounced off the walls, peppered with exaggerated impersonations of Damon's latest rant about professionalism.

They took their antics to a desk in the corner of the office, like it was a pool table at some dive bar, each holding out imaginary cues and narrating their shots in ridiculous, over-the-top Damon voices.

"Gentlemen," Jason said, puffing out his chest and squaring his stance like he was about to deliver a TED Talk on cue ball strategy. "You'll never get ahead in life if you're behind the eight ball."

Frank looked around, then grabbed a trailer hitch off the desk and held it up like it was the actual eight ball. "Wise words from our fearless leader," he said, nodding seriously. "Position is everything." He placed it carefully in front of him on the desk.

"Careful, Tiny," Jason snorted, chalking the end of his pretend stick. "If you miss this shot, Boss man'll have you reorganizing the entire parts department with nothing but a headlamp and regret."

Frank squinted, lined up a very dramatic fake shot, chanting under his breath like a man psyching himself up for greatness. "I will be in front of the eight ball... I *will* be in front of the eight ball..."

He took the shot—with flair, with confidence—and missed entirely.

He froze, let out a long, exaggerated sigh, then threw his hands in the air and collapsed against the wall like a man who'd just lost everything in Vegas.

"I'm *still* behind the eight ball, Bouncer! I'm *doomed!*"

The room cracked up. Even Eddy—peeked around from her desk, trying to keep a straight face but losing the battle. Her mouth twitched, and a tiny snort gave her away.

Alex, Andi, and the newest part-time addition, Rebecca, missed the spectacle, though they could hear the laughter echoing from the front office. They were out on the sales floor, each in their groove. Alex was helping a couple who were torn between two different camper models, walking them through pros and cons with that warm, approachable energy she had a knack for. A few rows down, Andi was walking Rebecca through a crash course in camper education—explaining the difference between fifth wheels, toy haulers, teardrop trailers, and all the confusing little quirks that came with them.

Rebecca listened intently, nodding along as Andi spoke, occasionally asking thoughtful questions and making notes in her little spiral notebook. She wasn't learning—she was absorbing. Fitting in.

Even in her first couple weeks, Rebecca had become one of them. She was a little shy at first, but her sweetness and sincerity drew people in quickly. She was the type you just knew was trustworthy. And once she relaxed, her sense of humor came out too.

She and her husband Theo were known around town—a fun, unexpected pair that somehow worked perfectly. He was the louder one, ex-military turned five-star chef, with a big laugh and an even bigger personality. Known for his over-the-top Hawaiian shirts and easy charm, Theo could hold court anywhere he went. Rebecca balanced him flawlessly—quieter, more reserved, but every bit as sharp and genuine. Together, they made an impression.

Andi liked Rebecca—respected her, really. She had a steady presence and a good heart. But it wasn't quite the same magnetic connection she felt building with Alex. Still, she was grateful Rebecca was part of the team. She brought a lot to the table.

Alex, meanwhile, hit it off with Rebecca almost immediately. Within a few conversations, they realized they had an absurd amount in common—three kids, gardening, natural remedies, food label conspiracies, a love of animals, and the exact same goofy sense of TikTok humor. More than once already, their lunches turned into full-blown laugh-fests, the kind where you nearly choke on your sandwich because the meme you're showing is just *that* dumb and *that* perfect.

It was nice having Rebecca around. She balanced things out. She had this calming way about her, like nothing rattled her too easily. It made everything feel more relaxed.

The three of them together just... worked.

It was Saturday, and as Alex and Walker pulled up to the VRBO house, Alex had to glance at her phone again to be sure they were in the right spot. The place was *huge*—tucked just outside of town, surrounded by trees, with warm porch lights twinkling across the railing like something straight out of Pinterest. Music was already thumping from inside.

And once they stepped in? Yeah—*wow*.

The smell hit first—smoked meats, roasted vegetables, fresh-baked rolls—the kind of scent that made your stomach growl in anticipation. To the right, a full wraparound bar was fully stocked and manned by some college-age guy in a crisp button-up who looked like he'd taken a blood oath to serve the perfect cocktail. To the left, the house opened into a massive rec room that looked like Chuck E. Cheese met a cool mountain lodge. There were pool tables, a whole wall of old-school arcade games, a Skee-Ball machine already spewing tickets, and dartboards—where Cora was currently trying to teach Rebecca how to throw without "accidentally stabbing someone."

People were already in full party mode. Drinks were flowing, laughter echoed from every corner, and the playlist was *chef's kiss*—pure 80s and 90s gold. Theo stood out like a human highlighter in his usual party uniform: a blinding blue-and-purple Hawaiian shirt covered in cats wrapped in tacos. He, Eddy, and her husband Steve had claimed DJ duty on the Alexa and were absolutely *killin' it*—belting lyrics, dancing like nobody was watching, and pumping up the crowd like it was their own private concert. And ya know, for a short, round woman in her late sixties, Eddy had *moves!* She was tearing up the living room like she'd been waiting all week for this exact moment. Spinning, laughing, completely in her element—her energy was infectious. You couldn't *not* smile watching her. It was the perfect start to the night.

Alex spotted Jason and Frank near the bar. Jason was wearing a ridiculous neon green shirt with pineapples on it—undoubtedly borrowed from Theo's collection. Alex grinned and hollered, "Hey look, it's Tiny Bouncer!"

The guys turned toward her with matching grins and exaggerated waves, already halfway to trouble. Frank held up two shot glasses like they were sacred relics and wiggled his brows. "Alright, girl—we're kicking things off right. You in?"

Alex raised an eyebrow, but her smirk gave her away. "Please," she said, snatching one of the glasses. "Tonight's milk: not FDA approved!" she added, laughing as she lifted it—because yes, she was still breastfeeding the twins, and yes, that meant she'd be pumping and dumping it later like a responsible party mom.

Walker hovered behind her, offering a polite hand wave of decline. Shots weren't his thing—but watching Alex cut loose? *Definitely* his thing.

They clinked glasses with dramatic flair, and Frank grinned like he was about to deliver a sermon. "I only drink on two occasions—when I'm thirsty and when I'm not."

Jason raised his shot high. "To taking hits—and hitting back harder!"

They tossed the vodka back, slammed their glasses on the nearest table, and threw their hands in the air like they'd just won the championship.

"I'm having so much fun!" Frank and Alex shouted at the same time, already cracking up before the burn even hit their throats.

Andi, true to form, was making her rounds like a woman on a mission—checking drinks, straightening snack trays, refilling coolers, gathering empty cups, and laughing with guests like she'd been hosting events her whole life.

She wanted everything to be perfect. *Needed* it to be. But more than anything, she wanted to relax. To have fun. Even if just for one night.

No matter how many people she stopped to chat with or how many rooms she wandered through, her eyes kept drifting back to Alex. It was subtle. Maybe no one else noticed. But Alex did.

At work, Alex and Andi kept things professional—especially with Damon always hovering—but nights like this gave their friendship room to breathe. And it had become exactly that: a *real* friendship. The kind that sneaks up on you and feels like it's always been there.

Alex wasn't used to being the one people leaned toward. She did great professionally, but close relationships? Those were harder. She constantly lived in her own head, always judging and second-guessing herself.

People often misread that as her judging *them*, which couldn't be further from the truth. She loved making people feel good. So she'd try too hard, overcompensate—and end up coming off as fake, even when her heart was in the right place.

But these people—these wonderful people—were different. Effortless. And Andi? She saw Alex for everything she *was*, and everything she was trying to be—and leaned in. Alex loved that. With Andi, she didn't have to be "on." She didn't overthink or second-guess herself. No pressure. Just... ease. When they were around each other, there was this subtle kind of safety—like they'd both been holding their breath for years and finally found someone they could exhale with.

Meanwhile, Damon was holding court in the corner of the main room, laughing loudly, retelling exaggerated stories, and handing out drinks like he'd been voted prom king. Alex was surprised by how people were responding to him—smiling, engaging, even enjoying his company. For the first time since she met him, Damon actually seemed... fun.

But as the evening went on, she also noticed something else. He was keeping an eye on Andi. Not in an overly obvious way, but he found his way to her side more than once—murmuring something in her ear, his hand ghosting the small of her back.

Alex wasn't trying to listen in, but one exchange slipped through the noise. She caught sight of Damon reaching for Andi's arm—nothing rough, but firm enough to draw her closer. He said something Alex couldn't quite catch, his mouth too close to her.

"I'm fine," Andi said softly, offering a small, half smile as she tried to turn away.

Damon pulled back just enough to study her face, his hand sliding beneath her chin, guiding it until her eyes met his. His tone shifted—controlled and clipped. "Two drinks. That's it. I don't want you embarrassing me."

Andi nodded, her expression polite but distant. She tried to look away for a moment, and Alex caught the flicker in her eyes—silent rebellion flashing before she turned back to him.

Damon lingered a beat longer, his voice low enough that Alex couldn't quite hear him—only catch the shape of his words as his lips moved. "And take your medicine tonight—like the doctor said."

Andi had mentioned some heart issues, and a few weird sleep and memory things she'd played off like it was nothing. But Alex could tell it wasn't nothing. It seemed to scared Andi—you could see it in the way she tried to act like it didn't. Little things she said didn't quite line up. And Alex couldn't shake the feeling that there was more going on than Andi was letting on.

Andi had been making her rounds for a while, but now she seemed content to settle in with Alex, Walker, Rebecca, and Theo. The five of them had clustered near the edge of the game room, trading jokes, stories, and laughter. Alex and Andi sat shoulder to shoulder, leaning into each other like they were attached.

It didn't go unnoticed.

Damon, across the room, sipped his whiskey and watched. Something in his jaw ticked as he saw Andi fully in it—more relaxed and light than he'd seen her in a long time. Laughing without hesitation, high-fiving Walker after a joke, raising her glass in an easy cheers with the group. Then she leaned in, gently grabbing Alex's hand as she smiled—soft, unguarded, like being there, in that moment, was exactly where she wanted to be.

Damon's eyes narrowed.

Out of nowhere, he jumped up and clapped his hands—loud enough to slice through the music and chatter, grabbing the attention of half the room. "Who's up for darts?"

It was casual, playful. But there was an edge beneath it—one only a few people caught.

Rebecca laughed. "Oh, no thanks. I'll poke someone's eye out."

Cora held up her hands. "Same. I'm good just watching. I got my round in earlier."

In the end, teams fell into place: Theo and Frank, Alex and Walker, Andi and Damon, and Jason paired up with Eddy's husband, Steve. The rest of the group—Rebecca, Cora, Eddy, a few other employees, and Meryl—Andi and Damon's 16-year-old daughter, who had stopped by with a friend—gathered around a nearby table. They made a lively cheering section, hooting over good shots and throwing in playful boos whenever someone missed.

The game started off light and easy. Laughter was constant, the mood relaxed. Everyone clapped for great shots, no matter whose team made them. When Andi nailed one right on target, Alex and Walker high-fived her, grinning.

"Nice one!" they called out in unison.

That didn't sit well with Damon. He played it cool at first, but Walker was getting on his nerves fast.

Walker was a machine—three perfect shots in a row, clean and calm like he'd done it a thousand times. The group was eating it up. So was Andi.

She was jumping, laughing, and clapping when Walker—or anyone, really—nailed a great shot. Her excitement was genuine—effortless—but all Damon saw was the way she bounced on her toes and the way her chest moved when she did it. In his mind, it wasn't innocent. He didn't see her joy. He saw a performance—for Walker's attention. Which couldn't have been further from the truth.

Then came the final round. All eyes were on Walker. He needed just one more to lock in the win for him and Alex. He let the dart fly.

Bullseye.

But before the group could cheer, the air was sucked from the room—so sudden and sharp it felt like a slap.

Damon spun on his heel like something had snapped inside him. He slammed his glass down on the nearest surface with a sharp *crack* that cut through the room.

"I'm done," he said—flat, cold, final.

Andi blinked. "What? What are you—"

"Cleanup time," he barked, storming toward the bar sink. He snatched up a stack of plates and hurled them into the basin. One shattered, the sound loud and jarring.

The entire room froze. Laughter died. Conversations stopped mid-sentence. Everyone exchanged a look—quiet, uneasy. They'd seen *this* side of Damon before. And they knew exactly what came next.

Frank leaned in and muttered under his breath, "That's our cue."

And just like that, the party was over. People grabbed their coats, murmuring thanks to Andi, avoiding Damon entirely. A few who had planned to stay in the bunk rooms quickly abandoned that idea.

Andi tried to apologize, her voice quiet but urgent. "I'm so sorry. I don't know what—"

"No worries, honey," Eddy said, offering her a soft smile. "It was a great night. Really."

Everyone echoed the sentiment, offering hugs, handshakes, and polite goodbyes.

Andi stood near the door, trying to smile, trying to salvage what was left.

As people began to file out, Andi caught Alex's eye. Her expression faltered. Tears shimmered at the corners of her eyes as she mouthed, *I'm sorry.*

Alex stepped forward, gently taking Andi's face in her hands and bringing their foreheads together in a quiet, grounding gesture.

"It's okay," she said softly. "We had a great time. This was amazing—and *you* are amazing. Don't forget that. I'll see you Monday."

Andi nodded, swallowing hard. She stood there in the doorway, bathed in the soft glow from the porch lights, watching Alex, Walker, and the others disappear into the night.

Even Meryl, who had planned to stay longer with her friend, stepped reluctantly to her mother's side. "I think I'm gonna head back to Taylor's," she said. "I already said goodnight to Dad."

Andi's voice was soft and aching. "You don't have to go. I'll fix it—I'll go apologize, it'll be okay, I can make it—"

Meryl stopped her with just a look. "Mom... don't you *dare* apologize. You didn't do anything wrong."

Andi blinked fast, brushing Meryl's hair behind her ear like she had when she was little. Her hand lingered for a moment longer than necessary. "Okay, baby. Text me when you get there."

"I will. Love you."

"Love you, too."

Andi watched her daughter go, the dread already curling in her stomach.

The house was quiet again.

She stood there, wrapped in a silent dread—and a sudden, crushing loneliness she couldn't outrun.

Five

Behind the Looking Glass

Monday morning, the dealership was quiet.

Too quiet.

Alex unlocked the front door like usual, flipping the lights on as she moved through the still, echoing showroom. The coffee pot was empty. No scent of perfume. No Andi humming along to her morning playlist.

She checked the time: 8:02 a.m. It wasn't like Andi to be late without saying something. Alex pulled out her phone and shot her a quick message:

> Hey lady, everything okay? You coming in today?

She waited, keeping herself busy—turning on the computers, getting the coffee going, restocking the brochure rack.

Still no reply.

Then her phone buzzed. But it wasn't Andi.

Damon:

> She's sick. In bed. Won't be in today. Maybe not tomorrow either. I told her to stay put.

There was no "good morning." No pleasantries. Just... cold facts.

Before Alex could type a response, another message popped through.

Damon:

> Hold down the fort for her. Handle what needs handling.

No please. No thank you. Just a command.

Alex stared at the screen for a beat, that uncomfortable flutter in her stomach growing stronger. She typed back:

> Sure. Hope she feels better soon.

No reply came.

She sighed, setting the phone down. Rebecca arrived a few minutes later, giving her a sympathetic smile when Alex explained the situation.

"I'll take the front desk for now," Alex told her. "If I need help juggling stuff, I'll holler."

But something felt off. This wasn't like Andi. No matter how sick she was—migraine, flu, stomach bug—Andi would be the one to text. Even if it was short. Even if it was just a "Hey, not feeling great today. I'll miss ya!" That was her. The only reason she wouldn't... was if she *couldn't.*

Alex pushed the thought aside—for now—but her gut was already whispering what her heart didn't want to admit. Something was very, very wrong.

No word from Andi that day. Or Tuesday.

But Wednesday morning, when Alex walked in with a fresh coffee and cinnamon roll in hand, Andi was there.

Only... it *wasn't* her.

Andi stood near the service desk, arms crossed over her chest, wrapped in a shapeless oatmeal-colored sweater that practically swallowed her. Her hair was tied back in a lazy knot, and her eyes looked heavy—like she hadn't slept in days.

"Hey...glad you're back." Alex stepped closer, voice strained with concern despite her effort to sound casual. "I brought you something."

Andi gave a small smile but didn't reach for the coffee. "Thanks," she said, her voice hoarse. "You didn't have to."

"Just happy to see you," Alex said. "I was starting to think you ran off to Mexico without me."

That earned a tiny breath of a laugh, but it didn't reach her eyes.

"Damon said you were really sick?"

Andi looked away. "I was. Still kinda am."

Alex hesitated, watching her fidget with the hem of her sleeve. She was *always* animated—talkative, expressive, warm. This was... off.

When the rest of the crew rolled in, Andi went through the motions—smiling politely, avoiding long conversations.

She barely reacted when Frank cracked a joke about his wife threatening to trade him in for a bulldog and shoot the bulldog. Even Jason's impersonation of a TacoCat-clad Theo didn't get more than a ghost of a grin.

The rest of the week slid by in a blur of small talk and unease. Andi stayed behind the front desk like a shadow, speaking only when she had to, flinching whenever her phone buzzed.

Then, Friday afternoon, Damon came strolling in and announced to everyone like he was doing them a favor.

"Packin' up tonight. Headed to Des Moines tomorrow for the RV expo. Back on Wednesday." He slapped the back of Jason's chair like they were frat buddies.

"Gotta see the new Winnebagos. Maybe I'll buy you one if you keep schmoozing the customers like that."

Jason smirked but didn't respond.

Andi didn't even blink. But Alex saw it—the tiny exhale of relief.

Later that night, Alex sent a text to Andi:

We need to hang out. I miss you. Come for dinner tomorrow? Walker's grilling. Gotta introduce you to our favorite game! You can help me kick his ass. You in?

The reply came back almost instantly.

He's leaving first thing. I'll be there.

It had been a week since the VRBO party—one that had started light and fun but ended with tension no one could quite put into words.

And still, no one really knew why Andi had missed work on Monday and Tuesday. She hadn't offered much, and the only thing anyone had heard—passed down vaguely through Damon—was that *"she hadn't been feeling well."* But what did that even mean? She'd come back midweek quieter than usual, moving through the days with a forced smile and tired eyes. She'd hardly spoken unless spoken to. No one knew what to make of it. Alex hadn't pushed—not yet. But her gut had been whispering all week.

So when Saturday night rolled around, it felt like a reset button—a chance to exhale and maybe see a glimpse of the old Andi again.

She arrived just before six, dressed in dark jeans and a stylish scarf loosely wrapped around her neck. Her hair was down, soft and clean, and her makeup was minimal—just enough to bring out the sparkle in her blue eyes. For the first time in days, she looked like *herself.*

Alex met her at the door and pulled her into a hug. "There she is."

Andi stepped in, her smile shy but genuine. She let out a soft sigh, kicked off her shoes, and glanced around. "I needed this."

Alex took her hand and led her into the kitchen, grabbing a couple of hard seltzers from the fridge. "Cranberry or mango?"

"Definitely cranberry," Andi said, snatching it with a grin.

Alex handed it over, her smile stretching wide. "I'm so glad you are here! I've missed you."

Andi cracked open the can and gave a wistful laugh. "Yeah... I've missed me too."

Walker came in from the back deck, still holding a pair of tongs and grinning. "Hey! It's the woman of the hour! You showed up at the right time. I'm making my *famous* grilled chicken."

"*Famous*?" Alex teased. "That's interesting because Harper and I have heard exactly zero rumors about it."

"That's because I'm humble," he shot back with a wink.

Andi turned to Walker with a warm smile. "Well, humble or not, it smells freaking *amazing*. I haven't eaten all day, so I'm seriously excited for this."

Harper, seated at the kitchen table coloring, chimed in without missing a beat. "He burns stuff sometimes," she said, pointing to the sign in the kitchen that read, *"Many have eaten here, few have died."*

Alex and Andi looked at each other, fighting to contain their giggles.

Dinner was loud and chaotic in the best way. Walker's grilled chicken was a hit—perfectly juicy and full of flavor, and despite his casual shrug, it was obvious he was proud of it. Alex had made her usual roasted potatoes and a simple salad, and Andi had picked up a store-bought cheesecake she apologized for—until Walker polished off two slices and called her a hero.

They laughed and lingered in the kitchen, cleaning up after dinner, picking at the last bites of food, sipping drinks, and reminiscing about the VRBO party—carefully skipping over how it ended. Like if they didn't say it out loud, it didn't happen.

"Oh my God," Andi said, half-laughing, half-choking on a sip of her White Claw. "Theo's taco cat shirt? I couldn't even look at him without losing it."

Alex grinned. "Seriously. That shirt needs its own Instagram account."

"I heard he has more than one of those shirts," Walker said, setting a stack of plates near the sink. "Like... taco pig, taco cow, even a taco emu wearing sunglasses."

Andi snorted, laughing. "Wait—he has a *collection*?"

Alex, still giggling, raised an eyebrow. "Who the hell makes those? Like... where do you *buy* something like that?"

Walker shrugged as he wiped down the counter. "Internet's a weird place, babe. You can probably buy a damn taco sloth riding a motorcycle if you look hard enough."

As the night went on, the fun only grew. They laughed until their stomachs hurt, watched a 2004 live performance of *"In the Air Tonight"*—Phil Collins behind the drums like an absolute legend—and played a few ridiculous rounds of Song Quiz on Alexa. It was one of Alex and Walker's go-to games—something they played often that almost always turned into a full-blown competition. Walker was usually the one dominating—and definitely not shy about it—but tonight... he was losing more than he'd ever admit. Andi, calm and casual, quickly proved herself to be a low-key music trivia assassin.

Later that evening, while Alex and Walker took turns settling the twins, Andi stayed back to help with Harper. There was something comforting about the quiet routine of it—brushing teeth, pajamas, the familiar dance of winding down. Harper handed Andi a worn copy of *Where the Wild Things Are* and climbed into bed without hesitation, scooting over and patting the spot beside her.

"Will you do the voices like Mommy does?"

Andi smiled softly as she sat down. "I can try."

She opened the book, falling into the rhythm of it without overthinking. Her voice shifted for each line, adding little inflections and quirks. Harper nestled in close, her head resting against Andi's shoulder as her eyelids grew heavy. By the time Andi closed the back cover, Harper was asleep. Completely still, completely safe.

Alex stood just outside the door, leaning against the frame. "She adores you," she said with a soft smile.

Andi glanced down at the small body curled into her side, brushing a piece of hair away from Harper's face. "She's so sweet," she whispered. "So trusting."

Alex stepped into the room. "Kids know good people. They always do."

There was a beat of silence, and then Andi nodded, just once.

They left the room together, pulling the door until it caught but didn't latch. The house had settled into a rare, peaceful stillness. In the living room, Alex handed Andi a soft throw blanket and sat beside her on the couch. The lights were low. Walker was still in with Corbin, who was stubbornly fighting sleep.

Andi pulled the blanket across her lap, twisting a corner of it between her fingers. Her eyes shimmered in the dim light, and her smile trembled like it couldn't quite hold itself together.

"This night..." she began, then stopped, trying again. "I didn't realize how much I needed this. To be somewhere... happy."

She trailed off, swallowing hard, her eyes dropping to her lap. The silence between them was heavy but not uncomfortable.

Alex reached over and took Andi's hand, grounding her with a quiet kind of steadiness.

Andi drew in a slow, shaky breath. "Being here... with you guys—it's the first time in a long time I've felt like I can actually breathe. Like I can just be... *me.*" She paused, her throat tightening. "Most days, I feel like I'm walking on eggshells—even in my own skin." Her shoulders gave a slight shiver, like she was trying to physically shake the feeling off, but it clung to her anyway. She let out a shaky breath, her smile holding by a thread. "I mean... to laugh. To sit still. To not feel like..." She hesitated, her eyes dropping to the blanket in her lap, her fingers twisting the edge as she blinked back tears. "... like someone's mad at me. Like I screwed something up and I don't even know what." She gave a small, helpless shrug. "I walk around all damn day wondering what the hell I did wrong."

Alex gave Andi's hand a gentle squeeze. "Listen to me. You are one of the most loyal, hardworking, beautiful people I've ever known—inside and out. And it's not just me. Everyone sees it." She paused, letting the words settle. "If anyone deserves to be happy... *you* do. Without apology." Alex didn't look away. Her voice was steady, her eyes full of quiet knowing. "I can feel it, Andi. Something's not right. I've seen enough to know the difference between love and control. I'm here. You can talk to me." She leaned in, her voice just above a whisper now. "What's really going on with you and Damon? What happened after the VRBO party?"

Andi pulled her hand away like it burned, her head turning as her shoulders started to shake. The tears came fast, silent at first. "I can't..." she choked out. "You won't believe... You won't see me the same..." Her voice cracked. "I can't lose you."

Alex didn't hesitate. She reached out and cupped Andi's face, her hands steady but gentle, guiding her to look up.

"Hey," she said softly, but with quiet force. "Look at me. You're not going to lose me," Alex said, her eyes locked on Andi's. "I'm here. And I'm *not* going anywhere."

Six

The Wicked Reflection

The silence between them was louder than any scream. It was the kind of silence that exists only after everything has cracked wide open, with the truth hanging in the air like smoke after a fire.

No more laughter. No more baby squeals. Just the faint sound of music still playing in the background. A slow, aching song drifted through the room—chillingly fitting for the moment. When Alex caught the lyrics, she blinked, the weight of it hitting her. Of course that song would be playing now, she thought. It was too perfect—sad and heavy in all the right places, like it already knew what was about to be said.

Andi was curled up in the far corner of the couch, her knees drawn to her chest, a blanket wrapped tightly around her like it might be the only thing holding her together. Her face was blotchy and tear-streaked, and her eyes wouldn't meet Alex's. She stared past her, through her, into something dark and distant—a whirlwind of memories she'd kept locked away for far too long.

Alex sat quietly beside her, not too close. She didn't reach out or press. She just waited, her heart pounding in anticipation, dreading what might be said, knowing instinctively it would change everything.

When Andi's voice came, it was hoarse and hollow. "So... after the party that night... after everyone left..."

Alex nodded slowly, her heart tightening in her chest. "Yeah."

Andi paused, pressing her lips together. She blinked once, slow and deliberate. "Damon told me I embarrassed him... that I humiliated him in front of everyone."

Alex's brows furrowed. "What? Why?"

Andi's chin quivered, but she forced the words out as if she had rehearsed them a thousand times in her head and still couldn't believe them. "He said I was flirting with Walker. That I was acting like some desperate little whore."

She swallowed hard. "He looked at me like I was disgusting."

Alex's stomach dropped. Her voice cracked before she could stop it. "What? You weren't flirting. That's insane."

"He said I betrayed him and that I didn't deserve to be there with him. That I should go sleep in the dirt where I belonged," Andi said, her voice beginning to shake. "Then he grabbed me by my hair and shoved me out the front door like I was nothing."

She closed her eyes, wincing at the memory. "He didn't even let me grab my purse. Just shoved my car key and phone into my hand and told me to get the hell out of his sight."

"Andi..." Alex exhaled in disbelief as her hand flew to her mouth.

"I didn't have my house keys," Andi continued, her tone hollow, a desolate look in her eyes, as if she were reliving the moment. "I couldn't go home. So I just drove around and cried. I didn't know where to go or who to call. I pulled over by the river, just trying to breathe. I thought maybe if I could calm down, I'd be able to sleep for a bit." She stopped herself, her voice suddenly rising, laced with panic and rage. "But I can't fucking sleep! Not by myself... because of this goddamn sleepwalking! It's getting worse, and it's not just weird anymore—it's completely freaking me out!" Her hands clenched the blanket. "I was terrified I'd wander off in the dark and fall into the river or walk straight into traffic. Like, I'd die out there, and nobody would even know until it was too late."

Her eyes went vacant, fixed straight ahead as if she were still there by the river—frozen in that moment, detached from the story she was telling.

She wiped at her face. "So, I sat there for hours, staring at the water, trying to breathe... trying to stay awake because I don't trust myself to fall asleep."

"It was almost three in the morning when he called me," Andi said, her voice growing smaller. "He sounded calm. Like nothing had happened. He told me he hoped I'd learned my lesson—that I could come back if I apologized."

Alex shook her head, bracing herself against the words she knew were coming. "No. No, Andi..."

"So I apologized," she whispered. "Because I needed to go back. When I got there, I tried to explain myself, told him I wasn't flirting...That I'd never do that. But it made him angrier. He said I was gaslighting him, manipulating the situation, and that I was refusing to admit what I'd done."

Walker had just come back into the room after settling Corbin. He paused in the doorway, immediately sensing that something was wrong. The air felt heavy, charged with unspoken tension. He didn't say a word—just stood still, watching from the shadows as the moment unfolded.

Andi's voice began to tremble, tears streaming down her cheeks as she stared into the distance. "He wouldn't even look at me at first. Just sat there, sipping his brandy like it was any other night—like he was waiting for me to walk into a trap. Then, out of nowhere, he exploded. He stood up, came straight at me, and wrapped his hand around my throat. He slammed me into the wall so hard I... I couldn't breathe—I thought he was gonna kill me."

Alex gasped, reaching out to hold Andi's hand. Her grip was firm, grounding.

"He dragged me into the kitchen. His fingers were so tight around my throat, like a clamp—I couldn't speak, couldn't scream. I saw his eyes look toward the knives on the counter, and I swear... I truly thought that was it. That I was going to die in that kitchen."

Her breath trembled, her voice cracking under the weight of memory.

"He threw me against the counter so hard—my hip hit—I thought I broke something. He ripped my clothes off. Just tore them."

Andi's face twisted, confusion and sadness flickering in her eyes. "And he had this look on his face... like... I don't know. His eyes were just... dark. He was crazy. He raped me. He slammed into me like he hated me. Like I was something he needed to break. He kept calling me names... horrible names. Telling me I belonged to him. That I needed to learn a lesson. That I ruined his night and *made* him do it."

Tears streamed relentlessly down Alex's face, her body locked in stillness as her fingers clung tightly to Andi's.

Walker hadn't moved. His body was rigid, fists clenched, the veins in his neck and arms bulging from restraint. He looked like a man holding back the urge to explode.

Andi's voice dropped to a haunted whisper. "He grabbed a beer bottle. Empty. Cracked along the side." Her eyes darted away, as if the words themselves burned to say aloud. Shame flickered across her face—raw, unspoken. "I begged him not to. I begged... Alex, I begged him," she sobbed, struggling to form the words. "But he didn't care. He rammed it inside me. The pain—God, the pain was..." She shook violently now. "The suction—it felt like it was ripping me apart from the inside. And the crack on the bottle... it kept cutting me every time he moved it. I was bleeding so badly, Alex. I thought I was going to pass out."

Alex pressed her hand to her mouth, her face pale, her whole body shaking with rage.

Walker stepped forward, fists still clenched. His voice was a low, seething growl. "He's a fucking monster."

Andi flinched, her eyes darting to him in fear and shame, as if she were the one who'd done something wrong. "Oh my god... I'm sorry. I shouldn't be—"

"No," Walker said, falling to one knee in front of her, his voice low but firm. "You *should* be telling us. Don't you dare apologize for this. *He* did this. Not you. None of this is on you."

Andi tried to nod, her breath ragged, her eyes distant. "When he was done, he just stood over me like he was proud of what he'd done. Then he walked out. A few minutes later, he came back with a towel, a glass of water, and my pills. He put them beside me on the floor, looked down at me like I was dirt, and said, 'Clean yourself up. Don't forget to take your meds.' Like nothing had happened."

Alex sat frozen, trying to make sense of everything she'd heard. Her nerves on fire, her stomach in knots. Then she asked a question she knew she needed to ask—but also knew she wasn't ready to hear the answer.

"Andi... has he ever... done anything like that before?"

Andi hesitated. Her eyes flicked away, and for a long moment, she didn't answer.

Finally, she nodded. "Yes."

Alex's stomach clenched. She felt like she was about to vomit. But she stayed quiet.

Walker and Alex listened as Andi continued to reveal things that sounded straight out of a nightmare. She spoke about the time Damon slapped her across the face so hard that she couldn't hear out of one ear for days. About the time he kicked in the bathroom door while she was hiding and held her against the wall with a knife to her throat. About how he once shoved her into the bathtub and held her head under the water until she passed out.

Alex felt paralyzed but forced herself to breathe. The cruelty of it twisted in her gut—how could someone do that to the woman they claimed to love? How could he be so deliberate, so vicious, and, even more disturbingly, do that to someone who was clearly unraveling right in front of him? Someone sick. Someone vulnerable.

Alex didn't understand it, but something deep inside her screamed that there was a connection between his violence and Andi's failing body. She didn't know how or why, but it wasn't just coincidence. She needed answers. She needed to understand what exactly was happening to Andi—what had the doctors said? Why hadn't anyone figured it out?

"I know you've said you haven't been feeling well for a while, and that the doctors can't seem to figure it out," Alex said. "But you've never given me details. I want to understand what's happening... like, what's really going on with that?"

"Yeah," Andi said, her voice raw. Yet there was a strange shift in her tone, almost as if she were trying to convince herself. "These episodes are getting so bad... it's scary. My heart races out of nowhere. I get dizzy—confused." She pressed her palms to her eyes, overwhelmed. "The sleepwalking... it can't be normal sleepwalking. It's like something takes over. I wake up in places I don't remember walking to. Sometimes I have bruises or blood on me, like I fell or ran into something, and I don't even know how the hell it happened."

Her voice trembled, just above a whisper. "One night, I woke up outside. Another time, I was halfway down the basement stairs, barefoot. I could've broken my neck. It's like

I'm living parts of my life I can't remember—like pieces of time go missing."

She let out a shaky breath and looked up, her eyes wide and almost pleading. "But... he's been helping me through all of this. He takes care of everything—schedules the doctors, gets my medications. He keeps track of my episodes and says he's the only one who understands what's happening to me. He says I need him. I know I do. He's caught me before anything really bad could happen. He's stopped me from hurting myself. He's the reason I've made it this far. If he hadn't been there... I honestly think I'd be dead by now."

Alex and Walker exchanged a knowing look, silent but filled with alarm. Alex had just heard the horrific things Damon had done to Andi—and now, somehow, Andi was starting to defend him. She was clinging to the very hands that were breaking her.

Alex's voice dropped, trembling with emotion. "Andi... this is not love. A man who loves you would not hurt you like this. If he was even capable of love, he'd protect you—not terrorize you."

Andi looked down at her hands, her brows drawn together as if she were trying to solve a problem she couldn't understand. Her voice was barely audible. "But he keeps saying he's the only one who sees the truth. That everyone else is just trying to turn me against him. And sometimes... I believe him. I don't know what's real anymore. I feel like I'm losing my mind. Like maybe he's right. Maybe I am the crazy one."

Walker and Alex exchanged glances, their faces tight with heartbreak and helpless rage.

Alex reached out and gently grabbed Andi's arm. "You are NOT crazy," Alex said firmly, her voice filled with emotion. "He's gaslighting you, Andi. That's what narcissists do. He's a manipulative, controlling asshole. I've seen how he treats you at work—everyone has. And now, knowing he's capable of all of this? You are not safe there! Meryl is not safe there!"

Walker stepped forward, his voice urgent. "You can't go back there. You just can't. You can stay here, Andi. We'll figure something out together. You can call a lawyer, get help. There are people—resources—"

"No! Stop!" Andi jumped up, her arms tight across her chest as she backed away a step. Her eyes were wild with panic. "I'm sorry. I didn't mean to make it sound that bad. He's not—he's not that bad! Yes, he got a little rough, but he wasn't going to actually hurt me. I'll talk to him. I'll fix it. It'll be fine."

"Andi," Alex said, standing cautiously, keeping her voice steady. "You don't have to fix anything. This isn't your fault. None of it is."

"Please just stop," Andi said, shaking her head. "You don't understand. If I just talk to him calmly—if I don't push—I can smooth things over. I know how to handle him."

Walker clenched his jaw but kept his voice calm. "And if it happens again? What if you can't talk your way out of it next time? What if he actually kills you, Andi?"

Andi's eyes filled with tears again, and she looked away.

Alex stepped closer. "Just promise us something, okay? That if things start to spiral—if anything feels off or scary—you'll get out. Call us anytime, day or night. We'll come get you, no questions asked."

Walker added, "We're here for you, Andi. You don't deserve any of this. You don't have to deal with it alone."

Andi nodded slowly, tears falling again. "Thank you... for tonight. I'm sorry for all the drama."

Alex shook her head, her voice soft but weighted, each word slow and deliberate. "Don't apologize, Andi. You have done absolutely nothing wrong."

Andi gave a weak smile, pulled her bag over her shoulder, and walked toward the door in a numb haze.

Alex stood in the doorway and watched her disappear into the darkness toward her car. The porch light flickered faintly against the night. The engine started, and the taillights slowly faded down the road.

The moment the sound of the car disappeared, Alex turned around and collapsed into Walker's arms. The tears came fast and uncontrollable.

"I'm so scared for her," she choked out the words into his chest, her voice breaking.

Walker held her tighter. "Me too."

Seven

Reflected in Red

It was Sunday. The kind of late fall day in Montana where the air had a bite to it, even with the sun shining. The trees were mostly bare now, and the breeze carried the smell of distant wood smoke and the soft crunch of dry leaves underfoot. It was the kind of day that asked for flannel layers and hot coffee—a day that made you want to stay busy, if only to keep the chill out—of your skin and your thoughts.

Alex, Walker, and the kids were spending the day at Sheldon and Melena's place, a small slice of quiet tucked on the edge of a gravel road, surrounded by old trees and open sky. It was a place that had always felt safe—warm and lived-in. But today, it was working overtime trying to hold all the emotions inside it.

Upstairs in the shed, Alex and Harper were helping Melena sort and organize what used to be the makeshift loft apartment—the space Alex, Walker, and the kids had lived in for over two months while waiting to close on their home. Now, it was being transformed into something beautiful—Melena's dream crafting studio. The smell of sawdust and fresh paint mingled with the faint scent of cinnamon candles and dried eucalyptus hanging in bunches by the window.

Melena, ever the creator, was completely in her zone. She moved between boxes and shelves with excitement, organizing her supplies and making the space her own. They were hanging pegboards for her tools, stacking bins full of ribbon and glue sticks, and setting up her Cricut machine near neatly labeled drawers filled with vinyl sheets, transfer tape, cutting mats, and weeding tools. A new laser engraver—sleek and compact—sat beneath the window, catching the afternoon light like a crown jewel, polished and perfect, waiting to be put to work.

The twins giggled from their oversized playpen near the back of the room, safe and happy. Harper would run over every now and then to make them laugh, then bounce right back into helping with whatever needed doing. It felt like a little pocket of joy in a day that was otherwise far too heavy.

Downstairs in the workshop, the sound of metal on metal clinked steadily. Walker was helping Sheldon with what could only be described as a labor of love—a full-on restoration of an old 1969 Chevy C20 pickup that had long since seen better days. Sheldon had always dreamed of bringing that truck back to life. It wasn't just about horsepower or looks; it was about something deeper, about building something strong, something that lasted.

He'd started with a beat-up shell and a vision: deep red paint, dropped suspension, drag radials in the back, and skinny street tires up front. The original 350 small block was long gone, replaced with a 383 stroker he was building from the inside out—all new internals, bored out, tuned to scream past 7,000 RPM and push close to 600 horsepower. The bench seat was gone, too, swapped for sleek black leather buckets stitched with red piping. A four-on-the-floor manual would make sure it drove like Sheldon liked it—old-school and unapologetic. The truck looked like something out of a dream, and it had started with a red toy truck that once fit in the palm of his hand. A lifeline, really—one he hadn't let go of even when the world around him had come undone.

Walker and Alex were still reeling from what they'd learned the night before.

Andi had finally cracked open the part of her life she'd kept locked away—the bruised pieces, the late-night panic, the loneliness that no one saw under her smile. She'd cried, not just from the pain of it but from the relief of actually saying some of it out loud. She'd admitted how bad it had gotten—the abuse, the threats, the way Damon could twist her reality until she doubted everything, especially herself. And yet, Alex could tell it was still just the surface, just the beginning. There were years of things Andi hadn't said yet—wounds she wasn't ready to show. The weight of what was still unspoken hung in the air like smoke.

And then there were the medical issues: the confusion, the blackouts, the anxiety, and the heart racing that came and went like shadows. She'd shared how terrifying it was not knowing what was happening to her body.

Alex had exchanged a few texts with her throughout the day—short check-ins, little lifelines. Andi had replied that she was doing okay. Nervous, but okay. Damon had called to say he was staying at the expo until Friday. Some buddies had convinced him to rent motorcycles and hit the road for a few days of "unwinding." He needed a break, he said. A mental reset.

Andi had acted happy in the text. Free. But there was hesitation between her words. She admitted she never knew when one of her episodes might hit. She didn't want Meryl to be alone with her if something happened.

Still, she felt good. Better than she had in days. She hadn't had an episode—no dizziness, no blackouts, no panic. Just a stretch of quiet, steady days. The kind of clarity that felt rare—like sunlight breaking through storm clouds. And the timing—too perfect to ignore.

Alex had jumped at the chance. She'd texted back:

> Let's do something Wednesday night. You, Meryl, and a few of us from work. A cookout at my place—burgers and brats, and some drinks. Grab coats, bring blankets. We'll get a fire going outside. Easy, fun. Just something to look forward to.

Andi had said yes, and even mentioned Meryl could help keep the kids entertained... so the adults could hang out worry free.

Later that afternoon, Alex wandered downstairs and caught Walker near the back of the shop. He was finishing up some wiring while Sheldon worked under the truck nearby.

She leaned in close. "I asked Andi over Wednesday after work. Damon is gonna be gone longer than expected—such a relief. So I figured we'd do a cookout... us and a few others from work. It'll be fun for her."

Walker's eyes lifted. "Good. She needs some normal."

Alex hesitated. "I've been thinking, though. Doesn't it seem strange that all of her health stuff—the heart racing, the sleepwalking, the confusion—it only seems to happen at night? Or on weekends? Never at work?"

Walker frowned. "You're right. That's weird. Yeah, you've never mentioned seeing anything like that at work."

"And now Damon's been gone for a few days, and suddenly she's doing fine?" Alex's voice dropped, shaky. "I don't know, maybe it's nothing. But it's just... odd, right?"

Walker's brow furrowed. "Yeah, it doesn't add up."

Alex hesitated, her voice etched with suspicion. "You don't think he's... doing something to her, do you? Like, maybe drugging her? Something subtle—just enough to mess with her head?"

Walker stiffened, the tension rippling through his shoulders. "I don't want to believe that—but honestly, I wouldn't put it past him. The guy's not just controlling—he's got something seriously wrong with him."

Alex swallowed. "But that doesn't make sense. How would a doctor not know?"

Walker's voice was low but firm. "No clue... but what *is* obvious is that Damon is doing whatever he can to control her. He's building fear in her to break her down. That's what abusers do."

Just a few feet away, Sheldon had stopped moving.

He hadn't meant to listen. But his ears were trained to pick up even the softest whisper when this was the subject. The way their voices shifted when talking about a man who hurt the people who trusted him most. A man who broke down the woman he claimed to love. That tone—he knew it too well. He knew what it meant. His hand loosened on the wrench. His chest felt tight.

He stood slowly, stepping back from the truck and walking toward the far window, needing air, needing space—but mostly needing to keep control of what was rising in him.

Then, a gust of wind hit the side of the shed, and a heavy board that had been leaning against the wall came crashing down. The sound split the quiet with a deep, violent *boom.*

Sheldon flinched hard.

His eyes shot to the window just in time to see two birds take flight, wings slicing through the air.

And in that instant, he wasn't in the shop anymore.

He was three years old.

Then.

Three-year-old Sheldon pressed his forehead to the rippled windowpane of the enclosed front porch, peering through a thin strip where the grime hadn't completely taken over the glass. The wood floor beneath his bare feet was splintered and warped, the boards creaking every time he shifted his weight. Hot air seeped in through a broken screen above him, carrying the distant scent of grass clippings and charcoal from a nearby grill. It mixed with the musty, sour smell of old wood and mildew that lived in the walls of the dilapidated little cottage.

He wasn't supposed to be out here.

Clarence didn't like it. "Keep the blinds shut," he'd bark, again and again, like it was gospel. "Ain't nobody need to know our business."

But today, the porch door hadn't latched all the way. And Sheldon, too young to know better but old enough to feel the difference between safe and afraid, had slipped into the hazy sunlight that cut through the porch windows like golden blades. His tiny fingers clutched a scuffed red plastic truck—the only toy he hadn't lost or had taken away. He held it like it meant something, like it could keep him safe.

Across the street, laughter rang out from the McKays' yard. Bright and free, it rolled on the breeze like music from a faraway world. Kids with grass-stained knees raced through sprinklers, squealing in delight. Mrs. McKay sat on the porch, sipping sweet tea and watching her sweet little Alexandra—barely two, maybe close to three—toddle around the yard, both of them smiling like they had nothing in the world to be afraid of. Sheldon watched them with wide eyes, his chest aching with a longing too big for his tiny body to contain. He didn't know the words for what he felt. He just knew he wanted to be over there. With them. Where the sun didn't burn so hot. Where people smiled without flinching.

The porch door creaked louder as it swung shut behind him, and the sunlight hit Sheldon full-on, lighting up his dark curls and soft cheeks. His little feet hit the hot cement, rough and warm against his soles, and for a moment, he stood perfectly still.

This was what he always watched from behind the window: the light, the air, the sounds of other people being... free. From across the street,

Mrs. McKay looked up. Her smile softened. She gave a small wave—gentle and warm, like she'd been waiting for him to come outside all along. She'd seen Naledi a handful of times—quick hellos when Clarence was at work. Sometimes Sheldon would walk alongside her down to the mailbox, his little hand wrapped around her fingers. Mrs. McKay would walk over to them, carrying banana bread or muffins wrapped in napkins. She never pushed conversation, just stood with a kind presence, smiling wide and sweet, like Naledi was the kind of neighbor she wished she had on both sides.

And she did wish that. Most of the neighbors did.

There was a quiet sorrow that ran through the block—a shared ache that no one spoke aloud. They all knew something was wrong in that little sagging house with the peeling paint and the drawn curtains. But they didn't know how wrong. They hadn't seen the bruises on Naledi's arms or the way her smile disappeared when Clarence's truck turned onto the street. They didn't know how deep the fear ran or how much of her light she had to snuff out to survive. They just knew she didn't come outside much. That the little boy they'd seen chasing dandelions one spring afternoon was rarely allowed out.

Still, when he did appear—on rare days like this—people noticed. Not with judgment. Not with hate. But with a hope that maybe, just maybe, he and his mama were coming out for good this time.

But Clarence... he never saw that. He twisted every look into a slight. Every smile into mockery. Every silent moment into judgment. The wrong kind. In Clarence's mind, the neighborhood treated him like dirt because he'd married outside of his race. Because he'd "fallen too far"—taken up with a Black woman, had a mixed son, and dragged himself to the bottom of some imaginary totem pole he believed everyone measured him by.

But none of that was true. He never understood that the neighbors liked Naledi. They liked her a lot. She was radiant. Regal. Her kindness lingered long after she'd gone. On the rare days she slipped out while Clarence was at work, the neighborhood came alive in quiet, hopeful ways—offering banana bread, folding chairs on porches, and gentle invitations to church picnics and neighborhood get-togethers. They wanted her to stay awhile, to know she was welcome, to see more of her.

And little Sheldon? They adored him. Shy and quiet, always clutching his mother's hand like it was the only thing tethering him to the earth. He was the kind of boy who made people soften when they saw him: polite, soft-spoken, sweet—perfect.

People avoided Clarence because of *who he* was. Yes, the neighborhood hated him. But they didn't hate him because of *who he* loved. They didn't care about skin color. They cared about character. They hated him because he didn't love them—his wife, his son—the way they deserved.

Clarence was a man whose fears were born from his own insecurities, not from the hearts of the people around him. He convinced himself they judged him for all the wrong reasons, never realizing that the only thing people truly disliked was the temper, the bitterness, the darkness he carried everywhere.

He had loved Naledi once—so deeply that it scared him. But instead of honoring that love, he buried it beneath resentment, anger, and regret. Loving her made him feel vulnerable. Weak. And the child they created—a beautiful boy with brown skin, soft curls, and wide, wondering eyes—reminded him every day of the love he had felt...and the shame he twisted it into.

So he turned it all into control. If he couldn't change the past, he could at least silence it. Keep them inside. Keep them quiet. Keep them his. And now, on that hot July afternoon, that control was slipping.

Sheldon took one more tentative step off the porch, the red truck dangling from his hand, the sun warming his skin for the first time in days. Maybe weeks. He looked like any little boy would—quiet, curious, full of wonder. Until the door behind him slammed open with a crash that rattled the frame.

"Sheldon!" Clarence's voice split the air like a whip—slurred, seething. Rage danced with panic in his bloodshot eyes as he stumbled onto the porch, sweat clinging to his neck. He hadn't expected to see his boy out there. In front of them. Where people could look. Judge. Laugh.

Sheldon froze.

"I told you—you don't fucking go out there!" Clarence barked, already moving toward him. His steps were unsteady, drunk and furious, but purposeful. His hand went to the small of his back—where the gun always was. The one he said he kept "just in case." Naledi had begged him to get rid of it. He wouldn't.

Sheldon took a shaky step back, clutching his red truck tight. "I want to play..." Sheldon whispered, his voice so small it nearly vanished.

Clarence's face contorted. "You don't get what you want!"

Inside, Naledi's scream cut through the thick summer air. "Clarence, STOP!"

She burst through the door barefoot, her dress fluttering in the heat, her eyes wild with terror and love. She didn't hesitate—not even for a second. Her body moved to protect her baby before her mind could catch up, instinct flaring to life as she sprinted across the porch.

Clarence didn't see her at first. He was focused on Sheldon—his jaw clenched, eyes blazing. He raised the gun. He never meant to pull the trigger. Not yet. He just wanted to scare the boy. Snap him back into obedience. Show him who was in charge. Like always.

But Naledi saw everything.

The boy.

The gun.

The rage.

She threw herself between them with a cry that shattered the sky.

And in that split second of chaos—Clarence's finger jerked.

The shot exploded. Naledi's body jolted in front of her son, and a crimson bloom spread across her chest as she dropped to her knees, arms still reaching for Sheldon. She fell forward with a soft gasp, collapsing at his feet—her body shielding him even in death. Her eyes, once full of fire and grace, were open. Still.

Clarence staggered back. The gun slipped from his hand and clattered to the porch. For a moment, he just stared. At Naledi. At Sheldon. At what was left of the only people he ever loved. He hadn't meant to kill her. Not her. God, not her. But it was done. And he couldn't undo it.

The wail that tore from his throat was part animal, part man, all broken. And before the neighbors could scream—before someone could run—he bent, picked up the gun again, and placed it under his chin. The second shot rang out across the street, sending birds flying from the trees.

And Sheldon...

He didn't cry.

He didn't move.

He just stood there in the grass, paralyzed, his mother's blood soaking into his tiny toes.

The smell of it thick in the summer heat. The sounds of the sprinkler still spinning, children still laughing—until they weren't. Until everything went quiet.

For Sheldon... time had stopped.

In that silence, the echo of her voice came back to him—soft and steady, like a hymn carried on the wind. *You are my gift from God, my sweet boy. I see His strength in you already. He is shaping you—little by little—so you can stand tall for others one day. You will be His soldier of mercy. I can see the man you will become—and I am so proud already. God blessed me when He chose me to be your mama—and I love you more than you will ever know... in this life and the next.*

He didn't understand the words then. But someday, he would.

Because that was the day everything changed.

The day the McKays came running.

The day he became theirs.

Eight

Echoes in the Mirror

After hearing what Damon had done—and being pulled back to the darkest day of his own childhood—Sheldon didn't hesitate.

Alex didn't want to tell anyone. She had guarded Andi's pain like it was sacred—because it was. It belonged to her friend, not the world. What Damon had done wasn't just cruel; it was monstrous.

But this was different. This was Sheldon.

If there was one person Alex could trust with every broken, terrifying truth, it was him. He had lived through the unimaginable and clawed his way out with the strength of a lion—not loudly, not for attention, but with the grit of a man who'd survived hell by holding on to his mother's voice, letting it guide him like a compass through the dark. Her faith had rooted deep in him, her words still steering every move he made, pushing him to be the kind of man she always knew he would become.

He didn't flinch when things got ugly. He didn't offer pity, only clarity. He didn't tell people what they wanted to hear—he told them what they needed to know.

After Alex's family adopted Sheldon, they stayed close to the people who helped him through that tragedy—especially a few officers who refused to disappear from his life. They checked in, showed up, and became something like extended family. Over the years, those bonds deepened into lifelong friendships built on respect and gratitude. Maybe that's why Sheldon kept those ties alive—through *McKay Motors & Fleet* Service, the shop he ran that kept patrol cars and local trucks running, and through his years volunteering as a reserve deputy. Staying close to the people who once saved him had become his way of doing what he could to make sure others didn't have to face what he did.

So when he asked what was going on—really going on—she told him everything.

Damon's behavior at work, the party, the medical issues, the rape, the way Andi was scared of him but still tried to make excuses for him, and how she still tried to take the blame.

Alex laid it all out, every ugly detail. And Sheldon didn't interrupt once.

He listened in silence, his eyes darkening with every word. When she finished, he stood up, kissed her forehead, and said only this:

"Give me two days."

Now, two days later, it was Tuesday evening—the day before Alex's cookout. She wasn't sure what Sheldon had found—or how much worse this was about to get—but she knew one thing for certain: they weren't going to look away anymore.

Alex sat at the worn pine table, her hands tightly folded in front of her, knuckles white. Walker stood behind her, one hand resting on her shoulder—steady, grounding.

Across from them, Sheldon leaned forward, elbows on the table, a small stack of manila folders laid out between them like an arsenal. His face was unreadable, but his eyes—those steady, storm-dark eyes—burned with a focus she hadn't seen in him in years.

"Hey," he said, glancing at Alex. "You remember Tommy?"

She nodded. "Of course. Thomas Callahan—he was one of the main cops who helped that day."

"Yeah," Sheldon said, a faint smile tugging at the corner of his mouth. "He's retired now, but he never really left the game. Still helps out on special cases, consults when they need a steady hand. We've stayed close all these years." His tone softened a fraction. "He's not some washed-up retiree, either—he's connected. Real connected."

Alex felt something tighten in her chest. She remembered Tommy—she'd been too young to recall the details of that day, but she'd grown up on the story. Tommy had been the calm in the chaos, the one who carried Sheldon away from that house. She'd always admired him and the others for what they did—for Sheldon and for their family. She knew how much he meant to Sheldon, and she was certain the feeling was mutual. They would do anything for each other.

Sheldon tapped the folder once, grounding the moment. "If there's something to dig up," he said, steady again, "Tommy'll find it. Doesn't matter how buried it is."

Alex nodded, her throat tightening. She glanced up at Walker, who gave her shoulder a small squeeze.

Sheldon flipped open the first folder. A black-and-white photo slid out—a young woman with pretty eyes. Hopeful. Trusting.

"Her name was Jenny," Sheldon said. "Damon's first wife. He married her when he was about twenty-two. They lived near the lake, in a small rental cabin."

Alex blinked. "Wait—he was married before Andi?"

"Yeah. Most people don't know. It was quiet. Didn't last long. She drowned. It was ruled an accident."

Walker shifted his weight behind her, arms crossing.

"She was afraid of the water," Sheldon went on, still looking at the photo. "Her sister told police she didn't even *own* a swimsuit. Wouldn't go near boats. But Damon said they went out all the time. Claimed it was a freak accident—said she slipped getting back onto the boat after swimming."

Alex stared at the girl in the picture. Jenny. Young, sweet, too trusting. There was something familiar in her—something uncomfortably close to Andi.

"He lied," Alex said confidently.

Sheldon nodded. "But there wasn't enough to make it stick. No witnesses. No bruises. Just his story. And Damon was... Damon. Charming. Clean-cut. Devastated husband. He played it perfectly."

"Jesus Christ," Walker muttered.

Alex didn't take her eyes off the photograph. "Do you think he killed her?"

Sheldon didn't blink. "I think Damon knows exactly how to get away with... whatever he wants."

The words settled like cement in the room.

"And get this," Sheldon added, flipping to another sheet in the folder. "Jenny had a small life insurance policy. Not much, but enough. Damon was the sole beneficiary. None of her family was listed. He collected everything—insurance payout, her car, all her personal belongings." He paused. "Sold it all. Kept the money. Moved on."

Alex felt a chill crawl across her skin.

Melena stepped into the room without a word, carrying a tray with a few mugs of tea. She set them down gently, then sat beside Sheldon. Her hand found his under the table, a small, steady gesture that said she was with him. She didn't speak—just nodded for him to continue.

"There's more," Sheldon said, flipping open the next folder. "Damon's parents—Patsy and Louis—they weren't just comfortable. They had serious money. Properties, investment accounts, old oil leases. Damon's dad had inherited a chunk of land outside Helena that turned into a goldmine when they put in a commercial development nearby." He gave them a second to take it in. "When Louis died, everything went to Patsy. Damon didn't get a dime—not at first," Sheldon said.

Alex glanced down at the table, already feeling the next shoe about to drop.

"But a few months later," he continued, "Patsy had an accident. She was out on the dock behind their lake house—conveniently, right after a few neighbors said Damon had been out there working on it. Cleaning it up, fixing boards, or so he told them. She almost died—ended up with a crushed leg, then had a stroke during her recovery. She survived, but she couldn't live alone anymore. That's when things started shifting. Damon stepped in, got power of attorney, sold the house, and used the money to buy the dealership."

Walker hissed under his breath, "Of course he did."

"No proof he did anything to cause it," Sheldon said, "but I talked to one of Patsy's old neighbors. Sweet lady, Lorraine—mid-eighties, sharp as ever. She told me Patsy had mentioned changing her will. Said she was thinking of leaving something for Meryl instead of everything going to Damon. She didn't think he deserved it."

Alex's stomach twisted. "She said that?"

Sheldon nodded. "Lorraine said Patsy told her she was meeting with an attorney the following week. Then boom—down the dock, crushed leg, stroke. No new will. Damon gets everything when she goes. He made sure of that."

Melena exhaled slowly beside him, shaking her head. "That's not a coincidence."

"No," Sheldon said. "It's not."

Alex didn't say anything. Just stared down at the photo of Jenny again. She felt the sadness in her eyes.

Melena followed her gaze. "She looks like Andi," she said quietly.

Alex flinched. "She does..."

Not in a way that would catch a stranger's eye. But once you knew what to look for—the softness, the unguarded warmth, the kind of vulnerability that made people like Damon feel powerful—it was obvious. Too obvious.

Jenny had trusted him. So did Andi. And now one was dead, and the other...

Alex felt the words scrape out of her, raw with disbelief and disgust. "He's been doing this for years."

Sheldon nodded, tone flat. "And getting better at it."

He pulled out another paper from the folder—a hospital intake form, the edges soft from handling.

"Medical records are tough to get. I'm working on more, but this one stood out." He laid it on the table. "This was from a few months into their marriage. Andi came into the ER with a head injury. Said she fell down the stairs."

He looked up. "Guess who signed her discharge papers?"

Walker didn't even blink. "Damon."

"Yep."

Sheldon reached for another page and slid it across the table. "And right around that same time, a life insurance policy was taken out in Andi's name. Damon's the sole beneficiary."

Alex's breath caught.

"It wasn't huge at the time," Sheldon went on. "Respectable, but nothing that would raise eyebrows. But once Damon brought her in as manager at the Outpost, he had the excuse he needed to bump it up." He tapped the paper sharply. "He's increased it steadily over the years. Between the company policy, a supplemental policy, and a few layered personal policies..." He flipped the page and tapped the total at the bottom. "She's worth millions to him now. If she dies."

Alex stared at the number, cold spreading through her chest. She didn't speak, couldn't.

Walker swore under his breath, taking a step back from the table. He ran a hand over his mouth, then started pacing in a slow, agitated circle, like he couldn't figure out what to do with the adrenaline suddenly rushing through him.

"That fucker has been planning this," Walker said finally. "This isn't just abuse. This is calculated."

Alex looked back down at the paper, Her voice was nothing more than a whisper. Tears rising fast. "Does Andi even know?"

"I doubt it," Sheldon said. "But Damon does. And that's all that matters to him."

Melena didn't flinch. "He's gotta be drugging her."

Sheldon nodded. "I know. Or I will soon enough. I've got someone digging through her prescription records, and I'm looking into every kind of substance that's hard to trace—shit that can mess with your head. Confusion, anxiety, memory loss, heart palpitations... all of it." His jaw tightened. "If he's putting something in her food or swapping out her meds, we'll find it."

Alex pressed her fingers to her temple, the weight of it all pressing down on her. "And if we don't? What if there's no proof?"

Sheldon didn't miss a beat. "Then we don't wait around hoping for it. We protect her anyway. We plan. We stay one step ahead of him. He's careful—but he's not untouchable."

Alex looked up, eyes clearer now, the sting of tears replaced by something harder. "She can't end up like Jenny."

"She won't," Sheldon said, and there wasn't an ounce of doubt in his voice.

Walker leaned in, both hands flat on the table, his jaw set. "Just tell us what to do."

Sheldon gave a short nod. "Then we start here. Quiet. Smart. We gather everything we can—financials, medical, personal. We keep eyes on him. We stay close to Andi. Make sure she's not alone as much as possible." He looked from Alex to Walker, then to Melena, whose gaze was locked with Alex's now—firm, steady, unblinking. They didn't have to say it. The room already knew.

"When the time comes," Sheldon said, "we finish this."

Nine

A Quiet Reflection

The Wednesday evening cookout was intended as a simple midweek reprieve—a chance for food and a little laughter with friends. But for Alex tonight, everything felt heavier, more urgent beneath the fragile veil of normalcy.

The air had a sharpness that nipped at skin and curled around ankles, even with thick socks. Alex had lit the backyard torches early, and two propane heaters flickered near the patio, casting pools of golden warmth. The sky above was clear, a deep navy canvas scattered with early stars. The smell of burning wood drifted from the fire pit, mingling with the comforting scent of grilled meat and crisp leaves.

Kids chased each other in puffs of visible breath, their laughter rising like smoke in the cold. Harper's cheeks were flushed pink as she tore across the grass in a fleece unicorn hoodie, her hair wild and tangled. Near the sliding glass door, Muttonhead barked at the two rescued kittens inside—tiny black-and-white troublemakers the family had named Thelma and Louise. The kittens batted at him through the glass, their tails twitching with mischief before darting out of sight. Muttonhead gave a playful whine and bounded off to join the chaos in the yard.

Meryl stood near the porch steps, hands tucked into her coat pockets, a soft knit beanie pulled low over her long hair. She kept an eye on Harper and Rebecca's little ones as they zigzagged through the yard—not hovering, just close enough to jump in if needed.

What struck Alex most was how relaxed Meryl looked. She wasn't just helping—she was enjoying it. Smiling. Laughing quietly when one of the kids tripped over their own feet and popped right back up. There was something light in her, something easy, as if this was exactly where she wanted to be.

Over by the grill, Theo—Michelin-starred chef turned backyard barbecue legend—stood wrapped in a puffy vest and his signature ridiculous apron that read *Grill Sergeant*. Tongs in hand, he flipped burgers with a flourish worthy of a cooking show finale, simultaneously searing perfection into every bite while barking faux orders to an imaginary sous chef. "Fire that filet, Johnson! This isn't amateur hour!"

Jason nearly dropped his beer laughing, and Theo didn't miss a beat—he pointed a spatula skyward and roared, "You're cooking like a bloody *donkey*, get out of my kitchen!"

Alex stood at the folding table, balancing Liam on her hip while scanning the yard with seasoned eyes. He was bundled in a zip-up fleece and a knitted cap, his cheeks red from the chill, a line of drool tracing the edge of his chin as he gnawed on his mitten. Corbin sat wrapped in a thick blanket in the playpen, kicking his legs and squealing every time the wind stirred the fringe around him.

The cold had settled in. Not brutal yet, but biting enough that the fire pit and propane heaters were doing real work. Alex adjusted her scarf with one hand and took a slow breath, letting her eyes land where they always did lately.

Andi—near the fire, talking with Walker, Frank and Cora, Sheldon and Melena—sat cross-legged in a lawn chair, hands wrapped around a mug of Bailey's and coffee, steam rising slowly into the cold air. She wore a pale green sweater under a tan jacket, her blonde hair tucked up beneath a soft gray beanie. The firelight painted her face in warm flickers, catching the edge of a smile that looked almost effortless.

She wasn't talking much, but she was present. And that mattered. Her posture wasn't as guarded, her face not as drawn. Whatever Melena had just said made her smile—and it wasn't a polite one. It was real.

Alex grinned.

This was why she'd wanted tonight. Not to distract Andi, but to *remind* her that there was still life outside the fog. That she wasn't alone. That she was wanted and still belonged.

"Hot chocolate. Heavily spiked—like responsible adults," came a voice at her side.

Alex turned to find Rebecca holding out a cup. Her cheeks were red, her breath fogging in the air. She managed a faint smile, but there was a quiet tension in her face. Something was on her mind.

Alex took the cup. “Well, thank you, ma’am. I knew I liked you.”

They stood shoulder to shoulder, not speaking for a moment, just watching the fire and the people gathered around it.

Rebecca shifted slightly. “I’ve been meaning to talk to you.”

Alex’s body tensed. She didn’t move her eyes from the fire. “Yeah?”

Rebecca hesitated, then said it. “It’s about work. About Damon.”

The name cut through the night like a blade. Alex glanced down at Liam, adjusting his hat, then nodded toward the porch. “Come on, let’s go sit.”

Alex lowered Liam into the playpen beside Corbin, tucking the blanket snug around both boys before straightening. The twins cooed softly, content in their little nest of warmth. With one last glance to be sure they were settled, she led Rebecca up the steps and toward the old bench. The boards groaned beneath them, and the air felt colder here—sharper—away from the heat of the fire and the noise out in the yard. The cup in Alex’s hands was still warm, but her fingers had already gone numb.

Rebecca glanced out toward the yard. “I hate that they switched my days. It seems like I don't even get to work with you anymore. It just felt... better when you were there.”

Alex exhaled, “Yeah. Same.”

Rebecca's eyes dropped, her voice cautious. "I don't want to jump to conclusions. I keep second-guessing myself. But Eddy and I... we've both noticed something. Damon's been... more difficult lately. It's like he's wound tighter. Meaner."

Alex didn't speak. She just listened.

Rebecca took a breath. "He's getting worse. More aggressive. I'm so sick of it. The second he walks in, it's like the air gets sucked out of the room. You know something's coming, but you don't know what. It's exhausting."

Alex's grip on the cup tightened.

Rebecca looked down at her hands. "And Andi's been... off. Like she's trying to hold it together, but it's not working very well. She's so quiet lately. And sometimes she just... drifts. Like she's not there. I think something's really wrong. I'm worried."

Alex turned to her, jaw tight. "Yeah, I know. You're not jumping to conclusions—you're right to think something's wrong." She paused. "Rebecca, I wish I could tell you more. It's just not my place right now. This isn't stress or mood swings. It's deeper than that. She's... surviving." She took a deep breath. "She needs people around her who see it. Who pay attention."

"I do," Rebecca said, without hesitation.

Alex nodded, then paused. "She's not okay. I can't explain why, but just don't assume she's fine because she shows up and smiles."

Rebecca's brow furrowed slightly, but she didn't press.

Alex met her eyes. "Promise me—if anything feels off, even a little, you call me. Don't second-guess it."

"I won't." A quiet breath. "I promise."

The wind picked up again, rattling the last of the dry leaves across the porch. The sound of Theo's guitar drifted up from the fire pit—soft, steady, familiar. The kind of sound that made you forget, for a minute, how heavy things actually were.

The yard had settled. S'mores. Laughter. Sheldon pretending to yell at the kids about marshmallow technique. Corbin babbling at Walker, who patiently helped him stack graham crackers.

Harper had curled into Andi's side, her head resting against her arm, small fingers absentmindedly twisting a piece of Andi's hair. Andi didn't move. She just brushed Harper's bangs aside, her hand lingering there for a beat. Her smile was small, but it stayed.

Meryl crouched nearby, tucking a blanket around one of Rebecca's toddlers who had started to drift off in a chair. She glanced toward Andi and Harper, her eyes lingering for a quiet moment. Then she looked up and caught Alex's gaze, offering a small, inviting smile—soft, unspoken, like a gesture that said *come join us.*

Alex and Rebecca made their way back toward the fire, settling in with the group. Alex eased down beside Andi, Liam nuzzled warm against her chest. The fire cracked. Overhead, the sky stretched dark and still, scattered with the most beautiful shimmering stars. For a while, nobody said anything. And that was okay. It was a good night.

But as the warmth from the fire reached her skin, Alex felt the other thing underneath—the thing that wasn't going away. The clock was ticking. And she knew it.

TEN

SHARDS AND SPLINTERS

IT HAD BEEN JUST over two weeks since Damon slithered back into town. On the surface, things at work had remained strangely calm—deceptively so. He'd made only a few brief appearances at the dealership, each one nauseating. He'd breeze in with that oily grin, reeking of overpriced cologne and superiority, slapping backs, cracking jokes, pretending to be the picture-perfect husband and charismatic business owner.

No one was fooled. Not the staff. Not the customers. And definitely not Alex.

While Damon played the part of a man in control, Andi was unraveling. She told Alex she had three more "episodes" since his return. That's what she called them now—*episodes*. As if they were a series of unfortunate blips instead of a descent into something terrifying. But the most recent one... scared Alex to her core.

Andi came in late that morning, slipping through the door like she was trying not to exist. Her movements were slow, stiff, like every step hurt. Her left eye was half-shut, already purpling, and a dark bruise swelled beneath her hairline. Cuts trailed down her arms, barely concealed by the sleeves of her cardigan. She looked like someone who'd been in a car crash—shaken, silent, shattered.

Alex saw her and froze. Something primal gripped her chest. She crossed the showroom in seconds and pulled Andi aside, her voice low but urgent.

"What happened to you!?"

Andi flinched at the question, her eyes glassy and evasive. "It was nothing. I... I fell. In the basement, I think. I must've passed out or something."

Alex's stomach knotted. The lie was weak, shaky, and laced with shame. She didn't buy it. Not for a second.

"Don't give me that shit," Alex snapped, her voice trembling with restrained panic. "You *know* I know better. Look at you, Andi. What the hell *really* happened?"

Andi looked away, biting her lip. Her shoulders rose in a silent, defensive flinch—but then dropped. She let out a shaky breath and sat down slowly, as if the weight of holding it in had finally become unbearable.

"I woke up during the night in the basement," she stammered. "I don't even remember going down there. I was on the floor... next to the metal shelves where I keep all my canning stuff. I guess the top shelf somehow collapsed—jars shattered. Green beans, broken glass, metal rings... it was *everywhere.*" Her hands twisted in her lap, knuckles white, as if she were reliving the moment in real time. "I couldn't move at first. I didn't even know where I was. My hair was soaked in brine. My face was wet. I thought it was water until I saw the blood." Her voice broke. "There was so much glass, Alex. It was stuck in my arms, my legs... even in my scalp. And the smell—the brine, the metal—it made me gag. I couldn't figure out what had happened. If I fell, if I sleepwalked, if something else—" she swallowed hard. "I woke up in it. Lying there—alone."

Alex felt like she couldn't breathe.

Andi continued, her words rushing out as if saying them quickly was the only way to prevent them from choking her. "This gash above my eye is so deep—I could feel it pulsing. I couldn't see straight—my other eye was swollen shut. And when I tried to stand up, I stepped right onto one of the metal lid rings. It sliced into my foot. I went down so fast I cracked my elbow on the concrete." She looked up, her eyes red, lips quivering. "I couldn't walk. I had to *crawl* to the stairs—bleeding, glass sticking out of my skin, my foot pouring blood."

She laughed then, a short, broken sound that didn't even pretend to be humor.

Alex's breath hitched. "Jesus, Andi..."

"I cried," she said, almost apologetically. "I didn't know what else to do. I didn't even clean myself up first. I just started scrubbing the floor because I didn't want him to see it. I didn't want him to come down there and—" Andi's voice dropped to a whisper. "When it was clean, I went to the bathroom, wrapped myself up the best I could, and crawled into bed... tried not to wake him."

Alex stared at her, tears stinging her eyes, fury boiling just beneath the surface.

Andi looked like a shell of herself. But the way she spoke—the numbness, the shame—told Alex everything she needed to know.

This wasn't some freak accident.

For the rest of the week, Alex couldn't shake the image of what Andi had described. It haunted her—flashing in her mind at random moments like a horror reel she couldn't pause. The thought of her best friend waking up alone in blood and broken glass, crawling across a cold basement floor, then climbing into bed beside the man who may have caused it—*it gutted her.*

Andi put on a brave face at work, especially with customers. Almost every one of them asked what had happened. She would laugh lightly and wave a hand as if it were nothing. "Just a clumsy moment in the basement," she'd say. "Banged myself up pretty good."

It was rehearsed. Polished. Perfectly dismissive.

No matter how hard Andi tried to act normal, she still looked bruised. She still looked *hurt.* And every time Alex caught sight of her limping slightly or gently touching the scab near her temple, it took everything she had not to scream—not to march into Damon's office—or house—and burn his whole damn world down. Staying calm around her was becoming harder by the hour.

By Saturday, the tension in Alex's chest had calcified into something heavy and constant. She hadn't stopped thinking about Andi all week. Every time she tried to focus on something else—her kids, work, even just folding laundry—her mind snapped back to that basement. The blood. The glass. So when her phone buzzed late that afternoon with a message from Andi, her heart stuttered.

Hey, I was going through Meryl's old clothes and found a bunch of stuff Harper could probably use. If you wanna stop by and go through it, I'll be home. Damon's out with his buddies tonight and won't be back until after midnight.

It felt like oxygen. An invitation. Thank god. Alex didn't hesitate. She didn't even ask Walker. She just texted back...

On my way

...then threw on a hoodie, and left.

She wasn't going for the clothes—not really. She was going for *her.* For the woman who felt like a sister.

Now, standing barefoot in the Roths' entryway, Alex felt a ripple of unease crawl over her skin. It was like walking into a memory she didn't trust. She was happy to see Andi—*really* happy—but every time she looked around, the house made her skin itch. Damon was everywhere. Not in person, thankfully, but in the clutter he left behind.

His piles were there, scattered across countertops and corners like landmines. Andi had clearly tried to keep them tidy, stacking things neatly and sorting what she could. But the mess had roots. The refrigerator and corkboard were plastered with old photos, faded paperwork, and outdated appointment cards. One yellowed page near the edge caught Alex's eye—a daycare flyer dated nearly a decade ago.

Nothing ever left this house; it just got buried.

Andi stepped into the room, a large gray tote in her arms, her sleeves pushed just high enough for Alex to catch the faint, healing marks trailing along her forearms. She lowered the bin onto the rug with a soft thud and straightened with a quiet exhale.

"Most of this is still in good shape," she said, brushing a strand of hair from her face. "Meryl barely wore half of it. She outgrew things overnight."

Alex knelt beside her and lifted the lid. Inside were stacks of gently used clothes—little jeans, soft cotton leggings, and faded tees with glittery designs. Mostly size 7s and 8s. Perfect for Harper, who seemed to sprout taller by the week.

Alex picked up a striped long-sleeve shirt and held it up. "That's Harper too. I swear, if she farts near a growth chart, she'll need all new clothes."

Andi nearly spit out the wine she'd just taken a sip of. "Well, that's the perfect way to put it," she said, still trying to contain her laughter. "There's some smaller stuff in there too—unisex clothes from when Meryl was a toddler. If the boys can wear any of it, take it."

Alex grinned, holding up a tiny yellow sweatshirt. "Heck yeah, this is adorable! I can already see Corbin wiping peanut butter all over it."

Andi laughed lightly, then paused. “You know, I never actually picked Meryl’s name.”

Alex looked up. “Wait, seriously?”

“Nope,” Andi said, letting out a dry laugh. “I wanted to name her Sophia—something classic and beautiful. Damon just looked at me and said, ‘We’re going with Meryl Heather,’ as if it were already settled. He’s obsessed with Merle Haggard—his favorite singer, of course.”

Alex's mouth dropped open. “You’re kidding me!”

Andi shrugged. “Somehow he thought naming a baby after an old outlaw country star was charming. I had just had a C-section and was too drugged up to argue. By the time I realized what had happened, it was already on the birth certificate. Surprise!” She laughed again—light, but with a bitter undercurrent. Then she pulled out a worn pink hoodie and paused, settling back on her heels. Her fingers drifted across the front, her thumb catching on the corner of the faded embroidered heart near the zipper.

Alex looked over. “What is it?”

Andi didn’t answer at first. Her eyes remained fixed on the fabric, and when she finally spoke, her voice was tinged with sadness. “It’s just... going through this. Thinking about how fast it all goes. And how much I’ve missed.” She stared down at the hoodie in her lap. "The last few years have been... a blur. I’m either working, at a doctor’s appointment, or just trying to keep my head above water. Half the time, I can’t even tell what’s real anymore, or if I’m just making it all up in my head."

She let out a quiet, bitter laugh and shook her head. "And Meryl..." Her voice softened. "She’s only sixteen, but she walks around like she’s thirty. Always watching, always bracing herself. She can read a room faster than most adults. That’s not something a kid should have to know how to do." She took a breath, shaky but sincere. "I want her to know she deserves to be happy. I don't want her growing up thinking she has to walk on eggshells constantly—especially not around the person she loves. I want her to feel safe. To relax. To be her perfect, beautiful self... always."

Alex's throat tightened.

Because Andi wasn't just talking about Meryl. She was talking about herself, about the life that slipped through her fingers. She was mourning the woman she might have been, the mother she wanted to be. And beneath every word was something deeper:

The fear that her daughter would become her.

Alex leaned back with a sigh, tilting her head as she searched for the right words. "Andi... you know you deserve that too, right?"

Andi looked at her, and for a moment, she felt the ghost of the girl she used to be. "Yeah," she smiled. "I know."

But Alex saw it—the flicker of doubt, the silent struggle behind Andi's eyes. It was as if she wasn't sure she had enough strength left to fight for it.

Then, the front door opened.

It slammed against the wall, hard enough to rattle a picture frame. The women looked at each other, eyes wide with panic. Then came heavy footsteps shuffling across the entry tile, uneven and loud. Keys jangling. A low whistle—tuneless and arrogant.

Andi's face drained of color. "Shit," she breathed. "He wasn't supposed to be home yet."

They both froze when he stumbled around the corner.

Damon.

Red-faced, glassy-eyed, and reeking of alcohol and sweat, he stood with his shirt half-untucked, the buttons misaligned as if he hadn't even tried. A whiskey bottle dangled from one hand, while the other dragged his belt behind him like a grotesque accessory.

"*Andriiiiaaaa!*" he hollered, his voice thick and sticky. "You ready to earn your keep tonight? 'Cause I brought the good stuff, baby!"

He stopped cold when he saw Alex. For a split second, confusion flickered across his face. Then recognition. Then something far worse. A slow, filthy grin spread across his face.

"Well, well, well," he drawled, his voice low and venomous. "Look who it is—Alexandra Halloway. Standing on my fuckin' living room rug. Damn, sweetheart, you're looking like the feast I've been starving for all night."

Alex stood slowly, her spine stiff but her stomach twisted. Her instincts screamed *leave,* but her legs felt cemented.

Damon swaggered closer, his steps uneven, the bottle swinging lazily from his hand. He looked her up and down—like he owned her. Like she was a thing.

"Goddamn," he slurred. "You always look that good, or did you dress up special for me?"

"Damon, *stop*," Andi snapped, stepping in front of Alex. Her voice shook, but she held her ground.

He didn't flinch. Didn't even blink. "Relax, sweetheart," he said, brushing her arm off like lint. "Just being friendly. No crime in looking."

Then his slimy eyes slid back to Alex, and his voice dropped to a growl. "Tell me something, Alexxxaanndraa... you and sweet little Andi ever get curious? Mess around after a few glasses of wine? Bet you two get real close. I think we should all take our clothes off right now—let you show me just how hot you are together. Shit, I'd throw down good money just to sit back and watch."

Alex's breath hitched, rage flaring in her chest.

Andi went rigid. "You're drunk," she said. "Go to bed."

He smirked at her like a child scolded by a kindergarten teacher. "Aww, am I in trouble again, mommy?" Then, to Alex, "She's *always* like this. No fun at all."

He stumbled forward another step. Too close.

Alex instinctively stepped back, knocking into the ottoman. Damon reached toward her arm—lazy but deliberate.

"Don't touch me," she said sharply.

Andi's hand shot out, gripping his wrist hard.

"I said *go to bed,* Damon."

His eyes flicked down to her grip, then back up to her face—slow and dangerous.

"You forget your fuckin' place, little girl."

"No," she said, her voice like steel. "You forget *yours.*"

For a moment, the tension in the room became electric. Alex felt it prickling at her skin, dancing between the three of them like a live wire. Damon stared at Andi as if he didn't recognize her, calculating what it would cost to knock her down. Then he laughed. Short. Loud. Mocking.

"Jesus. What is this? Girl power night? What's next—matching tattoos and promise rings?"

He turned back to Alex and winked. "You should come by when she's not here. She's always killing the mood. Bet *you're* the wild one... All that quiet, holier-than-thou shit? I know what that means." He let out a low, sickening growl. "Mmm... you'd be a fuckin' firecracker in bed. Ya know, poor Andi's been real sick lately. Shame, really. She might not be around much longer." He smirked, his eyes raking over Alex as if she were already his. "Guess I'll need somethin' new when she's gone. A girl like you, Alex—I could make you feel *real special.*"

Alex's jaw clenched. Her fists did too. Her hands shook—not from fear, but from fury. *Burning*, blinding fury. She grabbed the tote bag of Harper's new clothes, her heart pounding so loudly it drowned out everything else. She didn't say a word. Just moved—fast.

Andi reached for her arm. "Alex—"

"I have to go," Alex said, her voice choked. "You should come."

"I can't," Andi whispered. "I'm sorry."

Damon staggered toward them again. "Oh, let the bitch run off. Probably has some little church group to cry to, anyway."

Alex turned sharply. "I'm not running," she said, her eyes locking hard with his. "I'm leaving before I puke on your floor."

That hit.

For the briefest moment, Damon's mask cracked. His lip curled, but he didn't stop her.

She pushed past him, shouldering the door open with shaking arms. The screen door slapped shut behind her with a snap that echoed in the night air. The cold hit her like ice water. She walked fast, her bootsteps crunching down the driveway, her teeth clenched so tight her jaw ached.

Once inside her car, she slammed the door, locked it, and sat there in silence. Her pulse raced. Her chest heaved with adrenaline, disgust, and heartbreak.

Poor Andi's been real sick lately. Shame, really. She might not be around much longer. Those words seared through her brain like acid.

As she drove home, something inside her had finally, irrevocably snapped.

Alex had seen vile. She'd stared it in the face. She knew what he was capable of.

This was the line.

And he'd just crossed it.

Someone had to end this—had to be willing to step into the mess and finish what everyone else was too afraid to touch.

Conviction flooded her veins—sharp, steady, unflinching.

She was going to burn Damon Roth to the ground—and salt the fucking ashes.

ELEVEN

MIRROR OF THE DEAD

SUNDAY MORNING DAWNED BLEAK and heavy. The storm inside Alex hadn't let up since the night before. She sat curled at the far end of the couch, knees drawn up, Walker's worn flannel hoodie draped around her like armor. Liam and Corbin dozed in their swings, while Harper peacefully colored at the kitchen table. The house was still, but her mind was a churning sea of dread.

She couldn't stop hearing his voice. Damon's slurred, disgusting words echoed in her mind. The way his eyes had devoured her, claiming her like an object. The entitlement. The stench of alcohol and power. That moment was burned into her memory—undeniable and revolting.

But it wasn't just about her. It was about Andi.

Alex closed her eyes, swallowing hard. Andi had stood between them—shaking, pale, scared out of her mind—but she had still stepped in front of Alex, shielding her. Still trying to protect everyone but herself.

Her fingers quivered nervously as she reached for her phone and dialed Sheldon's number.

"Hey, sis."

She didn't bother with greetings. "Shel, I was over there yesterday. He wasn't supposed to be home. But he showed up—drunk off his fucking ass. Said disgusting things. Claimed Andi wouldn't be around much longer—like it was already decided. Like she was... disposable. And then he looked at me like I was next in line. It was a joke to him, Sheldon. Like the whole thing is funny."

Sheldon was silent for a long moment. Then he asked, "You okay?"

"No, I am definitely not ok," she said, a bitter chuckle escaping her. "But I will be. We need to move faster."

"I agree," he said. "That's why we're meeting today."

They decided to meet for lunch at the little diner out on Highway 12—the one that was never very busy, with quiet booths tucked in the back and coffee that tasted like it hadn't changed since the '80s.

When the call ended, Alex stayed frozen on the edge of the couch, the silence around her suddenly too loud. The idea of walking back into that dealership, pretending like everything was normal, felt impossible. She stood, almost on instinct, needing air—just a breath outside, anything to steady herself.

Then her phone buzzed.

Andi:

I'm so sorry about last night. He claims he blacked out—says he doesn't remember a thing. Now he's walking around like it never even happened.

Alex's hand hesitated over the screen.

Alex:

I need a few days. I'm sorry. What happened last night—it wasn't okay. I know it's not your fault, but I can't face him right now. I can't walk in there and pretend like none of it happened.

Andi:

I understand. I'll tell him you're sick. Take all the time you need. I'm so sorry.

Alex met Sheldon and Melena at the diner just after noon. Sunlight filtered through the windows like a bad habit—weak, intrusive, and impossible to ignore. Sheldon sat in the far booth, hunched over a manila folder that looked older than everything around it. It wasn't just the papers that weighed him down—it was what they meant. What they confirmed.

Melena sat beside him, hands wrapped around a cup of coffee gone cold. Her sandwich sat untouched, a smear of mustard drying on the edge of the plate. She didn't glance up until Alex got close. And when she did, there was something sharp in her stare—the look of knowing that lingers in your gut after you've heard too much and can't unhear any of it.

Alex slid into the seat across from Sheldon, her skin buzzing. Everything around her felt loud—the hiss of the coffee machine, the clink of forks, the cheap silverware scraping against worn plates. It all faded under the weight of what she knew was coming.

Sheldon didn't waste time. He didn't even look up. Just flipped the folder open and said, low and flat, "We've got more." He pulled out an old police report, yellowed at the edges, the corners curled as if it had been hidden too long. "Jenny Whitmore—his first wife. We knew she drowned. What we didn't know is what her sister tried to do after." He laid another page on the table, its header stamped with an old courthouse seal. "Sealed civil complaint. Filed by Stephanie Whitmore three months after Jenny's death. Wrongful death. She claimed Jenny was trying to leave him. That he knew. That he'd warned her."

Melena leaned in, reading the first lines of the complaint.

"She wrote that Jenny had bruises—on her ribs, her wrists. That she was scared of water and never swam. And yet Damon told police they went boating all the time. Said it was their favorite thing to do." Sheldon continued. "In her deposition, Stephanie said Jenny told her, 'If I disappear, it won't be an accident.' And Damon? He told her once, straight-faced,

'If you ever leave me, you won't make it to shore.'" He looked up. "The case vanished. Bought and buried. Stephanie disappeared—changed her name, moved across the country. "But get this—before she left, she went to the media. Had a meeting set up. Tried to tell someone. The night before, her car was broken into. Nothing stolen—except the files she'd planned to bring. And tucked into her visor was a single Polaroid... of herself. Sleeping. She backed off. Said she was done trying to be a hero. Said she just wanted to stay alive."

Melena leaned forward. "That was never in the official report?"

"Nope. Because Damon's daddy had a buddy who was a sitting judge at the time. Plus his damn family owned half the commercial real estate in the county. The deputy who filed the original report? Reassigned two weeks later—real convenient."

Alex felt her stomach twist.

"There's more." Sheldon shook his head, sighing as he pulled out another sheet. "Jenny wasn't the only one. Damon had a girlfriend before her—Danielle Carver. Small-town girl. College dropout. She disappeared in 1992. No leads, no trace. The case went cold."

Alex's voice dropped. "You think he killed her?"

"We don't have proof. But her car was found abandoned less than a mile from the Roth family's lake property—the same place Jenny drowned years later."

"Jesus," Melena muttered.

Sheldon continued, "And then there's the dock collapse with Patsy. Not just suspicious—deliberate, maybe. The EMT who responded made a note in the report about the wood looking clean-cut, like it had been tampered with. No rot. No splintering. Just a clean break."

Alex stared at the table, her hand tight around her coffee mug.

"I talked to Patsy—his mama—yesterday," Sheldon added. "She's different now. She says Damon never visits. Said the last time she saw Meryl was years ago—Andi tried to bring her, and Damon pitched a fit. Called Andi mid-visit, demanded she come home immediately. Patsy said she saw the look in Andi's eyes that day, saw how upset she was... and right before they left, she told her: 'Don't you let my boy boss you around. One day, he's gonna push too far—and when he does, you make damn sure it's not you he buries.'"

Melena blinked. "She said that?"

"She did. And for a long time, she defended him without question. But now? You can see it in her eyes—she's not so sure anymore. Still, there's a hesitation in her voice, like she's holding back. Like there's more she's not ready to admit out loud."

Alex's gaze went distant, fixed on her hand still gripping her coffee. "We need something. Something concrete."

"We might have it," Sheldon said, sliding over a newer photo. "Patsy had a live-in aide for a while. A young lady named Jessa. She quit suddenly. My contact tracked her down. She's willing to talk."

"Why'd she leave?" Melena asked.

Sheldon sighed. "It started with Patsy saying weird things. One night, she was heavily medicated, talking about a woman in the lake. Jessa asked her to clarify—trying to make sense of it. Patsy went quiet. Said things like, 'He watches too close' and 'We don't talk about that here.' She warned Jessa not to bring it up again. That same night, Damon showed up—no call, no warning. Just walked into the house and stood there staring at her. And then he said—quiet, calm—'People who ask too many questions end up missing things... like time. Like air.'"

Alex's blood ran cold.

Sheldon's expression was grim. "She packed her stuff and left before morning."

Melena gave a grim nod. "That's the break."

Sheldon looked at Alex, his eyes steady, voice quiet but loaded.

"Here's the hard part," he said. "We need samples—food, medication, anything from the house. A hairbrush, leftovers—whatever you can get without raising suspicion. I've got a private lab lined up. If there's something in her system, they'll find it."

Alex nodded, her throat dry. She didn't ask questions. She didn't need to. Whatever they needed, she'd get it. Whatever it took. She let out a slow breath. Not relief—just resolve. Whatever hope she'd been clinging to that this might end quietly had long since slipped away. This was the edge now. And the only way forward was through. "I'll go back at the end of the week. Pretend like everything's fine."

Sheldon met her gaze. "You sure?"

"No," she said, a laugh escaping like a reflex—dry, sharp, laced with everything she didn't want to feel. "But I'm going anyway."

Melena reached across the table and wrapped her hand around Alex's, steady and sure. Her voice was calm but resolute. "You're not doing this alone, Alex. We're right here. Every step of the way."

Alex drew in a breath, the weight in her chest easing just enough to hold herself upright.

Melena didn't look away. Her gaze locked on Alex. A grin emerged—slow, deliberate—etched with fire and promise. "That man has no idea what's coming. He's about to learn what it feels like to be hunted."

TWELVE

SHATTERED REFLECTIONS

IT WAS THURSDAY NIGHT. The holidays were coming—music in every store, glittering lights in windows, people making plans with hopeful hearts. It should have been a time of comfort, of connection—but for Alex, it wasn't even on the radar. Her mind was miles away, buried under the weight of everything else. She had already laid out her clothes for the next morning—she was going back to work. Or at least, that was the plan: a fragile attempt at normalcy. But beneath that quiet routine, her nerves crackled. Her stomach had been in knots all day. The thought of seeing Damon face-to-face again, pretending everything was fine when it wasn't, made her feel nauseous.

For tonight, however, Damon was out of the way—off picking up a camper from another dealership for one of his high-profile clients. It was yet another one of his ego-stroking errands he'd be sure to brag about later. Alex and Andi jumped at the rare opportunity to meet up while he was gone. Just two friends daring to break the "rules," chasing a little bit of freedom the way real friends should be able to. Nights like this had become their hidden sanctuary—not exactly joyful or carefree, but a small crack in the walls closing in around them. A chance to exist without the heavy, suffocating tension Damon always dragged into the room.

Tonight was supposed to be one of those nights.

Andi walked into the Blue Lantern, a cozy little pub with an amazing atmosphere and even better cheese curds—the kind of bar food that is beyond sinful but feels like an explosive orgasm in your mouth. She spotted Alex and Walker tucked away in a corner booth, holding hands across the table. It was a simple, beautiful gesture, and for a moment, it struck Andi. A flicker of jealousy twisted inside her—an ache for something she had never really known. She found herself admiring the effortless tenderness between two people who simply chose each other, without fear or strings attached. Damon had never looked at her like that, never reached for her just because he wanted to.

She shook it off and made her way over, a smile tugging at her lips. Being around Alex and Walker always made her feel better, like they were the glue holding her together—keeping her from falling completely apart.

The plan had been simple: meet up, grab a bite, put the phones on silent, and try to carve out a few stolen hours without Damon's shadow choking the life out of everything. Nothing heavy—just a little time for lighthearted conversation between friends. But Andi and Alex were still raw, carrying the weight of that awful night when Damon had stumbled in drunk, leaving wreckage behind as if the destruction itself was what he loved most. This dinner wasn't just about unwinding; it was about checking in, reading between the lines, and figuring out how to deal with whatever came next. Because Alex knew one thing for sure—if Damon remembered even half of that night, or worse, decided to up the ante, they had to be ready.

Luckily, Walker was there to lighten the mood almost immediately. He cracked a dry joke about how Alex had banned him from ordering "the nuclear hot wings" after a certain "incident" last year, which left Andi in full-blown belly laughter.

"It's not my fault!" Walker barked, throwing his hands up in mock indignation. "I'd only eaten two! Wiped my hands with a napkin—like a normal person. Nobody said I needed to scrub in like a fuckin surgeon *before* taking a piss." He turned to Andi with wide, desperate eyes, voice lowering into a dead-serious whisper. "I'm telling you... it felt like Satan himself reached up and put my junk in a chokehold."

Alex was already doubled over laughing, and Andi completely lost it.

"You turned purple and cried. In public." Alex turned to Andi, laughing. "He came out of the bathroom practically screaming!" she said, wiping a tear from her eye. "I don't think he walked normal for like three days after that!"

Andi burst out laughing, covering her mouth with her hand. "Oh, I wish I would've seen that!" she said, shaking her head, still laughing. "You, hopping around like your...uh... little buddy was on fire—that's the kind of video that wins ten grand on America's Funniest Home Videos without even trying!"

They chuckled, letting the warmth of the moment settle for a beat. But it didn't take much for the tension to creep back in. A man at a nearby table raised his voice at the bartender, and Andi flinched before she could catch herself, stirring her drink absently without taking a sip.

Alex noticed. She always did now—every glance over Andi's shoulder, every little freeze when someone laughed too loudly or moved too quickly. She reached over and brushed her hand lightly against Andi's. "Hey," Alex said softly, "you're safe here."

Andi's smile faltered, but she nodded. "I know," she said, almost convincing herself. "It's just... habit."

Alex didn't push. Some wounds just need patience—and presence.

Still, it gnawed at her—the secrets she was keeping from Andi. Every instinct screamed to be honest, to lay it all out: the evidence they were gathering, the danger they suspected.

She had tried once. Carefully. She asked Andi if she had ever thought—if only for a second—that maybe Damon was doing something to cause her illness. The reaction was instant: disgust and anger, as if Alex had slapped her across the face. Andi defended him with a kind of blind loyalty that made Alex's chest ache. That moment told her everything she needed to know. Andi wasn't ready. Not even close. The web Damon spun around her was still too strong, still too blinding. If Alex pushed again, if she forced Andi to see too soon, she wouldn't shut down—she'd run. Straight into Damon's arms. They couldn't risk that.

So Alex smiled when she wanted to cry. Laughed when she wanted to scream. Pretended everything was okay. Because pretending was the only way to keep Andi close—and maybe, just maybe, alive.

While Andi excused herself to the restroom, Alex moved. Her hands were steady and quick. Each movement was sharp with purpose, wired tight with everything she couldn't say out loud. She dug into Andi's purse, pulling free the brush she'd seen her use earlier. She plucked a single hair curled around the bristles, slipping it into one of the tiny evidence pouches Sheldon had given her.

She dug deeper. Her fingers brushed against a small plastic bag tucked into a side pocket—strange, unmarked pills. Her stomach twisted, but she didn't hesitate. One pill went into another pouch. She snapped a photo of the bag, fast and quiet.

The faint rattle of a prescription bottle caught her attention. Alex photographed the label without blinking: doctor, dosage, pharmacy. She didn't need to know the details right now—just needed the trail—adding a pill to the growing evidence.

She moved methodically, heart hammering louder with every second as she swabbed the inside of the gum canister—the container of Andi's favorite loose tea. Everyday things. Things that should have been safe. If Damon was drugging her, it wouldn't be obvious. It would be buried deep, tucked inside the places Andi trusted most.

By the time she zipped the purse closed and set it back exactly where it had been, a rush of cold relief flooded through her.

Thank God.

It was done.

And if she had her way, it was the beginning of the end.

When Andi returned, the conversation had definitely shifted. Dinner was winding down, laughter fading into something quieter, heavier. Walker leaned forward, his voice low and steady. "You need to start thinking about an exit plan, Andi. Not only for you—for Meryl too. Talk to a lawyer. Someone who knows how to handle this the right way, under the radar. I know you're not ready to make a decision about your marriage yet, but please—you need to know your options."

He paused, letting it sink in. "And get a burner phone," he added, his voice dropping lower. "Hide it somewhere safe. If Damon's the kind of guy we think he is, he might already be tracking your phone. You need a way to call for help if you need it—without him knowing."

Andi didn't argue. She didn't say yes either. But the fact that she didn't shut it down felt like a start.

Alex leaned in, her voice soft yet fierce with emotion. "Andi, listen to me. I know you don't believe it right now, but you *need* to know that you are absolutely amazing. You are loved. You are respected. And you are wanted—by so many people who would show up for you in a heartbeat if you let them.

Damon needs you to forget that. He needs you isolated. He needs you to believe he's the only one left who cares. That's how he keeps you."

Andi dropped her head, staring down at her hands, twisting the edge of her napkin until it shredded apart between her fingers.

Alex pressed on, needing her to hear this. "It's taken me years to figure this out, but I can tell you without a doubt—you and I, Andi, we're givers. It's just who we are. And with you, it's so damn clear. You love with your whole heart. You give every piece of yourself without holding back, and people feel it. They know you genuinely care. You can't fake that—it's real."

Andi swallowed hard, blinking rapidly as tears welled up in her eyes.

Alex slid her hand across the table and covered Andi's shaking fingers. Her voice thickened with the weight of it. "But that beautiful, giving heart of yours... it fell in love with a taker."

Andi let out a tiny sound—half sob, half laugh—like some part of her wanted to argue but knew it was true.

Alex didn't let go. "A taker doesn't just take; they consume. They don't have limits. They'll drain you dry and still look at you like you're the problem for running empty. No matter how much love, how much patience, how much forgiveness you pour into them, it's always expected and never enough. It never will be."

Andi squeezed Alex's hand back weakly, her knuckles turning white.

"And the worst part?" Alex said, her voice breaking. "Givers... we don't have limits either. That's why you're so tired. That's why you feel like you're disappearing. Because you have given him everything you had, and he just keeps taking."

Andi crumbled. She dropped her face into her free hand and sobbed, the kind of raw, broken sound that made Alex's heart shatter right alongside hers.

"I know you want to believe there's still a piece of him left—the man you fell in love with. But he's not there, Andi. He never was. He showed you exactly what he wanted you to see."

Andi stared at her lap, silent and frozen.

"He love-bombed you," Alex pressed, tears streaming down her face. "That's what they do. They drown you in attention, in affection. They make you feel seen like nobody else ever has. Like you finally found the one person who truly gets you." Her voice broke. "But it's all an act."

Andi's chin trembled. She didn't lift her head.

"You didn't fall in love with who he is," Alex said, voice steady now, merciless. "You fell in love with the mask he built for you. The version he knew you'd trust. The version you'd fight for."

The silence was brutal.

"And the real him?" Alex continued. "He's the one who cuts you down every chance he gets. The one who twists your mind until you can't even recognize yourself anymore. That's who he is. That's who he's always been."

Andi's voice cracked through a sob, small and wrecked. "He tells me... I'm the problem. That I'm the narcissist. That I need tough love. He's trying to make me stronger. That I don't listen like I should." She wiped her face with shaking hands. "Maybe... maybe he's right."

Alex shook her head, harder than she meant to. "No." Her voice was firm. "He's not! That's not love, Andi. That's gaslighting—manipulation. That's what narcissists do. They rip you apart and then hand you the pieces, blaming you for being broken."

Walker spoke up then, his voice gravelly. "He's terrified of you, Andi. Terrified of losing the grip he's had on you all these years. If he loses control, it shatters the fragile, fake image he's built for himself. That's what this is—pure fear. Insecurity. Nothing more."

Alex reached across the table, wrapping both of her hands around Andi's. "Do you *feel* like you deserve better?"

Andi's lips parted, but the words fought their escape. "I... I think so. But... I don't know."

Alex blinked hard against the tears burning her eyes. She squeezed Andi's hands tighter, grounding her, holding her there. Her voice dropped to a thick whisper. "If this were Meryl—if it were her living like this—what would you want for her?" She waited, heart hammering. "Would you want her trapped? Afraid? Wondering if she deserves better?"

Andi's face crumpled, a sob slipping out before she could stop it.

Alex pressed on, her voice shaking but steady enough to carry the truth. "The moment you even wonder if you deserve better... you do. Sometimes you have to make a decision that will tear your heart wide open—but save your soul."

She shifted closer, her forehead almost touching Andi's now. "You and Meryl deserve to be free. You deserve love that doesn't come with fear. Don't you ever let him make you forget that."

Walker's jaw tightened as his eyes caught something ugly flash across Alex's phone screen. He caught her attention with a sharp, quiet, "Al..." and slid her phone across the table toward her. "Look. All from Damon."

Alex's stomach dropped. "Shit," she said under her breath. She unlocked the screen, her
hands panicking as a flood of venom filled the display:

Why the fuck is nobody answering my call? That's a problem!

You're with her, aren't you?

She knows better than to be out this late. You know better too.

How dare you defy me!

She's sick because of choices like this. Every time she gets worse, that's on you. And when she breaks, I won't forget whose fault it is.

I'm giving both of you this one warning. This won't happen again. If she's not headed home in five minutes, there's gonna be problems.

Well, Miss Halloway... Remember this moment. You chose it. You don't work for me anymore. Stay the fuck off my property—and away from Andria. Try crossing me, and let's just say CPS will be getting a little tip. Would be a shame if your perfect little life got... complicated.

Alex felt the blood drain from her face. Her hand tightened around the phone as if she could crush it. She looked at Walker, then at Andi—whose eyes were wide, terrified, locked on her own screen as it lit up with messages. Andi's hands shook uncontrollably as she scrolled, tears slipping down her cheeks before she could stop them.

Why the fuck aren't you home yet?

Answer my Goddamn call!

You know exactly what this looks like.

You know the fucking rules!

You're dragging yourself lower every second, making a fool of yourself—and dragging me down with you.

Keep it up. Keep acting like you're fine. Every time you get sicker, remember—you did this to yourself.

You think you can ignore me? Keep testing me, little girl!

You have five minutes, Andria. If I don't see you moving, I swear—you'll find out what it means to cross me. And trust me... you don't want that!

Call after call. Text after text. Every message peeling back the mask Damon wore in public, exposing the monster underneath. Each word was a blade, carving another wound. Tightening the noose around Andi's neck until she could barely breathe.

Andi's face collapsed. Her body seemed to fold in on itself, shoulders curling forward as if she could make herself small enough to disappear.

Walker shoved back his chair, fire flashing across his face. "He's psychotic. You can't go back there. Not after this. You need to get out tonight, before he gets back!"

Alex turned to Andi, panic rising in her chest. "Yes! Andi, Walker's right. It's not safe. Get Meryl and come to our house. Or find a hotel—somewhere discreet. We'll pay so he can't track you there!"

Andi looked broken. Not just afraid—stripped bare, as if her soul had been emptied out and abandoned.

Then, without warning, something hardened in her eyes—sharp, cold, final. It was the look of someone who had already made up their mind. Someone who knew they were walking straight into hell—and was still going.

Her hands moved fast, frantically, yanking her purse, her coat, and her keys from the back of the chair. Before Alex or Walker could process it, Andi was out the door, like she was trying to outrun the fear clawing at her back.

"Andi, no—please!" Alex called after her, pushing back from the table so forcefully that her chair nearly toppled.

Walker stood too, waving frantically to catch the waitress's attention. "I got the check," he said, his voice tight with urgency. "Go after her!"

Alex didn't waste another second. She chased Andi outside into the freezing night air, her heart pounding, terror scraping at her throat.

"Andi, PLEASE!" Alex begged, reaching for her arm as Andi fumbled with her car door. "You can't go back there! Please listen to me!"

Andi spun around, wild-eyed and crying, her hands trembling as she gripped Alex's shoulders.

"I have to!" she sobbed. "I don't have a choice!"

"You do!" Alex insisted, her voice cracking. "Andi, you *do* have a choice!"

"I'm sorry," Andi cried, her voice breaking. "I'm so sorry, Alex. I'm sorry for everything..." She clutched Alex as if she were drowning, her body shaking so hard it nearly knocked them both over.

Alex hugged her tightly, feeling the fear radiate off her in waves. "Please, please don't go back," she pleaded desperately. "Please listen. You don't have to do this."

But it was like trying to hold on to smoke. Andi tore away from her, stumbling into her car. Tears blurred her vision as she yanked the door shut and fired up the engine.

Walker rushed outside just in time to see the headlights flare and Andi's car peel out of the parking lot, tires screeching against the pavement.

Alex and Walker stood there, frozen under the dim streetlights, their breath fogging in the cold air.

Their eyes met—and in that instant, they both felt it: the sick, hollow certainty. They had just watched Andi drive away for the last time.

Thirteen

Smoke, Mirrors, and Locks

Rebecca cursed under her breath as she swung into the Outpost's neglected lot, a good fifteen minutes later than she should have been.

Her morning? A total shit show, to say the least. No more than three minutes after Theo and the kids walked out the door, one of her many dogs had a sudden, explosive case of the runs—right in the middle of the kitchen—and then took off on a victory lap, tracking it through every room in the house. There were paw prints on the couch, the stairs, and somehow even on the wall. The stench was awful—thick, sour, and clinging to the back of her throat—but there hadn't been time to clean anything properly. She had roughly managed to corral the mess and shove a towel over the worst of it before bolting.

Now, as she parked, dread gnawed at her, knowing the disaster was still waiting for her at home.

Rebecca hadn't even looked at her phone until she bent down to grab it off the floorboard—her purse had tipped over during the wild drive, spilling half its contents. She caught a glimpse of the screen as she locked her car and hurried toward the door, and her stomach dropped.

Alex:

I NEED TO TALK TO YOU, PLEASE CALL ME ASAP! DAMON FIRED ME!

She blinked at the screen, stunned. *What the hell?* she thought, furrowing her brows in confusion. Then she realized Andi's car wasn't there; the dealership wasn't open yet. Her pulse ticked up a notch. Still, there was no time to call. She had to get the place open and figure out what was going on later.

Still reeling, Rebecca rushed inside, flicked on the lights, turned off the alarm, and flipped the "Closed" sign to "Open." Anxiety tightened in her chest. One by one, the crew rolled in—Frank, Jason, Eddy, and the warehouse guys—each yawning, joking casually, coffee in hand, peacefully unaware that the day was about to go completely off the rails.

Frank scratched the back of his head and looked around. "Wait... where's Andi?"

"That's weird," Eddy added, frowning as she pulled out her phone. "She's supposed to be here. Did anyone get a message that she wasn't coming in today?"

Rebecca felt the words rising in her throat like bile. She took a breath, rubbed her hands down the front of her jeans, and looked at the crew. "I don't know what's going on with Andi, but something's not right, you guys." Her voice softened, heavy with concern. "Alex texted me early this morning, but I didn't see it until I walked in here. Damon fired her!"

Everyone stared.

"Fired her?" Eddy echoed, bewildered.

"Yeah," Rebecca nodded, her words spilling out in a rush. "I haven't even had a chance to call her back yet. I saw the text as I was walking in, and my stomach sank. Something's off, you guys... seriously off."

She looked around at them, her voice soft but urgent. "Alex has mentioned some things to me lately, like there's something going on between Damon and Andi that she knows about. She said it wasn't her place to say much, but you could tell... she's been really worried. She seems almost scared. She never said it out loud, but you know when you can just tell? It was all over her face." Rebecca exhaled hard. "With that text and now Andi not showing up... I don't know; I just feel like this is bad."

Dead silence.

Jason stood there in total shock, his big frame frozen as the words sank in.

"You serious?" Frank asked sharply, his eyes narrowing. "So we have no idea what happened? I mean... Alex is one of the best salespeople we've got. Damon would be an idiot to let her go. There's no way this could be because of her!"

Rebecca shook her head, her voice full of concern. "Yeah, I don't think this has anything to do with something she did... it feels more like it's tied to whatever this thing is that Alex has been worried about lately."

"Jesus," Eddy groaned, rubbing her temples. "I'm about done with this shit. Damon's been acting like a damn demonic lunatic lately, Andi's been totally off, and now Alex gets canned out of nowhere? None of this makes sense."

Attempting to keep the morning routine on track, Eddy walked behind the counter to tackle the usual opening checklist. She pressed play on the blinking voicemail light, expecting a customer call or a delivery notice—anything normal.

The speaker sputtered, and then Damon's voice came through: "*Yeah... Andria's not coming in today. You guys need to figure it out. I don't want excuses. Get your shit together and handle it.*"

The sound of Damon's smug, demanding tone ignited something in them. Rebecca could see it on their faces—the irritation, the anger, the growing unease. There was no explanation, no professionalism, no reason for why the manager was just not coming in.

They all exchanged glances, thinking, *What the hell was that?*

Jason walked over to grab his job schedule for the day so he could head to the back and start working. He snatched the clipboard off the counter, muttering under his breath, "He's such a fucking dick."

Frank shifted out of his usual wide-legged, arms-crossed stance—the one he defaulted to whenever Damon's name came up—and grabbed his clipboard without a word. He looked as if he wanted to be anywhere else. As he passed Rebecca, he muttered, "Let me know when you hear from Alex, alright? I need to know what the hell is actually going on," then headed toward the back without waiting for a response.

Rebecca was about to sneak away and call Alex when a car pulled into the lot, immediately followed by the phone ringing. Eddy answered it and seemed like she'd be tied up with this customer for a while. Rebecca sighed—her window of opportunity was gone. For now.

The crew did what they always did: shook off the weirdness and slipped into work mode. They were good at compartmentalizing, but Rebecca wasn't. She kept checking the clock, her stomach tightening with each passing minute. Something felt wrong, and it wasn't going away.

Just before noon, she made her move—lunch break, quick call in the car. But as she reached the front door, a familiar, jarring sound stopped her cold: tires crunching hard on gravel.

Damon's truck.

Her heart jumped, pulse pounding in her ears. She turned back and darted toward the office. "Damon's here!" she hissed to Eddy. "Go tell the guys. Now."

Damon entered like a storm—heavy steps, a dangerous shade of crimson on his face, eyes seething and dark. The energy shifted instantly, thick and electric. Rage radiated from him in waves so strong it practically stole the air from the room.

"Front and center!" he barked, his voice shattering the uneasy quiet. It ricocheted through the building, echoing through the service bays, across the hallways, and into every corner where someone might have hoped to hide.

He didn't stop moving. He paced like a caged animal, breathing heavily and scanning faces that hadn't yet appeared. The staff crept out one by one—Frank wiping his hands on a rag, Jason keeping his head down, and Eddy clutching her clipboard like a shield. Rebecca froze mid-step near her desk, her heart thudding in her throat.

No one wanted to be there. No one dared to leave.

He jabbed a finger toward the front lounge, the motion so sharp it sliced through the tension. "Sit. All of you. Now."

They moved as if walking through wet cement—slow and cautious, watching his every twitch. No one was fast enough. No one ever was.

He let the silence hang for a beat, then detonated. "You think I don't know what's going on?" he snarled, his words already hot. "You think I'm fucking stupid?"

Every sentence struck like lightning. He was sweating, veins bulging, words tumbling over one another faster than his mind could organize them. But beneath the fury, there was purpose.

"I'm out here dealing with real problems," he snapped, sweeping an arm toward the door. "Andria's had another episode—doctor, specialist, hospital, whatever—and I'm the one who has to waste my time taking care of it while you clowns sit around like you don't give a damn. And what do I get in return? Disrespect. Laziness. People thinking the rules don't apply to them."

He let the next word drip like poison.

"Alex."

He waited, letting the name resonate through the room.

"Liar. Thief. Traitor." He paced, his voice dripping with venom, then leaned forward, eyes blazing. "She's been running her own little side operation—parts, electronics, who knows what—skimming off the top and blaming the rest of you when the inventory comes up short." He shot a sharp glance around the room, holding each of them in his glare. "That's right. Little Miss Goody-Two-Shoes has been trying to make me think one of you is stealing from me. She's been bad-mouthing me to customers, spreading poison, trying to wedge herself between me and Andria to make herself look like some kind of hero. But I'm not stupid—I checked the records, traced the numbers, and the trail leads straight to her drawer. She's not going to pull one over on me." He jabbed a finger toward the group, his voice lowering to a deadly calm. "I'm not saying any of you are involved, and I don't want to believe any of you would stoop that low, but she's been pointing fingers your way. So if you value your jobs—and if you don't want me calling the police—you'll stay the hell away from her. And I swear, if one of you is hiding behind her, helping her... there'll be hell to pay."

Rebecca felt her skin prickle. *What is he doing?,* she thought. *He's trying to ruin her. There's no way Alex did this.*

But Damon wasn't done. He prowled the room, feeding off their silence. This wasn't a rant anymore—it was theater. Punishment. "You think I didn't try to talk to her?" he barked. "I gave her a chance last night. I laid it all out—proof, right in front of her—and what does she do? Blames all of you! Throws her own team under the bus so she can look like a fuckin' victim. Well, I'm not letting her get away with that. Not this time."

He slammed his palm on the counter. "And Andria—she's been getting worse ever since Alex started here. You think that's a coincidence? Maybe Alex's sweet little hands have been doing things she shouldn't. She thought I wouldn't find out.

She thought I'd let her keep ruining my name—my family. She thought wrong!"

The crew shifted uneasily. The accusation was insane, but he delivered it with conviction, like a man desperate to make his madness sound like reason.

Then, without warning, Damon strode toward the glass doors.

Click.

The sound echoed like a gunshot.

He turned, jaw tight. "We're closed until I say otherwise." He yanked down the "Open" sign and flung it across the floor. It clattered against the wall and fell silent.

Rebecca froze. "Damon… why did you lock the door?" she asked carefully.

He spun toward her, his eyes like dark glass. "Because we're having a private conversation," he said. "And I don't need any interruptions. Not from customers. Not from Alex's little spies."

No one spoke. The air grew heavier. Eddy's face went pale; Frank fidgeted with his rag.

Rebecca slid her phone from her pocket under the counter and texted quickly.

Rebecca:

I don't know if I'm safe here. Damon locked us in.

Theo:

Do you need me to call the police?

Rebecca:

Not yet. I'll text again if it gets worse.

Damon clapped his hands together, startling them all. A strange calm came over him. "Alright, listen up. Here's what's going to happen." He stalked forward, his voice softened a bit. "I'm going to be gone for a while. Like I said, Andria's sick—real bad. So I have to waste my time taking her to some specialist. But I'm not leaving this place in the hands of a bunch of children who can't tie their own shoes." He scanned the faces in front of him, his voice dropping low and serious. "You want to keep your jobs? Then you'll do exactly what I say—exactly how I say it."

He paused, waiting. "Do we understand each other?"

A slow murmur of yeses drifted back—half-hearted, shaky.

"Good." He nodded once. "While I'm gone, this place will run like a machine. Showroom spotless. Service on schedule. Lot neat as a pin. No excuses. And if anyone asks about Alex—you tell them she was fired. You tell them she's a liar and a thief, and that I never want her name mentioned in this building again." He took a menacing step forward. "And if any of you so much as speak to her—or let her set foot in here—you're gone."

He continued. "And don't bother reaching out to Andria. She can't answer right now. If you need anything, email me or text me—I'll get to you when I can. No calls. Do you hear me? NO CALLS."

Eddy rolled her eyes. Frank stared at the floor. Jason clenched his jaw so hard that a vein bulged at his temple.

For nearly two hours, Damon kept them trapped in his twisted "meeting." He paced, barked orders, and repeated himself, his voice rising and falling in angry then calm waves. The message never changed: Andria was sick, Alex was poison, and he was the only one holding everything together—the hero in his own story.

When he finally stopped, he scanned the room, daring anyone to challenge him. "And I don't need anybody fucking with me about this," he growled.

Then he turned on his heel. "Boys—back with me. Let's go see what kind of shit's falling apart in the warehouse."

Jason, Frank, and a couple of the part-timers followed him, silent and stiff. Rebecca and Eddy just stood there, stunned.

Eddy exhaled shakily. "Holy hell," she said, dragging a hand through her gray hair. "So what the hell am I supposed to think right now? Alex stealing? Andi's sick and not coming back anytime soon? That's what he meant, right?"

Rebecca nodded, still staring at the door. "Yeah. I just... there's no way Alex would do that. And Andi—sick like that? I had no idea."

Eddy's eyes narrowed. "Yeah, we knew she wasn't doing great, but not like this."

"Neither did I," Rebecca said. "And now we're supposed to keep this place running without them? What if someone comes in with a return or something? I think they were the only ones with the codes to process those."

Eddy let out a bitter laugh. "Figures. Those two were the only reason this place didn't crash half the time. And now it's on us? This is gonna be a shit show."

Rebecca let out a dry laugh. "Yeah... worse than my house this morning."

They stood there for a moment, both overwhelmed and unsure what to say next. Then Eddy squared her shoulders. "Alright. Go grab something to eat before he comes back and starts another round. I've got the front."

Rebecca gave a small nod. "Yeah... I'll just grab a protein bar from my car. I don't want Damon seeing me heat up an actual lunch."

Outside, Rebecca hurried toward her car, passing Damon's truck—and stopped dead.

Inside, slumped against the passenger door, was Andi.

Rebecca's heart slammed into her ribs. She'd been out there the whole time—right there in the truck, while Damon went off like a lunatic inside? She rushed to the window and knocked softly, her hand shaking.

It took a moment, but Andi stirred, her eyes fluttering open. She looked to be dressed in nothing more than a heavy robe and a thin blanket. Her hair was matted, her face was pale and bruised. As she shifted, the blanket slipped, revealing a large wound on her neck, half-covered by a clumsily placed bandage.

"Oh my God, Andi... what happened?" Rebecca breathed.

Andi's lips were stiff as she managed to whisper, "I ran,"

Rebecca stared, struggling to comprehend. *Ran?* She wondered if Andi had run into something or had some kind of accident. What did that mean? She was about to ask more questions when Damon's voice boomed from inside.

"Shit..." Rebecca gasped. "I've gotta go."

"Wait," Andi rasped, her voice rough and faint. She reached out and grabbed Rebecca's wrist, her grip weak yet urgent.

Fumbling in the pocket of her robe, Andi's fingers trembled as she pulled out a crumpled, folded piece of paper and pushed it into Rebecca's hand.

"For Alex," she whispered, like it was the last bit of strength she had.

Rebecca froze, staring at the note in her palm and then at Andi's bruised, distant face. Her throat tightened. "I'll give it to her." she said, voice etched with confusion and sadness. "I promise."

The dealership's sliding doors whooshed open as Damon approached to leave. From inside, Eddy's voice rang out—sharp, furious. "Why do you have to act like such an asshole all the time?!"

Damon didn't bother to turn around. He just barked over his shoulder, "Might wanna watch that tone—I'm the one signing your fuckin' paycheck."

As they crossed paths near the door, Rebecca stepped slightly into his path, her tone cautious but genuinely concerned. "Hey, um... I saw Andi in the truck. Is she alright?"

Damon didn't slow down. He scoffed under his breath. "I told you, she's sick. Had one of her little episodes and fell or something. I had to take her to the hospital—wasted half my day."

Rebecca blinked, taken aback. "Oh... wow. She looks bad. Is she going to be okay?"

Damon stopped long enough to toss her a sideways look, cold and annoyed. "They gave her something to relax her. She'll be fine. Just needs rest. Like I said, we're gonna be gone a while, so you guys need to step it up and hold it down. Don't make me regret leaving you guys in charge."

And with that, he kept walking, as if none of it mattered.

He jumped into his truck and tore out of the lot, gravel spitting behind him.

Rebecca stood frozen, staring after him, her heart pounding in her ears. Maybe she should have felt relieved that he said they'd been to the hospital—but something about the whole situation felt off. Way off. His tone, the way he brushed it all aside like it was nothing. And that bandage on Andi's neck... that wasn't hospital work.

She looked down and realized she was still clutching the note. Her hands were sweaty as she unfolded it. With one glance, the blood drained from her face. Her knees nearly buckled. The words were short, shaky, but clear enough.

She clutched the paper tighter, her breath catching.

She had to get to Alex.

Now.

FOURTEEN

SHATTERED SILENCE

ALEX HAD TOSSED AND turned all night. The entire day was crawling forward like it was dragging chains behind it.

Walker was already at work, and with daycare and school closed for the holiday break, the kids were supposed to spend the day at Sheldon and Melena's. But at the last minute, Alex couldn't let them go. She'd told herself keeping them home would help—give her something to focus on, keep her busy, keep her grounded. But it wasn't working.

She was supposed to be at work today. Instead, she paced the kitchen floor like a caged animal, circling the island again and again like she might wear a path straight through the floor. She stared out the window. At the door. At her phone. She made coffee. Let it go cold. Made toast. Let it sit untouched. Still wearing the same hoodie and leggings from the night before, her clothes felt wrinkled and clung to her like the weight of the last day. Her eyes were raw from crying, her lids heavy, and her lashes matted. Her skin felt stretched too tight over her bones.

She reached for her phone again, checking it for the hundredth time, as if the next glance might finally break the silence.

She had texted Rebecca earlier that morning:

I NEED TO TALK TO YOU. PLEASE CALL ME ASAP! DAMON FIRED ME!

A little later, she sent another message:

Let me know if everything's okay. Please. I'm worried about Andi. Is she there?

Still, there was nothing.

Throughout the day, she messaged Andi repeatedly:

Are you okay?

Call me. Please!

I'm right here for you, always.

Nothing. No response. No read receipts. Just that crushing, breathless silence that felt like it was tearing the oxygen straight from her lungs.

She checked the time every few minutes. Looked out the window. Refreshed her messages. Backed out of the app, and reopened it, as if that might reset the reality she was stuck in. She even called Andi's number once—only once—because the silence was terrifying, but the thought of hearing Damon's voice answer was worse.

With each passing hour, her chest grew tighter. Still no answers. She tried calling the dealership from her home line. No answer there either. Eventually, she blocked her number and tried again—still no answer. *What the fuck?*

She moved restlessly from room to room, picking up clutter only to put it back down. She tried to fold laundry but ended up sitting on the floor, clutching a towel and staring at the carpet. Her phone never left her hand.

The kids, sensing something in the air, were unusually quiet. Harper had taken it upon herself to keep an eye on the boys—reading to them and handing them toys—like a little angel who knew exactly what Mommy needed. They were being so good, entertaining themselves and giving her space.

Alex couldn't stop picturing Andi, replaying every worst-case scenario like a horror film stuck on repeat. She could be anywhere—drugged, beaten, bleeding, or maybe worse. Maybe dead.

At one point, Alex gripped the sink and dry-heaved until her stomach twisted into knots. The sound that escaped her was more animal than human.

Just over twelve hours earlier, she had dropped the samples from Andi's purse into Sheldon's hands. He had promised to rush them to the lab, assuring her it would be fast. But time dragged like dead weight tied to her ankles.

Noon. 2 PM. 3:45. Still nothing.

She pressed her palms into her eyes and tried to breathe, but her chest felt tight, and her mind was fogged from exhaustion. The silence, the waiting, the not knowing—it was eating her alive.

Desperate for something to ground her, she wandered into the kitchen. Maybe a snack. Chips and salsa sounded good. She knew she'd bought a jar two days ago, but when she opened the fridge, it wasn't there. "Of course," she muttered, shoving containers aside and pulling them out one by one. Tupperware clattered against the counter. Milk, juice, leftovers—everything but the damn salsa. Her irritation spiked with each passing second until she was unloading the entire refrigerator like a woman possessed.

It wasn't about the salsa. It never was.

Frustration swelled like a wave in her chest as she turned and stalked down the hall. She found Harper sitting cross-legged on her bedroom floor, drawing a picture in crayon while the twins played nearby—Corbin babbling to a stuffed bear and Liam happily chewing on a block.

"Harper," Alex said, forcing her voice to stay calm. "Do you know where the salsa is?"

Her daughter froze. Those wide blue eyes flicked up, guilt flashing behind them. Alex recognized that look instantly—the *I'm hiding something* look she'd been reading since Harper was a toddler.

"Harper?" she pressed, her voice sharper now. "Where is it?"

Harper hesitated, then slowly pointed to the floor beside her bed. The jar sat there, almost empty, the lid half on. "I'm sorry, Mommy," Harper said, her voice small. "I was hungry last night. I forgot to put it back."

Something inside Alex cracked.

The exhaustion, the gnawing worry about Andi, the helplessness—it all broke loose. Her voice came out screaming, too loud. "You *know* the rule! No food outside the kitchen! What if one of the babies got into this? What were you thinking!?"

Harper's eyes began to well with tears. The twins stopped what they were doing, startled by the sound.

But Alex couldn't stop. The anger kept spilling out, hot and shaking. "You could have ruined the carpet! You could've made the boys sick! Do you ever—" Her voice broke. She grabbed the jar and slammed it down hard on the desk. The lid flew off, salsa splattering across the wall, the desk, and Harper's drawing. The smell of tomato and spice filled the air.

Harper pulled away and gasped, clutching her doll to her chest. The twins began to cry—high, startled wails that pierced straight through Alex's heart.

The sound snapped her back.

Her breath hitched. She froze, staring at the mess, the fear in her children's eyes, her daughter's trembling shoulders. It was like seeing herself from outside her body—rage distorted into something she didn't recognize.

Oh my God, she thought. *What the fuck am I doing? Stop!*

The shame hit her like a tidal wave. She dropped to her knees, scooping the twins into her arms, kissing their heads as they sobbed against her. Harper sat against the wall, silent tears streaking her cheeks.

"Baby, I'm sorry," Alex choked out, reaching for her. "I'm so sorry. I didn't mean to yell at you like that. You didn't deserve it. None of you did." Her tears fell into Harper's hair. "Mommy's just... tired. Worried. I don't know why I did that. I'm so sorry."

Harper buried her face in her mother's chest, crying quietly. The twins calmed, their tiny fingers tangled in her hoodie. Alex held them all—three warm, fragile little souls—and felt the full weight of her failure crush her chest.

This is how it happens, isn't it? she thought. *This is how pain turns into poison. One person carrying too much for too long until it spills over, hurting the people you love most.*

She pressed her forehead to Harper's and whispered, "I'll do better, baby girl. I promise."

When she looked up, the room was chaos: red salsa streaked across Harper's drawing, the twins' toys scattered, and the air thick with the sharp scent of tomatoes and guilt.

She pressed a shaky hand to her heart, whispering to herself, "You can't fall apart. Not like this. Not when she needs you."

And that's when her phone rang. She lunged for it. "Tell me," she gasped.

"I just got the results," Sheldon said, his voice taut with tension. "Alex, they found thallium."

Her vision tunneled as she hurried out of the room. "Okay. What does that mean?"

"Thallium. And a cocktail of benzos, sedatives, and plant-based toxins—stuff so obscure they wouldn't even test for them unless they had a damn good reason. This blend can mimic illnesses like chronic fatigue, neurological breakdowns, and confusion. But thallium? That shit builds up slow. Silent. It eats your body from the inside out."

Alex swayed as she walked back into the kitchen, her mind swimming.

"But how? Why didn't any of her doctors catch it?"

"Honestly, Al? I'm starting to wonder if she's even seeing a real doctor. Or if she is, maybe Damon's the one controlling the narrative, feeding the doctor whatever story he wants them to hear. You mentioned that a lot of her appointments are virtual, right? Or he's the one who talks to them?"

"Y-yeah," Alex managed, her throat tightening.

Sheldon's voice dropped, hardening. "Then maybe it's one of his buddies—someone he can sweet-talk or buy off. Even if she *is* going to a legitimate doctor, this shit's damn near impossible to find. Unless they know exactly what to test for, they won't see it."

He continued, "Thallium's not used medically anymore. It's straight-up poison. And those other drugs? They metabolize weird, leave barely a trace. Remember her sleepwalking?"

"Uh-huh..."

"Yeah," he echoed, his tone darkening. "I think he's staging it. Drugging her, then pushing her down the stairs, cutting her, hurting her. And when she wakes up? He tells her she did it. Tells her she's dangerous. Tells her she's broken."

Alex's voice cracked as the words sank in. "Why? Why the hell would he do this?"

"Because he's creating his alibi," Sheldon said, his voice edged with fury. "And he's damn patient; I'll give him that. He's writing the story before it even happens—the sick wife and the caring husband. So when she dies, everyone feels sorry for him. They'll call it a tragedy, not a crime. He pockets the life insurance, plays the grieving man, and walks away clean."

Alex stared at the floor, her mind spinning. "Jesus, Sheldon..."

He exhaled hard through his nose. "He's not just cruel, Al. He's calculated. Every bruise, every hospital visit, every little 'episode'—it's all part of the setup."

Alex's body went weak as she sat down, hands gripping her knees. "He's been... breaking her. On purpose!?"

"Yep, and now we have enough to move," Sheldon said. "They're fast-tracking the warrant. The judge is on standby—surveillance clearance should come through any minute."

"My god, Shell," Alex breathed. "I can't believe this is real. I mean... I can. But I can't."

"Shit, Alex, I've got a detective on the other line. I'll call you back. Stay close to your phone."

She had only a brief moment to catch her breath before her phone lit up again.

Rebecca.

Alex didn't even say hello. "Where's Andi? Are you okay? What happened?"

Rebecca's words tumbled out in a frantic rush. "Alex—holy crap, I wanted to call sooner. I'm freaking out. I got your text that Damon fired you, and then—then he came in saying all this shit, and the whole day just—a total nightmare."

Alex pressed a hand to her forehead. "I'll explain my text in a minute, I swear. Just—what do you mean it was a nightmare? Where's Andi?"

Rebecca sucked in a sharp breath. "Alex... Andi wasn't there this morning. Nobody knew why. Eddy checked the voicemail, and Damon had left this short message—just said Andi wasn't coming in and that we were supposed to 'handle things.' No reason, no details. It was weird as hell." She let out a breath. "Then around noon... he showed up."

Alex's stomach tightened. "What happened?"

Rebecca continued, air thin in her lungs, still reeling from the shock. "He came in—like a raging asshole from the second he walked through the door. He kicked that parts display by the entrance—the one with the digital screen—and the screen flew off and shattered all over the floor. And I swear, Alex, he looked at me like it was my fault. But he didn't say a word about it. He just stepped over the pieces and screamed for all of us to sit down—'front and center,' just like that—and then he totally exploded."

Alex's grip on the counter whitened.

"Alex, he *lost* it," Rebecca said. "He's making insane accusations about you. Like, totally unhinged stuff."

"About me?"

"Yes, he called you a liar and a thief, claiming you'd been stealing parts and electronics for months, trying to pin it on the rest of us."

"What!?"

"Oh, and he took it even further! He said you'd been manipulating Andi, implying that you might even be *making her sick.* Like he actually suggested you were doing something to her to make her worse."

Alex went silent, disbelief settling like lead in her chest.

Rebecca continued, her voice shaking. "He said you've been trying to destroy his and Andi's marriage, that you were obsessed with her, spreading rumors to customers, trying to turn everyone against him. He said he found 'proof' in your drawer and almost called the cops. Then he looked right at us and said if any of us ever talked to you again, we'd be fired—and that if he found out anyone was helping you, he'd press charges."

Alex pressed a hand to her forehead. "Holy Christ. He is fucking psychotic! Please tell me you know he's lying, Rebecca. You *know* I'd never—"

"Of course I know," Rebecca said quickly. "You don't have to convince me. But, Alex... he was *convincing.* The way he said it—it was like he rehearsed it. Everyone's freaked out. They don't know what to believe. They're scared."

Alex dragged in a breath, trying to slow her heartbeat. "What the fuck!?"

"He wasn't done," Rebecca said, her voice rising again. "Alex... he *locked the dealership.* Like actually locked the front door and said nobody was leaving until he finished. He kept pacing back and forth, ranting about how he gave you a chance to 'come clean,' but you turned on all of us. Then he said you were trying to ruin the business, tank his reputation, destroy his family—all this crazy shit."

Alex's stomach knotted. All of his bullshit about her stung—of course it did—but it wasn't surprising. A lying, manipulative piece of shit like him would burn everyone in his path if it kept the spotlight off himself. That wasn't what mattered. Her voice sharpened with urgency. "And Andi? What did he say about her?"

Rebecca swallowed. "He said she had another episode last night. A bad one. That she was so sick he had to take her to the hospital first thing this morning. And then—" she hesitated, as if even repeating it felt unreal. "—and then he said they're leaving town. To go see 'specialists.'"

Alex froze. "Leaving? For where?"

"That's the thing—I have no idea. He never said where. He didn't give a location, a time frame, or even sound like he knew himself. He just said they'd be gone 'as long as it takes,' and we're expected to run the entire dealership perfectly in the meantime. No excuses."

Alex sighed deeply.

Rebecca continued, "He told us Andi wouldn't be reachable at all. No calls, no texts, no checking in on her. If we need anything, we're supposed to email or text *him* and he'll 'get back to us when he can.' That's all he said."

Her voice cracked. "And then he told us that if anyone asks, we're supposed to say you were fired for stealing and lying. That's literally the story he wants out there."

Alex stared at the wall, her heart pounding in her ears. "Of course he's coming for me. I'm a threat—and he can't have that."

"Yeah," Rebecca agreed. "Completely."

"How long was he there?"

"Two hours, maybe more. He'd blow up, then suddenly get calm, like he flipped a switch. By the time he finally went to the back with the guys, we were all like... numb." Rebecca exhaled hard. "Eddy and I stood there in total shock. I told her I was going to grab something from my car, but really I just needed to breathe."

Her voice dropped to a whisper. "But Alex... holy shit, when I stepped outside..."

"I saw her."

Alex's breath caught. "Her?"

Rebecca's voice cracked. "Andi was in his truck. Right outside. The whole freaking time he was ranting in there."

Alex's hand flew to her mouth. "Oh my God."

"She looked awful—pale, bruised, totally out of it. There was a messy bandage on her neck, like she'd been cut. She was slumped against the window. I tapped on the glass, and she blinked at me and put the window down. But it seemed like she struggled to recognized where she was."

Alex's heart plummeted.

"I tried to ask what happened, but she could barely get words out. All she said was, 'I tried to run.' That's it."

Alex sucked in a sharp breath. "Shit. Shit. Shit. She said she tried to run?!" The words slammed into her chest, panic flaring so fast it made her dizzy.

Rebecca's voice broke. "I didn't know what that meant! Then I heard his freaking voice yelling inside, and I panicked."

Alex's heart was racing now, her thoughts spiraling. *She tried to run!*

"I told her I'd be back, but before I could move, she shoved a note into my hand."

"A note?"

"Yeah." Paper rustled faintly through the receiver. "It's for you. It says, 'You were right. He took my keys. I tried to run. I'm sorry. Tell Meryl I love her.'"

Alex's body went cold as every word sliced deeper than the last. She let out a heartbreaking sound—a jagged, panicked, grief-soaked scream.

"Alex!" Rebecca cried, her voice sharp and shaky now. The sound of Alex's distress hit her like a gut punch. "What the hell is going on? You have to tell me. Please—I need to know *right now.*"

Alex knew she was right.

So she did. She told her everything.

For the next fifteen minutes, Rebecca sat completely silent on the other end of the line while Alex poured it all out—the poisoning, the lies, the manipulation. The dead first wife. The insurance money. His mother's so-called accident. Every sick detail they'd pieced together.

When Alex stopped talking, the line remained quiet except for the faint sound of Rebecca's breathing.

Rebecca swallowed hard, eyes tearing. "He's going to kill her."

Alex's voice steadied, stripped to its core. "Not if we find her first. But you can't tell anyone, Rebecca. Not Eddy, not Frank, not anyone at the dealership. Sheldon's working with the police, but if Damon figures out we know the truth, he'll disappear. And if he takes her with him..." She stopped, voice faltering with panic and realization. "God damn it! That's probably what this is! He's already running with her!"

Rebecca inhaled sharply. "So what do I do?"

"Nothing," Alex said. "You don't know any of this. You have to act normal. Do what he told you to do. Act like you believe what he said about me. He needs to think he's still in control—at least long enough for us to find them."

Rebecca was quiet, then said, soft but firm, "Okay. I get it."

It felt wrong to pretend to believe his lies, but it was necessary. For now, Alex had to be the villain, and Rebecca had to play along. To everyone at the dealership—Damon's story was the truth. Andi would remain the devoted wife of a man claiming to save her.

Rebecca's voice wavered. "I hate this. I hate that everyone's going to think you're the bad guy."

"I know," Alex replied quietly. "But if it keeps her alive, that's a price I'll pay."

The call ended, heavy and hollow, filled with everything they couldn't say.

Minutes later, headlights swept across the driveway. Sheldon stepped out of his truck, a detective beside him.

Alex opened the door before they could knock.

"This is Detective Hale," Sheldon said. "He's our local contact—Tommy and I have been working with him. He's got a team on this."

They stepped inside, and Alex told them everything Rebecca had just told her—the tirade, the lockdown, the accusations, Andi's condition, the note.

Detective Hale listened intently, taking notes, his face unreadable. Then his phone buzzed. He turned away to answer, returning pale.

"That was one of my guys," he said. "They're at the Roth house."

Alex's voice squeaked out. "And?"

"Nobody's there. It looks like they left in a hurry. There are open drawers, things knocked over, spots where it looks like items were grabbed in a hurry. The house is shut down tight—lights off, blinds closed, thermostat turned way down. Everything is locked up like they're planning to be gone for a while."

Alex's knees buckled, and she hit the tile. "Where's Meryl?"

"With a friend," Sheldon said, placing a supportive hand on her shoulder. "She's safe—for now. But she doesn't know."

Alex stared at the refrigerator, the hum filling the silence like pressure in her ears. "She doesn't even know her mom's gone."

Her voice hardened, cold and steady. "He's running, Shel. He's taking her somewhere. We have to find her."

Sheldon nodded once, his jaw tight. "Yeah. And we're running out of time."

Fifteen

Shards of Truth

Alex stood in her kitchen, pacing between the stove and the sink, her arms wrapped tightly around her waist as if holding herself together.

No word. No location. No answers. The last time anyone had seen or heard from Andi was yesterday.

Melena moved through the house with quiet purpose, rocking one twin on her hip while handing Harper crayons and whispering stories meant to distract her from sensing the fear thick in the air. She was doing what she always did—holding the pieces together. Her voice stayed calm, her touch steady, her presence grounding. She offered drinks, murmured reassurances, and squeezed Alex's shoulder with a hand that had weathered its share of storms.

But it was no use. The storm wasn't out there—it was inside Alex, coiled tight in her chest and pounding in her skull. The reassurances bounced off her like pebbles on armor. Nothing could reach the part of her that knew—knew with a mother's instinct and a friend's heart—that something was horribly wrong. She kept replaying the last conversation in her head, Andi's broken voice and the fear in her eyes. Now—nothing. No leads. Just empty guesses.

"Anything yet?" Alex asked as Sheldon walked through the door, Detective Hale following close behind.

Sheldon shook his head, tension coiling through his shoulders and jaw. "We checked surveillance—major highways, side roads, gas stations, rest stops. Nothing. He's vanished."

Alex cursed under her breath. Her hand ran down her face as if trying to erase the feeling pressing in. "We're missing something. He's always five steps ahead. We need to think like him."

Detective Hale exhaled slowly, his tone cautious. "It's time... we need to talk to Meryl. She might know something—maybe a place he's mentioned in passing. A family cabin, an old property, or even something from when she was little."

Alex's eyes snapped to his, fire igniting within them. Not defiance—protection. "I know. But let me be the one to tell her. She trusts me. And this? It can't come from someone she's never met. I'll bring her here. She needs to hear it from me."

She didn't wait for approval. Dread coiled in her gut like barbed wire, every breath slicing a little deeper. She was about to take a sledgehammer to a girl's world—a girl who deserved truth, but not this truth. She would have to look Meryl in the eye and say the unthinkable: your mother is in danger, and your father is the reason. There was no version of this that wasn't cruel; no soft way to land.

She stepped onto the porch, the morning air cold and biting against her flushed skin. Her hand trembled as she pulled out her phone and dialed, each ring like a countdown.

Meryl trusted Alex—not because of time or circumstance, but because she felt it, the same way her mom had. There was something in Alex's presence that cut through the noise, anchoring her without demanding anything in return. It didn't matter that they hadn't known each other for long. Meryl just knew. Her mom had said it once, in a tone that left no room for doubt: "If anything ever happens to me, go to Alex. She's the one I trust to protect you if I can't." Meryl never forgot that.

So when Alex called, she listened.

"Hello?" Meryl's voice was soft, cautious.

"Hey, sweetie, it's Alex. I need to pick you up from your friend's house. Can you get ready?"

A pause. "What's wrong? Is my mom okay?"

Alex swallowed the lump in her throat. "I'll explain everything when I see you. Just... be ready, okay? Please."

Alex picked up Meryl, and on the drive back, the question came fast—raw and panicked. "What's going on?" Meryl asked.

Alex didn't answer right away. She couldn't. Instead, she redirected the question back to Meryl. "What did your dad tell you?"

Meryl's voice shook. "He said that Mom was sick. That he had to take her to a doctor. But when I asked what kind of sick or where they were going, he got weird with me—like I was being annoying. He told me not to worry about it. Said I had to stay with Ellery for the rest of the week. He said her mom already knew, that everything was fine."

Her eyes filled with tears, jaw tightening. "I tried calling her, Alex. Over and over. She didn't answer. She always answers me."

Alex hadn't said much during the drive. She could feel Meryl's fear radiating beside her. Every instinct told her to soften the blow, to protect what little steadiness the girl had left. So she kept her voice calm, her words few, and simply tried to be a steady presence. The truth would come soon enough—and it would hurt.

Now, standing in Alex's entryway, that pit felt bottomless. Meryl's eyes drifted toward the living room, where Sheldon, Melena, and a very official-looking man she didn't recognize sat waiting, their faces tight with concern. They didn't speak at first; they just watched her, silently bracing for what came next.

"Seriously, what's going on?" she asked, panic rising in her tone.

Alex stepped forward, her voice gentle as she ushered Meryl to sit down. "Meryl... your dad took your mom. Last night. And we don't know where he went."

Meryl blinked hard, confusion crashing into something colder. "Yeah, but... I told you he said he was taking her to a specialist. That she was really sick. I thought maybe it was serious—like cancer or something." She looked at Alex, eyes brimming. "He took her to the doctor, right?"

Alex lowered herself beside her, never taking her eyes off Meryl's. "It doesn't look like that's where he took her. We think he's hiding her—and we believe she's in serious danger."

Meryl hesitated, her eyes glassy, lips barely moving. "What do you mean? Why do you think he's hiding her?" she said, though her voice sounded like it had already given up the answer. It wasn't denial—it was dread. The kind that clutches your ribs and dares you to speak the one thing your heart can't bear.

Sheldon leaned forward, voice soft and steady. "We had some of your mom's things tested—like hair from her brush, her tea, the medication she takes, and some other things... Meryl, I'm sorry. But it's clear that your mom is being poisoned. Little by little. We think your dad has been making her sick. On purpose."

Meryl blinked, like maybe she hadn't heard correctly. Then she shook her head fast, wild. "No. No, why would he..." Her voice broke into splinters. "Yeah, he gets mad sometimes. He says messed-up stuff, but he wouldn't actually hurt her. Not like that. Not like really hurt her. That's not—he wouldn't..."

Alex knelt in front of her, holding her trembling hands. Her voice was gentle but firm. "Meryl, people like your dad—they get obsessed with control. And when they feel it slipping away, they'll do anything to get it back. Even things we can't make sense of."

Meryl narrowed her eyes, desperation etched on her face. "But he's not evil. He's just... intense. He yells, like everything has to be his way, but that's not the same as—"

Sheldon gently interjected, his tone steadying the air in the room. His voice wasn't loud, but it landed like thunder. "Meryl," he said, locking eyes with her, "you need to hear this, and I need you to understand—your mom isn't the first. Damon has a history. He's... done this kind of thing before."

He paused, allowing the silence to draw tight.

"Two women are dead." He paused again, letting the words sink in like anchors. "And it wasn't just bad luck or coincidence. We've uncovered things—about his past, about money, about how he's manipulated people and covered things up. There are too many similarities to ignore. Too many details that line up with what's happening now."

He swallowed hard. "We're still digging, but we're certain of one thing—your dad is not who he pretends to be. And your mom's life isn't the only one that's been at stake."

Meryl's mouth opened, but no sound came out. Her eyes filled and overflowed as the truth crashed into her, sharp, sudden, and final.

She collapsed into Alex's arms, her sobs tearing through the room—loud and raw, as if grief had clawed its way out from her ribs. Everything she didn't want to believe, everything she'd tried to push down, came undone in seconds.

"I knew," she choked out, her voice broken. "I think I always knew."

Suddenly, panic washed over Meryl, her face contorting as raw terror took hold. Her eyes widened, wild and unblinking, and she clutched Alex's arms like a drowning girl grasping for a lifeline. "You have to find her!" she cried, her voice shattering at the edge of hysteria.

The sobs intensified—full-body, choking sobs that made her shake. "Please—don't let him hurt her," she gasped, barely able to speak between gulps of air. "You have to get her back, Alex. Please. Please—bring her back."

Later that night, the house was still, but Alex's thoughts kept circling.

She had set up the spare room for Meryl—fresh sheets, dim light, a sweatshirt folded at the edge of the bed. Something soft in a world that had gone hard. Meryl hadn't said much since that breakdown. She'd just clung to Alex without asking questions, as if instinct told her it was the only place left to land.

She'd be staying with Alex now, for however long it took. Until her mom came home—safe. That was never in question.

Alex stayed with her until her breathing evened out, until the tension in her shoulders seemed let go. She sat there in silence, watching the slow rise and fall of Meryl's chest, hoping—praying—it would bring some kind of peace. When the girl finally slipped into a light, uneasy sleep, Alex eased out of the room, closing the door behind her with a soft click.

She walked down the hall with quiet steps, arms folded tightly across her chest. Her thoughts spun, sharper than they had been all day. Something wasn't adding up. Damon had vanished too cleanly. He was slick, yes. Careful. But he wasn't invincible. Ego made men sloppy, and Damon Roth's ego could fill a stadium.

She lay down beside Walker, who was already half-asleep. The mattress dipped as she curled onto her side, and his hand instinctively reached for hers.

"She asleep?" he murmured.

Alex nodded in the dark. "Barely. She cried herself there."

Walker squeezed her hand. "You're doing everything you can."

"Not enough," she muttered sharply. "Not until we find her."

They lay in silence, the weight of everything pressing down like something physical, thickening the air between them.

Walker let out a slow breath, his voice low and rough. "I still don't get how a guy like Damon can just disappear. He always ran his damn mouth about who he knew—backdoor deals, old favors, shady-ass friends. He's probably holed up with that guy... what's his name? Simon. Remember him? I swear they had to be fuck'n butt buddies. That guy was just as fuck'n slimy as Damon."

Alex's chest went still.

Simon.

She hadn't thought of that name in months. But the second it left Walker's mouth, something tightened in her gut. A spark. A shift. Like the first hint of smoke before fire takes hold.

She rolled onto her back, eyes locked on the ceiling as her mind kicked into overdrive.

Simon. Damon's so-called best friend—though it always felt more like a twisted kind of alliance. Alex had only met him briefly, maybe twice. That was enough to know she didn't want to meet him again. He had a presence you forgot the moment he left the room, but not before something about him crawled under your skin. He carried himself as if he were more important than he was, always hovering on the edge of conversations—listening, but never quite present. Socially awkward. Unsettling. The kind of guy who stood too close and never broke eye contact. And that look in his eyes—off. Like you were a target he hadn't decided what to do with yet.

She hadn't considered him once in all of this. Not until now.

And now she couldn't stop thinking about him.

A memory tugged at her—faint, unfinished.

That name.

That day.

That visit.

Her heart picked up.

Something had happened.
Something she hadn't realized mattered—until now.
She closed her eyes.
And the memory started to return.

Sixteen

Glass Houses

Alex couldn't fall asleep. She lay on her side in the dark, moonlight peering through the window just enough to catch the soft rise and fall of Walker's chest. He looked peaceful—his steady breathing moved like waves against the shoreline, unaware of the storm that had taken hold inside her. Her eyes were dry but wide, straining against the shadows in the room, every nerve pulled taut. Her body was still, but her thoughts spun in relentless circles, like a wheel she couldn't unhook herself from. In that restless spin, something dislodged.

A memory.

Something she hadn't thought about in a long time. Something small. But now, suddenly, it felt urgent. Important.

It had been a Saturday evening, a few weeks after she started at the dealership—before anything truly sinister had sunk its claws in. Back when the discomfort she felt around Damon could still be reasoned away as overthinking. Back when Andi still laughed freely, even if the sound held something distant in it. Before the bruises you couldn't see. Before the undertow pulled them all under.

Andi had invited her over that night, her tone light and eager. "We're doing something casual," she'd said. "A few friends, some food and drinks. Come hang out."

Alex had said yes without hesitation. She felt lucky—new to the job, unsure of her footing, and suddenly being included in what felt like the inner circle. Damon, after all, was successful. Commanding. Sure, he could be a little cold at times, but then again, most powerful men were. And Andi... there was something about her—something unspoken and beautiful, kind. She was the type of woman who didn't need to say much to make you feel completely at ease.

For Alex, who had spent most of her life feeling like an outsider, quietly jealous of women who had their friend groups and that seemingly effortless closeness—being invited meant more than she could admit. This was the kind of welcome she rarely received, and it felt amazing.

She remembered pulling into the curved driveway just after six, the sky warming with streaks of gold and coral. The house looked like something from a magazine—tall peaks, warm lights glowing through the windows, the smell of hickory smoke wafting from the backyard.

Laughter spilled over the fence. Music hummed low from outdoor speakers. Alex stepped through the gate with the giddy anticipation of someone who had just been picked to sit at the cool kids' table.

And there was Andi—tongs in one hand, apron dusted with dry rub, smile wide and genuine. That image stuck in her mind now like a photograph: a beautiful woman hosting a barbecue. But even in that moment, there had been something behind her smile.

Something Alex hadn't understood then—but did now.

"Hey! You made it," Andi beamed. "We're just getting started."

Alex smiled. "Smells amazing."

A few people were already scattered around the deck, and over by Damon stood two older neighbors with polite, reserved smiles, along with another man who stood out immediately. He was tall, broad-shouldered, the kind of man whose presence filled the space effortlessly. His hair was light with a heavy dusting of gray, and his face—lined and sunworn—seemed to tell stories he had no interest in sharing. Leaning against the railing with a glass of something dark in his hand, he appeared relaxed, but his eyes? His eyes were sharp. Watchful.

When Andi brought Alex over, the man offered a nod.

"This is Simon—an old friend of Damon's," Andi said, her smile polished yet slightly awkward, as if she were playing a part she wasn't entirely comfortable with. "They've been friends since they were kids."

Simon gave a clipped, "Hey." That was it. No charm, no small talk. Just a glance that lingered a moment too long. Not overtly inappropriate—more like... he was assessing her.

Alex gave a quick smile, reminding herself not to read too much into it. He was probably just shy. Or weird. Or both.

Still, she caught him looking again as she walked away with Andi, and this time, she couldn't shake the feeling. It wasn't threatening exactly, but it wasn't benign either. Like standing too close to a snake you hadn't seen yet, still and silent, aware of you long before you noticed it.

In the yard, Meryl and her friends played Cornhole, their laughter breaking the dusk like wind chimes in a gentle breeze. The trees filtered the last of the golden light, transforming the backyard into a watercolor wash of peach and lavender—the kind of evening that begged to be remembered.

Alex and Andi settled at the far edge of the deck, sitting side by side with their bare feet on the lower step. Their drinks sweated in their hands, condensation soaking through napkins. They talked the way women do when something clicks—cautious at first, then spilling out faster.

They talked about everything—the light stuff and the real stuff. Music. Old dreams. Their kids. About the kind of pressure no one warns you about—always being the default, the caretaker, the one expected to hold it all together. They talked about growing up poor and how that feeling of being behind everyone else never fully goes away, like a voice in the back of your head always waiting for you to fail. They talked about how exhausting it was to be underestimated, having to prove yourself before anyone gave you credit.

And still, they laughed easily, naturally—like two women helping each other breath again for the first time in ages. It was surprisingly effortless, as if they had known each other much longer than they actually had.

"You and Damon," Alex said at one point, her curiosity getting the better of her. "How'd you meet?"

Andi's smile was delicate, tugging at the corners of her mouth, soft and nostalgic. Her gaze drifted beyond Alex, toward the other side of the deck—settling on Damon, who stood with Simon, exuding an aura as if he were the center of gravity and everyone else was just passing through.

"He saw me at a diner," she said, her voice soft and laced with something Alex couldn't yet name. "I was waitressing nights, barely scraping by. He came in with a group of guys after some business thing, left a hundred-dollar tip and a note on the receipt." Her eyes flickered back to Alex. "It said I had the most beautiful eyes he'd ever seen."

Alex's eyebrows lifted in surprise. It sounded sweet.

Andi laughed lightly, but the sound felt distant. "The next night, he came back. By himself. Sat in my section, ordered the most expensive thing on the menu. He said he couldn't stop thinking about me. Started asking me all kinds of questions—my favorite food, music, what I dreamed about... He said he couldn't wait to really get to know me."

Alex smiled gently, not wanting to interrupt.

"By the end of the week," Andi continued, "he was sending me flowers, leaving little notes on my car. He took me out in his Corvette, opening every door, treating me like I was royalty. We got serious really fast. I had never been treated like that. I fell for him so hard. He took me on trips, bought me jewelry, all these extravagant gifts... and he'd always say the sweetest things, like, 'You're mine now. I'm going to take care of you forever.'"

Alex felt a twist in her stomach. The words were romantic—but also possessive. Obsessive. Still, she said nothing.

Andi looked down at her drink, slowly rolling it between her palms. "I couldn't believe someone like him wanted me," she said with a grin, though her tone was etched with heaviness. "All that attention... the way he treated me—it felt like a dream. I honestly thought I was the luckiest girl alive."

Alex nodded. "Wow... That sounds like something out of a movie."

Andi smiled, but there was a heaviness behind it—a kind of sadness she didn't try to hide. "It was. At first." She took a breath. "He used to call me ten times a day, just to say he missed me. He'd get so upset if I didn't text back right away—said it was because he loved me so much... he just worried. That it hurt to be away from me."

Alex's fingers tightened slightly around her glass. She didn't know what to say. Part of her was stunned by the intensity. Another part—the quieter, more discerning part—couldn't help but wonder why she'd never once seen that version of Damon.

Then the grill hissed louder, a sudden plume of smoke rising as the sauce began to bubble and char.

"Hey!" Damon's voice cut through the chatter. "Andria, don't be an idiot and let that food burn!"

Andi flinched. She stood quickly, brushing invisible crumbs from her lap.

"I got it," she said lightly, walking briskly toward the grill.

Damon didn't move. He just sat there, legs stretched out, one arm draped over the back of his chair like a king on his throne—entitled and untouchable. The flames from the grill flickered against his profile, casting sharp shadows across his face. He didn't offer help, thank Andi or acknowledge her effort. He simply tilted his glass in the air like a lazy monarch demanding more wine. "Simon and I need another round," he barked.

"I'll get it," Andi chirped, already moving, her voice upbeat in a way that felt automatic.

Alex stood, her instinct stronger than her politeness. "I can help—"

"No, no, you relax," Andi said quickly, turning back with a reassuring smile. "You're the guest."

But it didn't sit right. The tone. The posture. The dynamic. Damon hadn't lifted a finger since she arrived, while Andi flitted from the grill to the fridge to the drink cooler, dutifully managing everything as he lounged, waiting. The way he spoke to her—commanded her—wasn't just rude; it was demeaning. And Simon's smirk as Andi hurried past with two drinks in hand? That sealed it. There was something else simmering beneath all this. Something that had nothing to do with drinks or ribs.

Alex sat down again, legs crossed, her drink suddenly too sweet, too warm. Her skin itched with unease. She tried to push it aside and join the group conversation, but it all felt forced—like surface-level chatter about where she was from, why she decided to move this way, and what her husband did. Damon pretended to listen, nodding at all the right moments, but his eyes never really focused on her. His laugh, when it came, was empty—a hollow, rehearsed sound.

Then one of the neighbors turned to Simon and asked how he was enjoying his place up in the mountains, adding with a half-joking sigh, "We're all a little jealous—it sounds like the perfect escape. So quiet and remote."

Simon chuckled, a small smirk tugging at his mouth. "It is," he said. "The views are incredible... and the peace and quiet? You could scream at the top of your lungs out there, and no one would hear you."

The group smiled and laughed lightly, but Alex felt a chill slide down her spine.

She excused herself to use the bathroom, grateful for the lifeline. Her head buzzed, her skin prickling with the unspoken tension curling around the evening like smoke. She needed a moment—a minute away from the performance.

Inside, the house was quiet, dim, too still. The hum of the refrigerator seemed louder than it should have been. And the walls—God, the walls were too thin. Every word leaked through like poison.

From the hallway, Damon's voice stabbed the silence. "Jesus, Andria, they said they wanted Italian dressing, not ranch. Is that so hard? Get it right."

There was a pause—just long enough for the sting to settle—before a neighbor let out an awkward chuckle.

"Oh, don't worry about it. It's okay. She's working so hard... probably running on fumes."

Damon spoke again, louder this time and more smug. "She's running on fumes, alright—fumes and a few less brain cells. I swear, even dressing is a challenge these days. No wonder waitressing didn't work out. Lucky for her, she's got me to keep the ship afloat."

Laughter followed—uneasy and uncertain, as if no one quite knew whether it was okay or not.

Alex froze. Her hand hovered near the doorknob, her breath caught halfway in her throat. That wasn't teasing. That wasn't affectionate ribbing or tired humor. That was something else entirely. That was humiliation served on a silver platter.

She swallowed hard and turned, stepping back toward the patio. But the air felt unsettling now, as if the whole night had been silently tilting on its axis while no one noticed.

As she opened the screen door, she caught another exchange. This one was low, too low to be for anyone's benefit but their own.

Simon leaned in toward Damon, both of them grinning like wolves.

"You ready for a trip to Cryer's Edge yet?" he asked, voice slick with something that made Alex's skin crawl.

Damon's smile twisted into something predatory. "Just about. Time to get a new one."

They both laughed.

Alex blinked, disoriented for a moment. Cryer's Edge. What was that—some twisted joke? A place in the mountains? A metaphor? Time to get a new what? Something about the way they said it didn't sit right.

She smiled stiffly and kept walking, pretending she hadn't heard a thing. Just a weird guy joke. She'd heard plenty from Walker—dumb, exaggerated things like "I oughta trade you in for a new chainsaw—less whining, easier on my ears."

Men were just wired to push buttons, right? She used to think so. Until now.

Alex jolted upright in bed, her breath catching as if she'd surfaced from a nightmare—only the nightmare was a memory. Her heart thudded wildly, a deep, echoing panic that crawled into her chest and wouldn't let go. She wasn't just awake. She was aware.

Beside her, Walker was snoring loudly, sprawled under the covers in blissful ignorance. His rhythmic, unbothered rattle was almost comical in contrast to the chaos unraveling inches away from him. Alex stared into the darkness, her mind spinning, and felt the surreal loneliness of sharing a bed with someone who had no idea she was drowning.

Alex swung her legs over the edge of the bed, her feet landing on the cold floor like a jolt to her system. She reached for her phone, the pale blue glow illuminating her face as she typed in the name that wouldn't stop echoing in her mind:

"Cryer's Edge."

Nothing. No listings. No images. Not even a vague GPS dot. Just scattered noise from message boards and ghost story blogs that led nowhere. Her stomach tightened. What were they talking about?

She would call Sheldon and Detective Hale first thing in the morning. They needed to find Simon. And they needed to find Cryer's Edge—whatever that actually meant. Maybe it was a cabin. Maybe a cliff. Maybe just a name tossed around in so-called jokes that were never really funny. Whatever it was, it wasn't harmless. Alex could feel that in her gut. This wasn't just something they said; it meant something. And that something felt dangerous.

Seventeen

Through the Mirror

Over the Edge

Alex spent the night in a restless daze, her phone clenched tightly in one hand, the screen casting a pale glow across the sheets as she scoured the internet for any mention of Cryer's Edge. Forums, map databases, old news archives—she chased every lead she could think of, but nothing made sense. What the hell was it? A ghost town? A forgotten trail? Some remote, ominous landmark lost to time? The more she searched, the more elusive it became.

Frustration burned in her chest. By the time her eyes closed, her soul felt raw—bruised from needing answers the world refused to give.

As the sun peered in through the window the next morning, Alex's eyes jolted open. Her body had slept, barely—but her mind hadn't. A tight, unshakable urgency gripped her chest. She needed to call Sheldon and Detective Hale. Now. The memory from the night flickered like a warning flare in her brain. She didn't know exactly what it meant, but she knew it mattered.

But she couldn't make the call here—not with Meryl sleeping just down the hall. She didn't want to risk the girl overhearing even a fragment of what she needed to say. And honestly, Alex needed a change of scenery. She needed to get out of the house, out from under the weight pressing in on all sides. She craved movement, the sting of cold air—anything to clear her head and steady her nerves.

She left a quick note for Walker and Meryl on the counter, then grabbed her keys. The door clicked shut behind her, and a sharp breath of icy morning air hit her skin. She welcomed it. The roads were quiet, blanketed in a fine shimmer of snow. She drove toward town to pick up breakfast for everyone from one of her favorite diners, which, surprisingly, was still open today. She'd grab coffee, juice, and some warm egg sandwiches—something comforting. Something that said, *You're okay. I've got you.*

She placed the order and then sat in the car with the engine running and the heater blowing. As she made a conference call to Sheldon and Detective Hale, her hands nervously gripped the steering wheel. She relayed every detail she could remember—Cryer's Edge, Damon, Simon—the way they smirked about it, like it was some dark, twisted inside joke. Detective Hale promised to get his team on it immediately, digging into any references that might connect to the name or location. Either he or Sheldon would be in touch as soon as they found something worth chasing.

By the time she hung up, her food had been ready for fifteen minutes—luckily, they had kept it warm for her. Her coffee, however, had gone cold. Despite the hot breakfast waiting in the passenger seat, Alex felt hollow. She had hoped for an immediate reaction from Detective Hale—an instant light bulb moment, a breakthrough. But it hadn't happened. The news didn't spark anything concrete. Instead, she was told to wait. Again. The urgency inside her clashed violently with the stillness she was forced to endure, and for a moment, she sat there, feeling utterly defeated.

When she returned home, the snow had thickened into lazy, deliberate flakes, coating the driveway and dusting her windshield in icy lace. She stepped inside with breakfast bags in hand, nudged the door closed with her hip, and stopped.

Meryl was curled into the corner of the couch, clinging to a throw pillow as if it were keeping her from falling apart. Her face was pale and blotchy, the skin beneath her eyes bruised with exhaustion. She looked like she hadn't slept, and judging by her swollen eyes, she'd cried most of the night.

The truth wasn't just hard for her to hear—it was devastating. Meryl had lived with shadows for years, nagging doubts she shoved into the far corners of her mind, convincing herself they were just noise. Not real. Not possible. Because facing them meant facing something far darker: that her father wasn't just strict, moody, or complicated—he was dangerous. The man who taught her to ride a bike, who straightened her shoulders with a cold palm and a stern look, the man she twisted herself into knots trying to please—was capable of things she'd only ever read about in headlines.

And now, he might be trying to kill her mother.

Coming to terms with the fact that the thoughts she'd buried all these years weren't crazy after all, was almost too much to bear. A heavy wave of guilt hit her hard. She had felt these things deep down before, but she'd ignored them. If she hadn't, maybe things would be different.

The questions pressed in, stealing the air from Meryl's lungs.

Was her mom alive? Would she ever see her again?

She felt like she was suffocating under the storm inside her head.

Alex handed Meryl a warm breakfast sandwich and a bottle of juice, the steam still rising faintly from the wrapper. She offered a small smile, keeping her tone light as she chatted about the snowy roads and how packed the diner had been. It was an attempt at distraction—one she hoped would loosen the weight pressing down on Meryl's chest.

Meryl nodded, grateful for the gesture but still locked in her own storm. Her fingers curled around the sandwich as if she wasn't quite sure what to do with it. As kind as the effort was, it didn't fix the ache. All she wanted was to go home. To her mom. To the version of life that existed before the last few days unraveled everything.

The soft creak of the front door opening and closing kept interrupting the stillness as Walker moved in and out, loading the last of the kids' things into the car. Alex knelt to help Harper zip her coat, lovingly wiping a smear of breakfast from her cheek with distracted tenderness. The kids were going to be gone for a few days, off to the warmth and simplicity of their grandparents' house.

It was Thanksgiving—a time that was supposed to be filled with family, food, and laughter. But today, there wouldn't be a big dinner around their table or any casual joy echoing through the walls. Alex and Walker didn't want that heaviness to touch the kids. Thankfully, Walker's parents understood. They knew something serious was unfolding and had lovingly stepped in, offering the children a special holiday all their own—snow play, cocoa, and stories by the fire.

For Alex, it was a much-needed reprieve. A few precious days to face something darker without letting it spill into her children's world.

Walker stepped back inside, brushing snow from his shoulders. He gave Alex a wink and a warm smile—his silent way of saying, *I've got it from here. Go talk to her.* Alex crouched down to give each of the kids a kiss, hugging them for a moment longer than usual. "I'm going to miss you so much," she whispered, tucking a curl behind Harper's ear. "I want to hear everything when you get back. Every single thing."

Alex lingered in the doorway, her hand lifted in a final wave until the taillights disappeared around the snowy bend. There was no room for sentiment today. As the silence settled, so did her resolve. She turned back into the house, her thoughts still tangled around the scraps of memory and what they might mean. Meryl sat quietly, eyes lowered, fingers idly swiping at her phone, though her expression said she wasn't truly seeing anything on the screen. Alex watched with a mix of worry and restraint. She didn't want to overwhelm the girl, but the clock was ticking, and she thought Meryl might be able to help.

Alex poured herself a cup of coffee. "I remembered something last night," she said, glancing toward Meryl. "It might be nothing—a weird memory maybe—but several months ago, I overheard Damon and Simon joking about something they called Cryer's Edge. I think it might've been a place."

"I've been trying to figure out if it is a real place or just some bizarre code they used. I've searched through old maps, online forums, everywhere I can think of on the internet. Nothing. Sheldon and Detective Hale hadn't heard of it either—total blank. Does that sound familiar to you at all? Ever heard of it?"

Meryl blinked, looking uncertain. "I think... maybe? I don't know. When you say that, it kinda feels familiar—like it makes me think about something I saw before."

Alex remained silent, allowing her space to think.

"I mean, I was a little kid, so I might not remember this right. But I swear, I saw a picture in my dad's desk that freaked me out. There was a cabin, trees all around, and behind it..." — she paused, trying to pull it back — "there was this huge drop-off or something."

Alex's breath caught. "Did you ask him about it?"

"I think I remember that he was really mad at me for going through his desk. He told me it was a fun place he and his friends liked to go—but it wasn't for kids."

Alex's stomach turned. "Would you let me look in his office? There might be something still there—old photos, paperwork, or even just a note scribbled in a drawer."

Meryl didn't hesitate. "Yeah. I'll let you in."

They arrived at the house less than an hour later. Snow clung to the rooflines and hedges like a warning left behind by ghosts. The kind that didn't scream but whispered. As Alex stepped from the car, a chill sliced through her coat, threading down her spine. It wasn't just cold; it felt wrong. The house stood too still, too dark—a hollow shell.

Meryl stood beside her, arms crossed tightly over her chest. Her face had gone colorless, lips pressed into a thin line. The driveway beneath them was the same, the sidewalk unchanged—but the home itself felt violated, as if someone had ripped out its soul while they were gone.

They stepped inside.

Silence.

No lights. No noise. No echo of life.

Meryl's jaw tightened until it ached. "This is so weird," she said through gritted teeth. "I hate this."

Alex rested a comforting hand on her shoulder. "We'll be quick. Just what we need, then we go."

Meryl led her to Damon's office and quietly said, "I'm gonna grab some stuff from my room."

Alex pushed the door open. The hinges groaned in protest, as if even they didn't want her inside. Stepping in, a chill washed over her. The office was a mess—typical Damon. Papers were scattered everywhere, old coffee cups littered the surfaces, boxes were stacked in corners, and random junk covered the desk. It looked like no one had touched it in weeks, maybe months. Her instincts coiled tight.

She moved quickly, her eyes scanning the bookshelves, the desk, and the filing drawers. Her hand paused on a stack of dusty folders—old bills, insurance notices—and just behind them, she found something thicker: a leather-bound binder.

She pulled it free.

Inside—handwritten notes. Photos. Names. Clippings. Her fingers trembled as she flipped through it.

Then she froze.

A photo.

Simon stood stiffly in front of a run-down cabin. Behind him, a cliff jutted sharply into a misty sky. The trees twisted along its edge, as if trying to crawl away. Simon's expression was off—his grin crooked, his eyes too wide. And beside him...

A woman.

Her face was streaked with tears, her body rigid, her expression locked somewhere between terror and surrender.

Alex's stomach turned cold.

She flipped the photo over.

Scrawled across the back in unfamiliar handwriting was a chilling note: "Another cryer claimed. Every one of 'em—weak and pathetic."

Above it, stuck to the photo like a trophy label, was Damon's unmistakable handwriting: Cryer's Edge.

Alex let out a sharp, grating breath that caught in a growl at the back of her throat. Her hand flew to her mouth as a tremor ran through her chest. "I knew it!" she gasped. "It's a place!"

Her pulse hammered as she stared back at the picture—its image swallowed in fog, the trees bent in retreat.

"It's a fucking cliff," she said under her breath, the words seething out of her. "And they call it that for a reason."

Down the hall, Meryl moved through her old room like a ghost. Her fingers closed around her favorite sweatshirt, her makeup bag, and a pillow. Then, in the corner—her koala blanket. She hadn't thought about it in years, but suddenly, the smell of home—the memory of her mom's arms, the couch, cartoons—rushed up and nearly knocked her down. She clutched the blanket to her chest.

As she walked out, tears threatened again, following the faint trace of her mother's perfume down the hall into the master bathroom.

The toothbrush still sat on the counter, along with makeup and a perfume bottle, as if Andi would be back any second. A wrapper lay discarded on the sink. Meryl picked it up, reflexively tidying, thinking, *Mom will want the house clean when she gets home.*

The trash was full. Of course. Her dad never took it out, always "too busy," always leaving it to Mom.

She sighed and reached to pull the bag from the can when something fell out.

A pink box.

She stared.

Early Response Pregnancy Test.

Her eyes darted back to the trash. A stick peeked out from the tissues.

She reached for it, her hands suddenly cold.

A plus sign.

Her breath left her.

She stared at the stick and then at the box, back and forth. Her knees went weak, and her fingers clenched the doorframe.

"Alex!" she cried out, her voice panicked. "You need to come here. Now."

Alex's footsteps thundered down the hall. "Meryl?! Where are you?!"

"In my parents' bathroom!" Meryl shouted back.

Alex skidded into the doorway, her face pale, her breathing shallow from what she'd just discovered in the office.

Meryl was perched on the edge of the marble tub, a plastic stick gripped in her hand.

The silence that followed was vacuum-sealed.

Alex's gaze dropped. A pregnancy test. Positive. Unmistakable.

"What does this mean?" Meryl's voice was a jagged whisper, her eyes brimming.

Alex didn't speak. She couldn't find the air.

She looked at the test, then back at Meryl's pale face.

Their eyes locked—shock overtaking them.

And just like that, everything changed. Again.

Eighteen

Shattered Mirrors Lie Here

Andi's fingers frantically gripped the house key as she approached the front door. The porch light flickered once, then steadied, casting a pale yellow hue over the chipped wood of the steps. She hesitated, inhaling the chilled night air that clung to her skin like regret.

The dinner with Alex and Walker had just ended in chaos—Damon's text messages exploding across her phone like grenades. First came the accusations, then the threats, and finally that cruel, final blow: he fired Alex over text.

Alex's voice replayed over and over in her head—raw with desperation as she begged Andi not to go back home. But she'd left anyway, and now the sound of her boots clicking on the hardwood floor inside the quiet house echoed with an unsettling finality.

Her phone buzzed. Damon:

You're home, right? You better be!

Andi's heart jolted. Her thumbs moved automatically.

Yes.

Three dots appeared. Then:

Good. Take your meds. I'll be home soon. This is all on you, little girl. You had to stir up shit tonight, didn't you? Don't think for one second I'm letting this slide. I'm done with your games. DONE!

Her body went cold.

She set the phone down on the counter fast, as if it had scalded her. The silence in the house was suffocating, pressing down on her chest with invisible hands. She glanced around—dirty dishes still in the sink, clutter on the table, an old throw blanket bunched on the couch. She moved quickly, wiping, folding, straightening—anything to keep her from thinking, from feeling.

But it was impossible to outrun the thoughts.

Alex was gone. Just like that. Damon would never let her see her again. Never let her have that friendship back—the one lifeline that had pulled her from the darkness she'd lived in for years. She had been drowning before Alex. Smiling on the outside, but dying a little more each day inside the walls of this perfect house, with its perfect husband and perfectly disguised hell.

She walked to the bathroom, stripped off her jeans and sweater, and turned on the shower. Steam rose, fogging the mirror, but she didn't step inside. Instead, she stared at her reflection. Her eyes were red and puffy. Her skin looked tired—old. She wrapped a towel around herself and sat on the closed toilet, gazing at the calendar on the wall. Damon made her keep it there to track everything: her meds, work shifts, her cycle, even how she felt each day.

She blinked.

Her period.

It was late.

A few days wasn't unusual, not at her age. *Perimenopause?* Plus, the doctors had told her after Meryl that her chances of having another child were slim to none. Still, something gnawed at her.

She shut off the water, steam curling around her as she knelt down and opened the cabinet beneath the sink. Her hands moved through the clutter until they landed on a crumpled pink box shoved behind a bag of cotton balls. A pregnancy test. Old. Probably expired. Still—what the hell.

She unwrapped it, peed on the stick, and set it on the counter like it didn't matter. Like it didn't have the power to shatter what little foundation she had left. She didn't need to look at it. Of course, it would be negative.

Back in the kitchen, she went through the motions: cleaning, straightening, placing her pills on the counter like she always did. She poured a glass of water and glanced at the bottles.

Then she heard it.

Alex's voice, clear and sharp in her mind: *"Do you pick up your prescriptions? What pharmacy? Are you sure you know what you're taking?"*

A chill slid down her spine.

No.

She didn't pick them up. Damon always did. He claimed it was because he couldn't trust her to stay on schedule—that she'd forget or screw it up somehow. He always said he was trying to protect her and help.

Was he?

Her hand hovered over the pills.

If there was even a tiny chance she was pregnant...

She dropped the pills into her palm and stared at them.

Then she walked to the bathroom and flushed them—she had to. Damon would count the pills, like he always did. If they weren't gone, he'd know. And if he knew she hadn't taken them, well, there would be consequences.

Her hands gripped the counter as the toilet swirled.

The test stick was still lying there. She reached for it with a nervous, detached kind of curiosity, as if it belonged to someone else.

Her breath caught in her throat.

A plus sign.

She stumbled backward like she'd been hit. A sharp gasp escaping her lips—dry, broken, the only sound her body could muster. Her emotions had been thrown in every direction tonight, and now she was left hollow, frozen in disbelief. She clamped her hand over her mouth. *This can't be true.*

Andi stood there, staring at the stick as if it might change if she blinked hard enough. Her hands shook as she wrapped the test in a wad of tissues and shoved it deep into the garbage. The box followed, folded and wedged beneath the pile. She snapped the lid closed. Damon would never notice. He never touched the garbage—that was beneath him. That was her job.

She moved on autopilot, crawling into bed and pulling the covers up to her chin like armor. Maybe if she was asleep when he got home, he'd leave her alone. Maybe he'd see her steady breathing and decide to wait until morning to destroy her.

But her thoughts refused to slow. The plus sign burned in her brain. There was just no way. The test had to be wrong. It had to be. But if it wasn't...

Andi swallowed hard, her hand resting protectively over her abdomen. *If it was a boy...* Maybe that would change things. Damon had been angry when they found out Meryl was a girl, saying it wasn't what he wanted. He'd never said it again, but Andi felt the resentment linger—like something unsaid, rotting between them. He'd wanted a son.

Her heart raced. Her body felt... different. Normally, after taking her pills, the world tilted. Her head got fuzzy. Her limbs felt heavy. She'd chalked it up to her illness. But tonight, without them, she felt clear, stable, present.

That was unsettling.

She hardly had time to process the thought when she heard the low grind of the garage door.

Her blood went cold. He was home.

She shut her eyes and slowed her breathing.

Footsteps shuffled through the house—drunken, heavy, predictable. She heard the clink of ice, the cupboard door slam, the bottle. Brandy. Always brandy.

Then the bedroom door creaked open. She felt him more than heard him—his presence a dark, electric weight hovering beside her. The scent of him. The sour breath. He lingered over her like a storm.

Then... he was gone.

Ten minutes passed.

The door creaked again. This time, he mumbled under his breath—rambling, words she couldn't quite make out.

"...let this go on too long... it's time..."

Her breath hitched.

"...Meryl might miss you for a little while... but she'll get over it..."

She didn't move.

Then he said it, clear as glass:

"I'll be back in a minute little girl. It's time to go to your new home."

What?

Her eyes flew open.

What the hell is he saying?

Terror surged like ice water through her veins. That tone—flat, purposeful, and calm—was foreign. Final.

She slid out of bed as quietly as possible and pulled on the sweatpants by the nightstand. Tennis shoes in hand, phone shoved into her pocket. Purse in the kitchen—no time. She had to move.

She always kept the key in the car. If she could just make it to the garage, get inside, and drive...

Thank God Meryl's at a friend's tonight, she thought. Meryl had been doing that more and more lately. She hated being home when Damon was around.

Andi crept to the door leading to the garage. Her hand trembled as she turned the knob.

Creeeeak.

Shit.

She darted out, bare feet slapping against the cold concrete. Her heart raced as she reached the car, yanked the door open, and scrambled inside. She reached for the key in the console.

Gone.

Where's the fucking key??

Behind her, the door to the house opened.

Damon stepped out, silhouetted by the light, smirking like a man who'd been waiting for this moment.

"Where do you think you're going?"

She slammed the lock button. All doors clicked.

He sauntered up to the driver's side, leaned down, and stared into her soul through the glass.

"Someone didn't take her medication tonight, like she was supposed to. Are you seriously trying to make this worse for yourself?... I guess you are."

He hit the window hard with the flat of his hand.

She jumped.

"You either open this door now, or I'll open it for you!"

She looked away, tears slipping down her cheeks.

He straightened up and growled, "Fine. I'll be back with the key—and then we'll sort this out."

He disappeared into the house.

This was her chance.

There were a few houses about a mile away. If she could make it there—get help, call someone, disappear—

She threw the car door open and bolted, barefoot and in the dark.

Out of the garage she ran, propelled by sheer survival. Her footsteps crunched across the gravel, then gave way to the soft, brittle layer of icy snow blanketing the grass. She couldn't feel the cold—couldn't feel anything—just the fire of adrenaline flooding her veins as she ran blindly into the night.

Then—

Her foot struck a sunken patch of frozen earth.

Crack.

Pain shot through her ankle. She collapsed.

FUCK!

Behind her—footsteps. Running. Fast.

She scrambled to her feet, limping, panicked, crying, adrenaline flooding her system.

He was gaining on her.

He's gonna catch me... this is gonna hurt...

Then she felt it—impact.

A crushing blow to her back.

The ground rushed up.

Darkness swallowed everything.

When Andi started to come to, the pain was the first thing she registered—an unrelenting, throbbing pulse behind her eyes and a pounding in her skull that made her groan softly. Her eyelids fluttered as everything remained blurry, the world around her a haze of light and shadow. She could hear clinking—glass against wood—and something else, something soft and domestic, like the faint stir of a spoon in a glass, the quiet thump of a cabinet door. Ordinary morning sounds. Familiar. Harmless.

Her vision slowly began to clear.

Damon.

He stood near a small kitchen area, moving about as if it were just another morning. Like nothing had happened.

Andi blinked against the sunlight slicing through the window, sharp and blinding. She winced. The room was small, wood-paneled, and unfamiliar. A cabin? She was lying in a bed—quaint, cozy, all wrong. Her head throbbed harder as she sat up slightly, every muscle in her body aching, her skin hot with confusion.

She coughed.

Damon's head whipped toward her. He stepped into the doorway with a too-wide smile.

"Good morning, sleepyhead," he said, his voice syrupy. He held out a steaming mug. "I brought you some tea."

She didn't take it.

He moved closer, knelt beside the bed, and guided her hand around the cup like she was a child. "C'mon now, sweetheart. You did a number on yourself this time. I bet you're not feeling so great."

She fought to get the words out. "No... I'm not. Where... where are we? How did I get here?"

Damon let out a long, exaggerated sigh as he sat down on the edge of the bed. "Well, my dear... you had one hell of an episode last night. Scared the shit out of me. I came home and couldn't find you anywhere—looked through the house, called out your name, and turned on all the outside lights. Then I spotted you lying outside by the woods near that big rock. You must've hit your head good this time, and twisted your ankle. You were rambling—saying the strangest things. Like you were caught in some weird hallucination. Talking about me like I was some kind of monster and babbling Alex's name over and over. None of it made sense. It honestly scared me."

Andi stared at him in silence. Her instincts screamed *liar*, but she said nothing.

He gestured toward the wall. "Look over there."

A mirror hung crookedly beside the door.

She turned her head quickly and recoiled.

Her reflection was unrecognizable—bloated, broken, barely human. One side of her face was grotesquely swollen, an angry mix of purple and red, with dried blood matted in her hair. Her eye was nearly shut. A jagged wound sliced across her neck, sloppily covered in gauze and crooked strips of tape that loosely clung to her skin. She looked like someone caught halfway between a horror film victim and a ghost.

She glanced down. Her right leg was propped up, the ankle bulging and marbled with deep, purplish bruises. Raw scrapes and crosshatched cuts lined her skin like she'd been dragged through a tangle of thorns.

"Oh my God... do I need to go to the hospital?"

Damon shook his head calmly. "Don't worry about that. I already sent pictures to your doctor and had a long chat with him. He said you just need rest. No stress."

His grin widened. "So, I did something special for you. Meryl's staying with a friend for a bit, and I brought you here.

Figured we could enjoy some peace and quiet together while you heal."

Andi's heart raced. "Where is this?"

"Remember I told you Simon and I own some properties here and there? This is one of our favorites. I can't believe I never brought you before—it's beautiful. Private. Secluded."

She shook her head weakly. "I don't want to be here."

He gave a dismissive laugh. "Nonsense. This is perfect. Just what you need."

He stood and brushed his hands together. "Now hey—we need to run a quick errand. I want to pop into the dealership to let everyone know we'll be away for a bit so they don't worry. I'll make sure they know how to reach me. They'll be fine."

He turned toward the bathroom. "I'll run you a bath and help you freshen up before we go."

Too tired. Too confused. Too broken. She said nothing.

She took the bath. He helped her into soft sweatpants, a t-shirt, and a robe. Then came the pills. He handed them to her in a little paper cup.

"Here. The doctor says it's important."

She hesitated.

He raised a brow.

She took them.

They drove. Time blurred. She drifted in and out, the medication thick and heavy in her veins. When she opened her eyes again, they were parked. She was still in the passenger seat. Her vision swam.

The dealership.

But Damon wasn't in the truck.

She tried to move. Couldn't. Her body wouldn't respond the way it should.

Panic flared. *Think. Think.*

She needed help. She had to tell someone. Warn someone. But how? She spotted a crumpled piece of paper on the floor and a pen in the console.

With weak trembling hands, she scribbled a note. She didn't know what she was going to do with it though—toss it in the parking lot and hope someone found it? She had no plan. Just desperation.

"Alex you were right. He took my keys. I tried to run. I'm sorry. Tell Meryl I love her."

As she wrote, she felt herself fading again, her vision dipping at the edges. She tried to fight the pull, gripping the paper tighter as she stuffed it into her robe pocket, clutching it like a lifeline.

Tap. Tap.

The sound pulled her from the fog, light and urgent against the glass. Her head lolled toward the window, vision swimming. A shape. Then a face.

Rebecca.

She stood outside the truck, eyes wide and horrified, as if she were staring into a nightmare.

Andi fumbled to press the window button. It inched down slowly.

Rebecca leaned in, eyes wide with alarm.

"Oh my God, Andi—what happened?"

"I ran," Andi said, her voice a mere whisper.

Rebecca's face tightened with confusion, eyes searching Andi's like she was trying to understand a language she couldn't hear.

Andi fought with everything she had to stay conscious—to force her drugged limbs to move, to shape her lips around the words that screamed inside her head: *He's trying to kill me. Get me out. Call the police. Please—save me.*

But nothing came out. Her body wouldn't respond. Frozen. Trapped.

Rebecca glanced over her shoulder. The second her gaze shifted, her entire expression changed.

Panic.

"Shit... he's coming. I've gotta go."

"Wait," Andi rasped, her voice dry and broken. She reached up, fingers dragging like dead weight across Rebecca's wrist, barely catching hold. With a shaky breath, she fumbled into her pocket and pulled out the crumpled paper.

"For Alex," she said, the words fragile as thread. "Please."

Rebecca nodded, her eyes brimming with tears. "I'll give it to her. I promise."

Then she was gone.

Damon slid into the driver's seat. Calm. Casual.

"Alright," he said cheerfully. "We're good to go. Let's get you back to the cabin."

Andi stared out the window, dazed.

He turned to her with that smile she'd learned to fear.

"You're gonna love it there. I've gotta show you out back. There's a big, gorgeous cliff overlooking everything. Cryer's Edge, they call it."

He smirked. "Trust me, babe. Once I show you, you'll *never* want to leave."

Nineteen

The Reflection She Stole

The snow had thinned to a ghostly dusting, whispering against the kitchen windows before settling into silence. Inside Sheldon's kitchen, the table was a battlefield of evidence—photographs, notes, and printouts layered over one another. Alex's hurried handwriting scattered across the pages, each note jagged and frantic, mirroring her racing thoughts. Meryl sat small and wordless on the couch, pale as the light outside, while Walker and Melena murmured quietly by the window, their silhouettes tense as they watched the driveway and the restless world beyond. Their hushed voices carried tones of disgust and disbelief as they spoke about Damon—his cruelty, his sickness—and their growing concern for poor Meryl, trapped beneath the weight of everything he'd done.

And now, the unbelievable possibility that Andi might be pregnant… a thought that turned something already unbearable into something even worse.

Alex's hands were tense as she lifted the photograph again—the one of Simon, his arm draped around a woman whose eyes were red from crying, her face drawn and fearful, as if she'd been caught in something she couldn't escape. The top edge bore two smeared words in black ink: *Cryer's Edge.*

"Who the hell is she?" Sheldon questioned, leaning in. The photo caught the overhead light, glinting off his watch as he studied it with the detached focus of someone accustomed to analyzing crime scenes. "And why would he have this picture?"

Alex exhaled shakily, brushing her thumb across the woman's face. "She looks… young. Early twenties, maybe. And she's wearing a shirt with a logo—see that?" Her voice caught, soft and uncertain. "What does it say?" She leaned closer, squinting in the light. "*Hotel Mar y Montaña?*" She tapped her phone, her fingers unsteady as she searched. "That's in Liberia, Costa Rica."

Walker looked up from across the room, his brows pulling together. "Costa Rica?"

Alex nodded, still staring at the photo. "Yeah. I wonder if that shirt actually means something—or if she's from there."

Sheldon rubbed his chin, thoughtful. "Good catch. I'll dig into Simon's past, see if he ever traveled down there or had any contacts from that area. Hale's been trying to get ahold of him for questioning, but the bastard's nowhere to be found."

Walker stepped over to the table and leaned over the photograph, squinting at the words like they were taunting him. “I’ve run this God-damn name through every database I can think of—public, private, old, new—and not one of them has a single hit on ‘Cryer’s Edge.’” His voice sharpened. “I hate this shit. When something should be there and it isn’t? We gotta be thinking about this wrong.”

“I agree,” Sheldon said, tapping his fingers once against the table. “If it were the real name of a place, we’d have found it by now. Has to be a nickname—something only Damon and Simon used. If it were anything official, we’d have found it by now. But we’ll pin it down.”

“And this—” Alex reached for the small plastic bag on the table, her expression heavy with worry. Inside sat the pregnancy test they’d found at the house, its faint plus sign still visible beneath the plastic. Her throat tightened as she spoke softly, “If it’s Andi’s... if she really is pregnant—and if he knows—”

Meryl didn’t want to hear it, but she couldn’t block it out. She turned away, burying her face in a pillow.

Sheldon leaned forward, his large hand settling gently over Alex’s. He tried for calm, for reason, even as his eyes betrayed what he really felt. “If she is,” he said, “and if he knows... then maybe that means she’s safer. For now, at least.”

The silence that followed was heavy, filled with the hum of the refrigerator and the faint sound of sleet ticking against the glass. Meryl shifted on the couch, wrapping her arms around her knees. Her voice, directed toward the kitchen, was broken and numb. “I—I’m not totally sure,” she said, hesitant, “but... I swear I remember my dad talking to my grandma about some place she didn't like. She got all weird about it, and he just laughed. I think—” she swallowed, “I think he said something about Cryer? Or... Cryer’s something. I don’t know.”

Alex's eyes widened as she met Sheldon's. "You need to talk to Patsy again," she said. "And I need to know who that woman in the picture is—there's something about her that feels important. I want to go with you when you talk to Patsy."

Sheldon nodded, his jaw tightening with resolve. "I'll call and see how soon we can get in."

The smell hit first—disinfectant, wilted flowers, the faint trace of old coffee. The halls hummed with quiet conversation and the squeak of nurses' shoes. Sheldon moved ahead, his shoulders squared, while Alex followed close behind, her heart thudding as they turned down the corridor.

Patsy Roth sat near the window of her small room, her wheelchair angled toward the muted glow of an overcast afternoon. She looked thinner than Sheldon remembered, her cheeks hollowed, her hair a tangled silver cloud. Her skin had taken on the fragile gray tone of fading life. It was clear she was deteriorating rapidly.

But when she looked up and saw him, her eyes snapped into sharp focus.

"I figured you'd be back," she said, her voice like sandpaper. "My boy's not gonna like that you're asking more questions."

Alex froze mid-step as Sheldon stepped ahead of her, positioning himself carefully beside Patsy's chair. He maintained a respectful posture, aware that any sudden shift might startle her drifting mind.

"Patsy," he said, lowering his voice, "this is my sister, Alex. She's Andi's good friend. And... we need to talk to you because Damon and Andi are both missing. No one has heard from them in days." He kept his tone soft and careful. "Meryl's beside herself. We're just trying to find them."

He shifted a little closer, still respectful, still cautious. "We found a picture—Damon's friend Simon with a woman. Someone we don't recognize. The words 'Cryer's Edge' were written on it. We're hoping you might know something about that. Anything at all that could help us understand why Damon would have it—or what, or where this place 'Cryer's Edge' even is."

Patsy's lips twitched into a warped, uneasy grimace—part disgust, part memory surfacing from some dark corner. "Such a horrible man," she muttered. "Such a horrible place."

Her gaze drifted to the window. For a long moment, she was silent. Then, in a low, broken murmur, she said, "He's not even mine."

Alex blinked. "I'm sorry—what?"

"I took him," Patsy said with quiet resolve, her hands unsteady in her lap. "Stole him. That's the sin I'll die with."

Sheldon's expression flickered, a mix of confusion and dread. "Patsy, what do you mean?"

Her eyes glistened as she stared into some invisible distance. "There was a park... out by Mill Road. I saw him there—a little boy, maybe two or three. Dirty. Kneeling by the swings, holding a dead kitten. I thought he was crying." Her voice cracked. "But he wasn't. He was laughing." An unusual chuckle escaped her as she recalled the memory.

Alex felt her stomach twist. The air in the room seemed to drop ten degrees.

Patsy continued, her words unraveling between coughs and fragments of thought. "I'd wanted a child so badly… God never gave me one. My husband was so angry. And he was just there. Alone. No one came for him. So I took him. Told myself it was fate." She paused, her voice unsteady. "But I knew, deep down… something was wrong. No empathy. No guilt. Cruel to animals… to people. I thought, in my foolishness, that I could set him right. But love don't mend what's born wicked."

She leaned forward suddenly, eyes blazing. "Should've taken him back. God help me, I raised the devil himself."

Alex's pulse pounded in her ears. She glanced at Sheldon, whose jaw had gone rigid, his eyes wide with disbelief. "Are you saying you kidnapped Damon when he was a boy?" she said, the words struggled free from her throat, thick with shock.

Patsy's gaze darted between them and the ceiling, her words coming faster now, unraveling in uneven bursts. "You think I don't know what that makes me? A thief. A liar. I told myself it was meant to be," she said, her voice pitching higher, words tumbling over one another. "Like some sign from above—my chance to be a mama. But it wasn't fate. It was madness. I know that now."

She gave a small, eerie laugh that dissolved into a trembling sigh. "I told myself his real mama never wanted him, and I fancied I was doing him a mercy, poor fool I was. I remember that laugh… that awful little laugh at that dead kitten." Her fingers twisted in her lap. "I still see that park every night. Thought I was saving him, I did—but I only fed the demon, brought it into my own home. The Lord saw fit to punish me for it the very day I carried him across my threshold. Worst mistake I ever made. My gravest sin. I see it every time I close my eyes."

As shocked as Alex and Sheldon were by everything she had just confessed, they couldn't ignore what she'd said leading into it about Simon and Cryer's Edge. She had just called it horrible—said he was a horrible man. Why? Alex's voice tightened with disbelief as she asked, "Patsy, what do you know about Cryer's Edge?"

The woman's expression shifted—something between fear and trance. Her voice dropped to a whisper. "That's a bad place. His place. His and that filthy friend's. They call it that. Up by Raven's Reach." Her eyes darted toward the window, as if afraid someone might hear. "People go there and don't come back. He told me the only sound louder than the gunshots was the crying from the edge."

"Crying from the edge?" Sheldon repeated, leaning in. "What does that mean?" He and Alex looked at each other, shocked, both realizing it might mean something far more sinister than they had imagined.

But she was slipping now—her focus dissolving, her hands shaking slightly. "That sound," she murmured. "That awful sound. Should've known then what he was..."

A cough hit her hard, wracking her frail body until the nurses rushed in, calling for help. One of them gently but firmly guided Sheldon and Alex toward the door.

"She needs rest," the nurse said, her tone firm but kind. "You'll have to come back another time."

In the hallway, the two of them stood in silence, the fluorescent lights buzzing faintly overhead.

Alex's pulse still hammered in her throat. She looked at Sheldon, her face pale, her eyes searching his. "Did she really mean what it sounded like?"

Sheldon's jaw flexed as he stared down the empty corridor. "I think she did." His voice was rough, shaken. "And if she's right about that place..." He trailed off, meeting Alex's gaze again. The realization between them was wordless but heavy—whatever Cryer's Edge was, it was darker than they'd ever imagined. But at last it seamed, Patsy just gave them something tangible. A direction. A thread in the dark that finally felt like it might lead somewhere.

Relief rippled through Alex's chest—thin, shaken, but real. If Cryer's Edge was just what Damon and Simon called it... then Raven's Reach was the ground it sat on.

They didn't waste another second. As they walked to the car, Alex was already pulling out her phone, her fingers flying as she sent the information to Walker:

Raven's Reach, possible connection, see what you can't find out!

Beside her, Sheldon typed just as fast, forwarding every detail to Detective Hale. "He'll jump on this immediately," he said, voice low but steady. "If there's anything out there worth finding, Hale'll dig it up."

They pushed through the nursing home doors and stepped into the cold. The wind needled at their coats, sleet slipping sideways beneath the streetlights, each icy tick against the pavement sounding sharper now—more deliberate.

Alex paused beside the car, her breath curling into the air. "Shel... if this is the place he's taken her—" She closed her eyes, forcing out a sharp, unsteady breath through her nose, the rest of the thought too heavy to speak aloud.

Sheldon snapped his fingers sharply, the sound cracking through the cold as he pulled her attention back to him.

When her eyes finally lifted, he met them—steady, grounding, unshakeable. "Hey. Don't go there. If this is the place... then at least we know where to start looking."

The storm gathered around them, eerie and restless, as if the world itself sensed what lay ahead.

For the first time in days, the darkness didn't feel endless. It felt like it was pointing somewhere.

TWENTY

THE SHATTERING

SNOW HAD FALLEN ALL afternoon—thin, gray flurries drifting from a colorless sky. It piled against Detective Hale's office window like cold ash, turning the world outside into a blur of motionless silhouettes. His desk lamp flickered, the only light competing with the bluish glow of the computer screen that cast restless shadows across his face.

He'd been at it for hours—records, transfers, bank trails looping through countries that promised secrecy but delivered sin. Beside them, notes from interviews sprawled across his desk: neighbors, former coworkers, Patsy Roth's old health aide, anyone who had brushed against Damon or Simon long enough to sense something was wrong. His coffee had gone cold an hour ago, but he didn't notice.

Then a file name caught his eye.

R & J Ventures LLC. Later renamed Diverse Horizons Group.

He sat back, a slow exhale escaping his chest. Roth and Jahner. Damon and Simon.

The cursor blinked over the names like a pulse. Hale leaned forward, scanning page after page—warehouses in South Dakota, rental cabins across state lines, properties tucked into the folds of tropical maps. Liberia. Costa Rica. One hotel in particular—*Hotel Mar y Montaña.*

The paper trail was too polished, too consistent. The kind of clean that smelled like bleach and blood. He didn't need proof to know what his gut already told him. This wasn't business. It was cover—a lattice of shell companies shielding predators who wore suits instead of shackles.

He hit *print*, grabbed his phone, and dialed.

Sheldon answered on the second ring. His voice carried that edge—tired but braced.

Hale drew in a long breath, his eyes still fixed on the monitor as he connected the last of the dots. His voice was steady when he finally spoke, carrying the weight of what he'd uncovered.

"Sheldon, I think I found your guy's skeleton closet—and it's got passports in it. Roth and his partner, Simon Jahner, built themselves a smokescreen. They've been in and out of Costa Rica for years. Every time they go, people seem to disappear. Different names. Same pattern."

He forwarded the files.

A faint *ding* from Sheldon's computer echoed through the farmhouse kitchen. Melena came up behind him, her hand settling on his shoulder. Together, they read.

Hale continued, "There's one case that stands out. The woman in the photo Alex and Meryl found—her name is *Mariela Rojas.* She was twenty years old when she was last seen. Costa Rican. Vanished nine years ago."

Melena's fingers tightened on his shoulder, nails digging into the cotton of his shirt.

Hale's voice filled the silence, measured but heavy with disgust. "Nine years ago, Simon Jahner took a 'business trip' to Costa Rica—officially, to scout resort properties. He met two sisters, Mariela and Isabel Rojas, barely more than girls, raising four younger siblings after their parents were lost in a fire. Simon promised Mariela the world. He said he'd marry her, bring her to America, and send money back home to take care of her family. She believed him—because when you're desperate, hope is its own kind of poison."

His voice dropped to a dry, clinical whisper. "The first wire transfer arrived. Then another. Then nothing. Fourteen months later, Isabel received a single letter. The envelope was filthy, edges torn, the handwriting shaky as though written in fear. You'll see a copy attached."

> *"Isabel, hermana... Simon lied to me. He said he loved me, but he's cruel. I am in a cold place, a cabin near a cliff. The wind never stops here. I miss the ocean. I hear them outside, laughing. They do bad things, Isa. His friend with the dark hair watches everything. They hurt me... it's getting worse. I'm not the only one. If I don't come home, please tell the little ones I tried. Tell them I love them. Don't wait for me. Pray for me. I'm so sorry. Te quiero mucho, de verdad."*

"That was the last trace of her." Hale's voice was grim. "Interpol couldn't prove a murder. But records show Simon returned to the U.S. with one companion—Mariela. She never resurfaced. We believe he held her captive for over a year... at this cabin by the cliff she talks about. Sounds like Roth was the dark-haired friend to me."

Sheldon's jaw flexed. The air in the kitchen felt smaller, sharper.

Melena's voice shook with fury and disbelief. "Those two... *monsters.* They've been doing this for years, hurting women like it's nothing. God, they make me sick."

Hale's tone hardened as he continued, the weight of what he'd uncovered pressing through every word. "There's more," he said. "Their company owns property near Raven's Reach—mountain land, isolated. No access roads. Same corporation on the deed."

The room tilted for Sheldon, memories clicking into place like a loaded magazine. Patsy's voice from the nursing home echoed in his head—*Raven's Reach. Cryer's Edge.*

Sheldon's voice emerged rough with realization. "It's the same place," he said. "She was trying to tell us. That's where he's got her."

At Alex and Walker's house, they were doing their best to pretend it was just another winter evening, holding on to whatever pieces of normal life they could. They had done everything possible for now. The authorities were combing through the new information, following the leads, chasing whatever thread might break this open. All that was left was waiting, and waiting had a way of fraying nerves.

So, Rebecca and Theo came over, because that's what friends do when things get heavy—they show up with warmth and something steady to cling to. Theo walked through the door with a huge bucket of fried chicken cradled in his arms, and Rebecca followed with another bag packed full of sides from the local restaurant.

The moment the smell filled the kitchen, Alex felt herself breathe for the first time in hours. It was a small, unexpected mercy—not having to think about cooking tonight, not with her mind stretched thin in a dozen directions.

The kitchen light glowed softly against the frost-webbed windows, doing its best to keep the cold at bay. Plates and half-empty coffee mugs littered the table, scattered among papers and notes that none of them had the energy to organize. They ate together, talking about anything but the heaviness sitting quietly between them.

But Damon had a way of slithering into everything.

It was Rebecca who broke the fragile bubble, mentioning the email she'd received earlier—the one Damon sent to the entire dealership. Just a short message about "keeping an eye on things" and asking for an update on the next shipment of parts. Harmless on the surface. Menacing in every way that mattered. His reminder that he was still out there. Still watching.

The sound of Alex's phone dinging cut cleanly through the space, making everyone flinch.

Sheldon:

Got something. On my way now.

The air shifted immediately—subtle but undeniable. No one said it, but every person in the room felt the same cold weight drop into their stomachs. Conversation faded. Plates were pushed aside. Even the furnace seemed to quiet itself, as if bracing for what was to come.

So when the door opened and Sheldon and Melena stepped inside, the room was already wound tight as wire.

Sheldon didn't sit. He didn't speak. He simply pulled a folder from under his arm and let it fall onto the table. A photo slid out and skidded to a stop in front of Alex.

Rebecca pressed closer to Theo, her fingers twisting nervously. Walker leaned back, arms crossed, jaw clenched. Alex looked like she hadn't taken a full breath since the text came through.

Sheldon pointed to the photograph—a young woman with dark eyes and a soft, hopeful smile. "That's Mariela Rojas."

Alex's breath caught as her eyes locked on the photo. "Shel, that's her!" she said. "The same woman from the picture we found... with Simon."

Sheldon gave a short nod, one born more from exhaustion than agreement. "Yeah. It is." His voice was steady but strained as he began to tell them every horrible detail Detective Hale had uncovered. He pushed through the explanation with visible effort, each sentence weighed down by how wrong it all was. When the last word left him, the table fell silent.

Walker leaned forward, elbows on his knees, disbelief roughening his voice. "So we're not just talking about some psycho husband. This is trafficking. Murder. Cover-ups that cross borders."

The words hit him hard. He smacked his hands against his thighs and stood abruptly, muttering under his breath what he thought a man like Damon *truly* deserved. He raked both hands behind his head and paced twice, sharp and restless, before stopping at the window to breathe and stare into the dark.

Rebecca pressed a hand to her mouth, her fingers digging into her skin as if to keep a sickness down. Her expression tightened, the muscles of her face freezing into a mask of cold realization. Her eyes remained fixed on the photo, glassy with disbelief

Theo let out a long, ragged exhale that seemed to grate against his ribs. He looked away, leaning back with his mouth open, searching for air as the atmosphere in the room felt suddenly thin—poisoned by a reality you only read about in headlines.

The silence in the room was heavy with a stunned horror. This was the kind of depravity most people never experience this close to home. This visceral.

Alex reached for the photo, her hand cold as her thumb brushed across the woman's face—so young, so full of life. "She was real." she uttered, laced with disgust. "They tortured her. Took her from her family and killed her."

Sheldon dragged a hand over his face, his voice rough. "We don't know for sure what happened to her. There's no body—no proof yet, but it looks bad." His words settled over the group like dead weight, carrying the stagnant, hollow chill of a funeral they were being forced to attend. The furnace hummed. The wind pressed against the house. No one moved.

The stillness wasn't empty though—it pulsed with anger, fear, and a shared determination to do everything in their power to stop him, to end this, and to make sure justice finally caught up.

Then Hale's call shattered the quiet. Sheldon answered immediately.

Hale's voice came through electric, steady yet thrumming with adrenaline. "We've got the warrant. That property near Raven's Reach—cabin, generator, off-grid. I've got a team mobilizing for first light, heading straight for that cabin where we believe Damon and Andi likely are. Another unit's already moving in to pick up Simon. They found him. That's happening tonight."

Sheldon's eyes lifted from the phone and swept across the room. No one moved. No one breathed.

Then his gaze found Alex's.

Something cold and certain pulled tight in her chest.

This was it—the moment everything shifted, the moment the fight turned real.

Later, the house had gone quiet. Meryl had been downstairs all evening, keeping to herself—trying to focus on homework, texting friends, watching a movie—anything that felt normal. She'd fallen asleep on the couch, the low sound of the TV filling the room with a familiar kind of noise she could handle—better than sitting upstairs, listening to the storm of worry unfolding above her.

The adults lingered in the living room, the air charged and heavy. Every whisper felt like it could crack the silence in half. They knew what was coming. They could feel it—like static crawling under their skin. And the worst part? There was nothing left to do but wait. The not knowing was its own kind of torture, the minutes dragging like hours.

Still, they couldn't stop themselves. They leaned in close, voices sharp and hushed, dissecting every possibility like soldiers studying a battlefield they'd never step foot on. Walker and Theo's military instincts took over—quick, efficient, precise—mapping out how they thought the police would move in. Sheldon paced the floor, talking through scenarios as if he were right there beside Hale, the rhythm of his boots matching the beat of a war drum.

They weren't part of the raid. They knew that. But in that moment, none of it mattered. Their minds were already there, out in those mountains, bracing for the sound of doors splintering and the first shout in the dark. Because when you care about someone that much, you fight however you can—even from a distance.

Alex slipped out to the porch. The snow had turned to a biting sleet, the air sharp and icy enough to sting. She gripped her phone, thumb hovering over Andi's name. God, she wanted to hear her voice. To believe she was still out there.

The door slid open. Melena stepped out first, followed by Rebecca, wrapping Alex in a blanket. For a while, none of them spoke. Just the hiss of wind through frozen pines.

Finally, Melena broke the silence, her breath clouded in the cold. "They're *gonna* get her out."

Alex nodded. She narrowed her eyes toward the mountains. The darkness out there pulsed with a lingering threat; the storm was picking up, and the wind and the cold felt like him—just beyond the tree line. She could almost feel his eyes, that cold, manipulative stare she'd come to loathe, watching from the shadows.

She took a breath, letting the burning in her lungs anchor her, forcing the frantic beat in her chest to steady. She stared into the black and spoke with the calm intensity that comes when you've finally realized that being scared doesn't change what has to be done.

"He thinks this is a game—that he's the one moving pieces on the board. He doesn't know who he's up against anymore."

The wind caught her words, carrying them into the night. Somewhere out there, beneath that shifting sky, Damon Roth was still trying to play God—clinging to the illusion that he was untouchable.

He was wrong.

People weren't cowering under his storm anymore. The storm was coming for him now, silent and certain. Alex could feel it in the air—the sudden, terrifying shift in the atmosphere.

Damon wasn't the one pulling the strings this time. He wasn't the hunter anymore.

He was the one being hunted.

Twenty-One

The Cruel Illusion

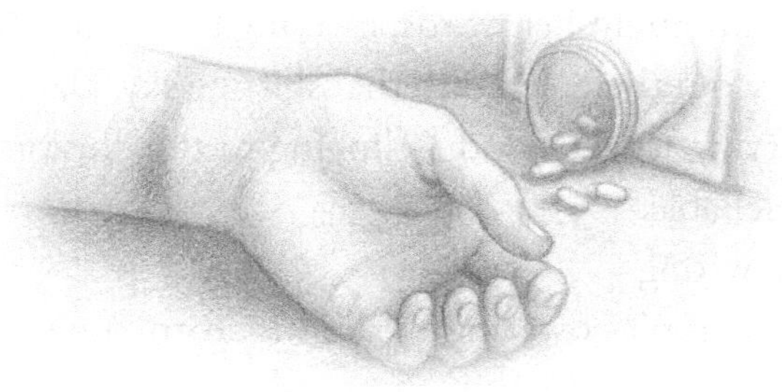

The cabin breathed around her—slow, damp, and sour. Andi woke once more in its belly, her lungs filling with the same stale air. Maybe it was Tuesday. Maybe Thursday. It didn't matter. Time had stopped meaning anything; it was just another weapon Damon used against her. The blinking 12:00 on the stove was the only thing that proved she hadn't died. It pulsed in the dark like a heartbeat—steady and indifferent. Not hers. The room felt suspended, waiting—watching—that endless maddening blink marking the seconds of her captivity.

Her mouth tasted like metal. Her head pounded, temples throbbing with every slow thump of her pulse.

Her body ached in places she didn't want to think about, deep in the joints, a soreness that felt earned somehow, as if she'd been fighting in her sleep. The blanket clung to her skin like a wet animal, sour with damp wool and Damon's cologne—a smell she now associated with control. With sickness. With danger.

When the drugs didn't have her pinned down, the silence did. It wasn't quiet; it buzzed, a low vibration under her skin, in her teeth, her skull. Sometimes she whispered just to hear her own voice, to prove she still existed.

The pills stole everything—hours, thoughts, memories. They dulled her into something compliant. Something obedient. She learned how to play her part: whisper that she loved him, thank him for every cruelty dressed up as care, smile when he called her fragile or broken. When he said he was taking care of her, she nodded and folded her hands neatly in her lap like a child—head bowed, eyes lowered—pretending to be grateful, pretending to believe him. And when he wanted more—when his touch turned rough, his voice commanding—she learned not to flinch, not to cry, not to show fear. Fear made him excited. She just endured it. Her compliance kept her alive. The act was her armor. Lies were oxygen.

He'd stand over her when she took the pills, eyes hard and searching, waiting for proof of submission. She'd choke them down when she had to. But when she could—when the lock clicked and his footsteps faded into silence—she would crawl to the one window he hadn't managed to seal. It only opened an inch, just enough for a thin slice of cold air to sting her face. She'd spit what she could hold in her cheek into her weakened palm and push it through the narrow gap, watching the poison tumble into the snow and vanish beneath the crust of ice—her small rebellion dissolving into white silence. It wasn't escape, but it was resistance. A secret. A promise to herself that he hadn't broken everything.

The room smelled of chemicals and loneliness. The toilet in the corner reeked. The windows wore a skin of frost, and the double-locked door cruelly taunted her. Freedom was just on the other side. Sometimes the generator coughed awake, lights flickering across the walls in flashes that made her flinch, her heart hammering so hard she could taste it. Each pounding heartbeat reminded her she was still here—raw but alive. Survival was the only thing she still had power over.

When she woke this time, the same haze clung to her mind. The wood stove. The chair in the corner. The broken table. The bottles of pills.

A faint sound—floorboards settling—made her cringe. She stared at the door, waiting.

The knob didn't turn.

No Damon. Thank God.

She let her shoulders sag with relief—only to tense again when she noticed what she hadn't before.

Someone else stood beside the stove.

Simon.

"Morning," Simon said, his tone disturbingly casual, as if he were walking into a friend's kitchen instead of a prison. His eyes dragged over her like grease—slow, deliberate, assessing. "Poor girl," he crooned. "Trying to get better. Damon wanted me to check on you, so I'm here. To make sure you're not alone."

Andi's heart jerked awake. She pushed up on her elbows, her muscles weak and trembling. For a moment, relief flashed through her—thankful it was Simon; he'd always been strange, but maybe—maybe he would listen.

"Simon... could you—please—help me? I need this to stop." She nearly said *I need Alex,* but her throat closed before the name could escape.

Simon tilted his head, that serpent smile stretching wider. "What you need," he said, "is to take your meds like Damon said. He's worried sick."

"He's not," she rasped. "You know he's not. Please, I can't take them."

He didn't flinch until she said, "It's not good for the baby."

The air seemed to shatter.

Simon's grin faltered, his gaze narrowing until his face looked carved from something cold and wrong. "Baby?" he said, softly at first, like the word itself was a sin. Then his smile returned, curling at the edges. "You're pregnant?"

"I think so," she whispered. "I'm not sure."

He stepped closer, his shadow crawling over her like an animal. "Do you know who the father is?"

Andi blinked, confusion flashing through her dazed mind. The question didn't make sense. She frowned. "Damon, obviously."

Simon laughed—a wet, ugly sound that made her stomach turn. "You sure about that?" he murmured, his tone soft but wrong, the words slithering through the air. "Because when you get sick and have your little episodes... well, you've been known to do some pretty wild things. Things you don't remember at all."

Something in his voice peeled back the last layer of denial she had left. Her pulse roared in her ears. "What are you talking about?"

He just smiled, eyes gleaming with perverse amusement. "Sit up now," he said, shaking two pills into his hand. "Take your medicine." When she hesitated, his patience snapped. His hand shot out, clamping around her arm with bruising strength. "I said take it, Andria."

She cried out, the sound small and strangled. He pressed the pills to her lips, forcing the glass to her mouth. The water spilled down her chin as she swallowed. It felt like swallowing glass.

"Good girl," Simon said, the words grazing her like velvet sandpaper. He stood and carried the glass to the counter, placing it down with quiet precision. A soft chuckle escaped him—directed at nothing, as if he were enjoying a private joke. "Funny thing... Damon never did care for that little four-leaf clover of yours, sweetheart."

He turned to look at her, his grin sharp and wrong.

"But I sure as hell do."

Her body went rigid. The words didn't make sense at first. Her mind scrambled, trying to place memories that no longer felt like dreams but something darker.

Then the meaning hit her—like a blade between the ribs. The clover. The small birthmark only a lover would know. A mark no one else had seen.

Her stomach churned violently.

Simon's voice dropped to a gravelly whisper. "Brought me luck," he said, almost tenderly. "More than once."

Her vision blurred as realization crashed through her. He *knew.* He had *touched* her.

Simon saw it register and grinned wider, teeth yellow under the flickering light. "You can be very entertaining."

The world reeled. Her heart pounded in horror, bile rising in her throat. Memory fragments tore through her—the sounds, the aching between her legs, the shame she couldn't explain. The missing hours. The bruises. All of it.

Simon leaned in close enough that she could feel his breath hot and foul on her cheek.

"Rest up," he murmured, voice slithering through the air. "We've got plans for you, sweetheart." His tongue flicked across his lips before he laughed—an ugly, broken sound that scraped against her skin as he turned for the door.

The lock clicked. The snow swallowed his footsteps.

Andi collapsed onto the mattress, shaking so hard her teeth chattered. Her sobs came silent at first, then deep and raw, her hands clutching her stomach as if she could shield the child inside from the horror that had touched her. "I'm sorry," she whispered over and over—to the baby, to herself, to the woman she used to be.

The generator stuttered, the lights dimming to a dull orange glow. Her world tilted, slipping out of focus as the drugs surged through her veins. Somewhere in the dark, she made herself a promise—thin and desperate but real.

If morning came, she would survive it. She would endure. She would make them both pay.

Outside, a bird cried once in the cold distance, a lonely echo swallowed by the wind. Andi clung to the sound until the dark finally dragged her under.

Twenty-Two

A Mirror for Monsters

The night had warmed just enough to become treacherous. Ice had softened into a greasy sheen on the county roads, and the air carried a metallic tang that warned of more ice before dawn. Sleet tapped on the mobile command trailer like fingernails on a tin coffin—steady and impatient. Out on County 9, the pines leaned into the wind, as if they knew what was coming.

Simon Jahner left the cabin like a man stepping out of his own reflection—admiring, satisfied, and certain of the image. He took the same route he always did, as if ritual could make him bulletproof. The heater in his truck wheezed, the vents hissing against the fog on the glass. He turned the radio low; an old song from another life drifted up and loosened his shoulders. He never sped at night. He didn't need to. Power was better savored than rushed.

He glanced at his phone. Missed call: Damon. He smirked, letting it ring like a silent victory lap—a small, deliberate act of dominance.

He had already decided not to return to the cabin for a couple of days. The girl would be fine; they always were, at least in the beginning. He knew which pills blurred hours and which erased them, how to make time vanish without leaving marks. She'd sleep—deep, dreamless, and obedient. The thought steadied him, made him feel in control. Besides, whatever happened next was Damon's mess, not his.

Inside the command trailer, technology pulsed beneath the hum of LED panels. A panoramic wall of ultra-high-definition monitors displayed a 3D holographic map of the county, with every movement of Simon's vehicle marked by a glowing pulse. Interactive touch tables projected heat signatures, weather fronts, and synchronized drone feeds tracking him in real time like a digital heartbeat.

Lieutenant Briggs stood before it all, broad-shouldered and motionless, his reflection fractured across the glass screens. He watched the drone feed merge seamlessly with autonomous traffic data and satellite imaging. The rail crossing at Dunbar Creek glowed red on the overlay—Simon's habitual route whenever he left the cabin.

"Crossing in three minutes," an analyst said, eyes on the GPS tracker. "Wind is shifting northwest. Visibility will drop when the sleet hits the ridge."

Briggs nodded once. "He's not sliding past us tonight." He touched the radio at his shoulder. "Units Two and Four, stage at Dunbar Crossing. No contact until I call it."

"Copy." Two voices, one male and one female, overlapped in his earpiece. Engines idled to life, unseen. Out there in the dark, tires rolled over slush with the patience of predators keeping to the tree line.

Simon flicked his blinker out of habit, even though there wasn't another vehicle for miles. The night pressed in, heavy and close. He could smell creosote before he saw the crossing lights. That scent—railroad wood soaked in oil and time—carried him back for a moment to when he was a boy: his father's hand firm on the back of his neck, guiding him toward the tracks, a coin balanced on the rail, a freight train screaming past in a blur as his father said, "See that? Power always wins." He shook it off. Sentimentality was a poor man's luxury.

The bells started before the lights. Their thin, insistent ding-ding-ding bored into his skull, and a moment later, red strobes swept across the dark—a quiet warning slipping past a man who believed consequences were for other people.

Suddenly, everything broke open behind him—blue and red lights flashing out of the dark, two vehicles rising up in his mirrors. His heart didn't lurch. He didn't panic. The first thought that arrived was stupidly ordinary: headlight out? Speed trap? He downshifted, eased onto the shoulder just before the tracks, and put the truck in park as the crossing arm began its mechanical descent.

The loudspeaker crackled like lightning.

"Simon Jahner! Step out of the vehicle with your hands up!"

He blinked, thrown off. *What the hell?* He'd been pulled over before—nothing about this made sense.

He huffed a laugh. *Too cold for the damn cop to walk up to the window like normal?*

He lowered the window halfway, sleet blowing in.

He stuck his arm into the cold, license in hand. "Here!" he shouted. "But you'll have to come get it!"

The loudspeaker hit again, firmer: "Step out of the vehicle, Simon. Hands where we can see them."

His irritation flared. With a snarky smile, he leaned his head out into the freezing air. "Why? What's the problem?"

Still no explanation. Still no officer approaching. That, more than anything, put a hairline crack in his confidence.

Simon sat still, anger rising at the absurdity of it all.

A thin silence followed—heavy enough that the air itself seemed to hold its breath. Then the loudspeaker crackled back to life, heavy, loaded, irreversible, a fatal truth gathering weight.

"We know about R & J Ventures and Diverse Horizons Group. We know about Costa Rica. We know about the girls. We know about Mariela Rojas."

Another breath. Not hesitation—condemnation.

"We know what you and Damon Roth have been doing."

The smile didn't so much fall as empty, like a photograph left in the rain until the ink ran. Heat drained from Simon's hands. The train bells drilled the air, louder now, faster, because the train was nearer—because time had finally changed speeds on him.

Inside the mobile command trailer, no one breathed. On the rightmost monitor, the truck sat angled on the icy shoulder just before the crossing arm, snow-muck caked on its wheel wells. Beyond it, a smear of light on the curve—headlamps from the locomotive. From behind the bank of screens, Briggs watched the way Simon didn't move, listening to every word through the trailer's audio feed.

"Don't rush him," Briggs said. "Keep your cover. He's calculating."

Out there, Simon's calculations fell apart like wet ash.

He saw it all rupture at once—as if the night had torn open and forced him to look. The perfect web he had spun for years snapped strand by strand: shell companies he thought untouchable collapsed like cheap paper; wires crossing borders and oceans that suddenly felt like nooses; Mariela's face—God, Mariela—rising out of the dark with that soft mouth that once said his name like it meant something. He saw the cabin. The cliff. The choices he'd buried for years—every lie, every threat, every bruise he'd dismissed as collateral—rose up in a single, merciless wave.

Then Damon's smile—those polished, empty teeth—flashed in his mind, not as a warning but as a final mockery. Simon had built the whole operation so that Damon would be the one to burn, the perfect fall guy, the shield that kept Simon untouchable.

How the hell did this happen? This wasn't the plan. This wasn't even in the realm of possibility. He had constructed every piece, every layer, every contingency—Damon was supposed to take the hit, not him. Not him.

The thought crashed through him, raw and vicious: This is wrong. All of it. Wrong.

And then, like a blade sliding through the dark, he remembered the rule he'd built his entire empire around—the one promise he'd made to himself if it ever came to this.

They'll never take me in.

The train's horn let loose—a long, predatory sound that made the pines shake their shoulders. The rails thrummed beneath the roadbed. The crossing arm shuddered as if what was coming had weight enough to bend metal.

"Hands where we can see them!" The voice ordered from the SUV behind him. "Step out now!"

Simon's fingers curled around the steering wheel until tendons flicked across the backs of his hands like wires pulled taut. He let go.

Slowly, deliberately, he opened the door. The cold slapped his face, wet and raw. The bells sounded like a drill bit now. The horn layered over them—a god's voice, vast and unyielding—reminding him that the world no longer moved by his will, that fate had taken the wheel and was roaring straight through him.

He stepped out, boots scraping slush, and lifted his hands shoulder-high. He could feel the eyes on him—the scopes, the breath cloud of the officer to his left, and the way the woman to his right set her feet as if he might charge. He looked past them—to the smear of light that had become a spear, to the clean brightness on the steel where wheels scoured a path like a blade through bone.

A thought came, clean and perfect:

I decide.

Even now, he could shape this into the story he told himself. He would not be walked. He would not be caged. He had said it once in a bathroom with the faucet running, a pistol on the counter, and his reflection asking if he meant it. He had meant it then. He meant it now.

"Simon," the loudspeaker said, the first time it used his name like a man's voice rather than a charge sheet. "Don't do anything stupid. We're past that."

He almost laughed. *Past that?* Past that was all he had left.

He took a step toward the track. The officers shouted, their voices blending with the horn, bells, and weather. He took another step. The light from the locomotive shifted, catching the ice on the road like scattered diamonds—dazzling and cold. He knew exactly how much space he had; the stupid child-memory snapping back—coins flattening into shining ovals, the way energy looked after it decided what it wanted to be.

"Stop! Stop where you are!"

He didn't.

He filled his lungs not with air, but with refusal. He moved with the sudden, decisive grace of a man who had already left his body and jumped. The surge of the train's presence hit him—wind, vibration, the massive certainty of it.

The world telescoped: a flick of coat, the slice of metal, the thunder of weight. The impact was cataclysmic—force screamed against bone, glass exploded like gunfire. A spray of red mist caught in the headlight beam, then vanished into sleet. For an instant, a single arm, torn free, arced up like a broken bird wing before the train swallowed it whole. Flesh and fabric scattered across the rails, a grotesque constellation that disappeared beneath the blur of steel.

Sound shattered and then snapped into a terrible, ringing quiet. The horn carried on alone, hanging in the air like an aftershock in the dark, while the train tore past—before the brakes could bite, before physics remembered mercy.

Silence landed like ash, thick and final.

For a moment, no one moved. Their breath clouded the air, shaky and uneven, as if the shock had stolen something fundamental from them—breathing, thought, the ability to comprehend what they had just witnessed. The night felt heavier, the silence louder. An officer near the lead SUV stumbled back two paces and found the front bumper with the backs of his legs, as if his bones had failed him. The female officer kept her arms raised, her sight line fixed on a space that now held only snow flurries and fragments of light.

In the trailer, the drone feed jumped, stuttered, and returned to an empty stretch of crossing, sleet drifting through headlight glare. No one spoke. The monitors cast their cold light onto faces gone pale and hard.

Lieutenant Briggs took off his headset like it suddenly weighed too much. He set it on the table. In the distance, he could faintly hear the rail company dispatcher's voice trying to rise in his earpiece, the way official voices do when they realize the script has changed.

"One down," Briggs said, his tone flat and tired—neither triumphant nor relieved, as if he were merely marking the end of a long equation. "One to go."

Outside, the last cars of the train shuddered past, and the bells finally, mercifully, fell silent. In the ensuing quiet, an unsettling feeling settled in; it was as if a noise had been holding the night together, and now everything across the valley might come undone.

"Secure the scene," Briggs said, his voice returning to steel. "Body recovery will coordinate with rail ops. No statements. Not a word about the companies or the names until I clear it. Unit Two, approach the vehicle. Unit Four, canvas the shoulder for any discarded devices."

"Copy." Boots crunched on the gravel. Flashlights angled low. The SUVs idled, their engines rumbling under the silence like animals that understood blood without needing to see it.

Briggs stepped to the trailer door and gazed into the darkness that had claimed the man he'd been hunting. He had wanted the man in cuffs. He had wanted the trial, the testimony, the truth dragged into the light in a way that could not be denied or spun.

Sometimes, justice arrived like that. Sometimes, it didn't.

The sleet thickened, drumming on the roof like a ticking clock, counting down the hours between a man's last decision and another man's reckoning.

Twenty-Three

The Shattered Edge

Damon woke to a full bladder and a sour mouth. Cheap hotel air clinging to him. A stranger's mascara smeared the pillow. He rubbed his eyes and reached for his phone on the nightstand. No texts. No calls. He scrolled back to his last message to Simon and frowned. Still no reply.

"Figures," he said under his breath. "Useless son of a—"

He stopped himself, swung his legs off the bed, and stood. His head throbbed as he stumbled to the bathroom to take a piss, pop a painkiller, and splash cold water on his face. He raked a hand through his hair and stared at his reflection—bloodshot eyes, hollow under the cheekbones, yet still slick enough to sell anything to anyone. He smirked.

He scrolled through the screenshots again—insurance language highlighted in yellow. His stomach fluttered with a familiar, greedy certainty. The smaller policy would pay out without a hitch. The bigger one might raise questions, sure—a death that could be seen as suicide always did—but with Andi's medical records, her confusion, her declining motor function, the story practically wrote itself. He had hours of video to back the story: Tragic as hell. A horrible misstep. A sick wife disoriented on a cliff. An accident dressed up like despair. And he'd be the grieving husband, cry on cue, devastated but dignified. Poor Andi. Poor Damon. The kind of tragedy people rallied around. The kind insurers eventually signed off on. And when they did, the payout would be massive.

He dressed quickly: wallet, keys, phone. The girl in the bed snored. He didn't look at her again.

Downstairs, he grabbed hotel coffee, two apples, a couple of pastries, and a plastic knife. The lobby TV murmured about the weather. He pushed through the sliding doors into the chill of the morning, walked across the lot to his truck, and balanced the coffee on the roof while unlocking the door. He typed out a text to Meryl.

> Hey sweetheart. Just checking in. Hope you're having a great time with your friend. Wanted to let you know Mom is doing great here at the hospital. I'm so glad we came. The doctors are great, but

your mom is still pretty weak and can't talk. She wants me to tell you how much she misses and loves you. Have a great day, honey. Talk to you soon. Love, Dad.

Send.

He smiled. People believe what they want to believe.

He drove toward the cabin, one hand on the wheel and the other drumming a rhythm. The country radio played softly in the background. He hummed along, botching the lyrics as he sang off-key, feeling like he was the king of the road—king of everything. He pictured Andi on the bed. He pictured the cliff. Not much longer. Push a little harder. Before long, Cryer's Edge would start to look like mercy—the final, easy way out. He could almost see it in her eyes already.

He felt good. Settled. In control.

Detective Hale sat in the mobile command van parked on the narrow service trail overlooking the valley, blue screens illuminating his face. The smell of hot coffee and damp earth lingered in the air. Drones hovered on standby, their live feeds flickering across multiple monitors—heat signatures, audio spikes, GPS tags. He kept one hand on the mic and the other on his tablet.

"Damon Roth's cell signal is live," one operator reported. "Moving northbound. ETA fourteen minutes."

Hale's jaw clenched. "Copy. All units, prep and lock in. Drones one and two, stay low and quiet. We don't move until he's on-site." He paused, watching the red dot crawl across the digital map. *Here he comes*, he thought.

He picked up his phone and dialed a saved contact. "McKay," he said when Sheldon answered. "We're in position. Tracking Damon's car now. You tell Alex we've got eyes on him, and we're bringing Andi home."

"She's a wreck," Sheldon replied, his voice cracking. "She can't sit still. She wants to drive out here."

"Then you hold her back," Hale said firmly. "Neither of you shows up here, you hear me? If Damon spots you, this goes bad fast. I need you steady. Let me do my job."

There was a long, heavy pause. "You better bring her out," Sheldon said.

"That's the plan," Hale replied. "I'll update when I can."

He hung up, shoved the phone back into his vest pocket, and turned to his team. "Last checks—rifles, drones, med kits, tasers, cams, restraints. Everything tight. If something's gonna break, it won't be our gear."

He scanned their faces, making sure every eye was on him. "We've run this three times already, I know," he said, voice firm. "But areas like this have eaten our comms before. New towers, unpredictable weather, magnetic interference—this whole area is a dead spot waiting to happen. If comms fail once Damon's here, we're blind. We do not get another chance at this."

The van rocked as the wind picked up outside, rattling the metal frame. Hale tugged his vest closed, pulled down his headset, and adjusted the mic with practiced precision.

"Comms check," he said, voice crisp. "All units—sound off."

"Sniper One online, clean lane," came the first reply. "Sniper Two locked on. Entry ready and waiting. Thermal reads stable. Drone Three hovering at seventy-five feet."

"Copy all," Hale said, eyes fixed on the monitors. "No shots unless I call it. I want her breathing, and him alive. Clear?"

"Copy," the replies echoed.

Hale leaned over the tablet showing a lone heat signature from the drone sweeping over the cabin. Then he zoomed in on the red dot approaching from the road. "Six minutes out," he said, voice steady but sharp. "Team, that's your window. Keep the drones low and quiet—no noise until I say."

He met the eyes of the operators packed into the van with him, the weight of the moment settling into the silence. "All units on my count. We roll on my mark. Let's bring her home."

Sheldon made a beeline for Alex's house and walked straight in without knocking. The kids were still asleep—thank God. He needed to see her. To be her shoulder. To make damn sure she didn't do anything stupid.

Alex sat at the kitchen counter, staring into her coffee as if it might tell her how this was going to end. Her hand hung limply as she tapped the mug over and over, eyes distant and raw. She looked wrecked—drained past the point of tears. Walker stood behind her, half a piece of toast in his hand, watching her like a man trying to hold a storm together with his bare hands. He met Sheldon's eyes. No words—just a silent nod that said it all: *She's breaking. Help her.*

She looked up when she saw him, eyes swollen, skin blotchy and pale. For a moment, she didn't move—then she fell apart. Sheldon bolted across the room and pulled her into him, arms locking around her like he was keeping her from shattering. She sagged against his chest, shaking.

"What did Hale say?" she asked with a frail voice.

Sheldon exhaled hard and sat beside her, trying to sound reassuring. "They're in position," he said. "They're tracking him in real time, waiting for him to pull in. The second he shows, they move. Hale promised he'll call the moment anything changes."

Alex's lips moved, but the words came out like broken breath—prayers, names, pieces of hope. Her fingers twisted together in a strained, unbreakable clasp she couldn't seem to loosen. Walker came around the counter, placed a hand on her shoulder, then the other on her cheek.

He leaned in, trying to ground her, give her something solid to hold on to. "This is almost over, you hear me? Hale's got this. She's gonna be fine." His words landed with both weight and warmth. He stayed there, steady and unflinching, while Sheldon stood nearby, tense and waiting—everyone braced, everyone just wanting this nightmare to end.

The command van vibrated faintly as Damon's truck came into view on the overhead feed. Hale's pulse quickened. "Eyes on target," he said. "Wait for my signal."

“Copy,” the sniper replied. “Target slowing.”

Damon’s truck rolled to a stop outside the cabin. He paused for a moment, scanning the clearing, then killed the engine.

Hale's voice spoke, tight with focus. “Alright. He’s here. Team Two, hold the perimeter. Entry, you move on my go. We grab him the second he steps out—don’t let him get inside—he doesn't touch her.”

The team shifted into position—boots silent, weapons drawn, moving like shadows through the pines. A sudden gust of wind slammed through the clearing, rattling branches and jolting the van. Hale raised his mic to give the command—

—and then, in an instant, the comms went dead.

A sharp burst of static hissed through the headset, followed by silence. “Team, do you copy?” Hale barked. Nothing. He tapped the earpiece and switched channels. “Entry team, confirm visual!” Still nothing. The operators in the van exchanged alarmed glances.

“What the hell just happened?” one asked.

Hale’s jaw locked. “God damn it. We just did a com check three minutes ago.” He toggled the radio—dead again. “Shit.” He slammed his fist against the console. “You’ve *got* to be fucking kidding me.”

On the drone feed, Damon was already stepping out of the truck.

“Move, damn it,” Hale hissed, pounding the console. “Take him *now!*”

But the team didn’t move—they couldn’t hear him. Damon walked straight to the cabin door and slipped inside.

“Son of a *bitch!*” Hale shouted, ripping off his headset. “We lost the window.”

The cabin sat quiet when Damon pulled in. He cut the engine and listened. Wind. Birds. No cars. No voices. He unlocked the cabin door and stepped inside.

Andi lay on her side, right where she was supposed to be, eyes half-open but unfocused—like her mind had gone somewhere far away just to survive the room. Her skin looked waxy against the pillow, lips dry, the faint rise and fall of her chest barely noticeable. Bruises patterned her arms and ribs in the shapes of his temper—small, round, linear—like a calendar of every time she'd slipped, stumbled, or simply failed to please him.

"Morning," he said, warmth layered thick for the camera. He set his phone against a jar on the counter, adjusting until the shot framed her perfectly: Proof. Always proof. He plated the pastries, cut the apple with a plastic knife, cracked eggs into the pan with performative calm.

"You're doing great," he said to the lens, his voice gentle and rehearsed. "Doctors said rest. I've got breakfast." He always narrated for the imaginary audience—hospital staff, insurance adjusters, anyone who might watch later and see a man devoted to his dying wife.

Andi stirred, her eyes flicking toward the phone before darting away. She swallowed hard and whispered, "Thank you." The words were automatic, worn down by fear. Her fingernails dug into her palms beneath the blanket.

“Hey, baby,” he murmured as he walked to the bed. He cupped her cheek, thumb pressing a little too hard. She flinched. His eyes warned her: Don’t.

He fed her a forkful of eggs. She gagged, swallowing against her own body’s protest. “Good girl,” he purred with cruel satisfaction, dabbing her mouth with a napkin like the perfect loving husband.

A noise cut through the stillness outside—a sharp crack of a branch. Damon’s breath hitched. Every muscle locked. He turned toward the sound, eyes narrowing. “Deer?” he muttered, but the word felt wrong in his mouth.

He moved toward the window, his boots silent on the old wood floor. Leaning forward, he peered through the glass, searching the tree line. Nothing. Just branches swaying, shadows playing tricks. He exhaled and forced a smile back on, masking the flicker of unease.

“Ya know,” he said as he faced her again, “the doctor said fresh air would do you some good. Maybe we can take a walk later—get you outside, check out the overlook.” A smooth tone, too smooth.

Andi’s gut clenched. She could feel it—the shift, the edge sharpening beneath his voice. Whatever he was planning, this was it. She shook her head, trying to sound soft, loving, careful. “I just want to spend time in here with you,” she pleaded. “I miss you when you’re gone.” The words trembled out, her mind scrambling to buy time. Time for what, she didn’t even know. Just more time.

He smiled without warmth. “Nah. I think we should listen to the doctors,” he said. “A walk’ll be good for both of us.”

Another noise outside—louder this time. He froze again. Birds burst from a tree, scattering in a rush of wings. He cocked his head, narrowing his eyes as he tried to separate the sound from the wind. Moving to another window, he scanned the area. Nothing. Then again—something. Branches moved. A shift of shadow that wasn't just a shadow.

"Simon?" he hissed. *It better be him. He was supposed to be here, not me.* His lip curled. *Figures he wouldn't answer. Useless piece of shit.*

Damon stepped closer to the glass, his heart picking up pace, eyes straining into the distance—and then he froze.

There—just past the trees. A flash of matte black. A man. Gear. Rifle raised, sightline aimed straight at him.

For a second, his brain refused to accept it. He blinked hard and took a step back. "No... no, no, no." He looked again, heart hammering now. The man shifted slightly—confirmation. The barrel tracked with him.

He stumbled back from the window, chest heaving. "What the fuck..." His voice cracked. "What the *fuck* is this?" He turned to Andi. "What did you do?!" he roared. "You fucking bitch! What the hell did you do?!"

Andi flinched back, terrified. "I didn't—Damon, I swear to God, I didn't—"

"Shut the fuck up!" he snapped, pacing the room. He grabbed his phone and tried to call again. Still no response. He slammed it on the counter. "Simon!" he shouted at the empty air. "Simon, pick up the goddamn phone!" Nothing.

He yanked open drawers, ripping one so violently it tore past its stoppers and crashed to the floor. Junk. Old receipts. Batteries that didn't work. Nothing he could use. "Fuck!" he exploded, slamming another shut with so much force the wood splintered.

His breath came fast and sharp. He spun, scanning the room—wild, frantic—searching for anything with weight, anything with teeth. His eyes landed on the hunting knife. Big. Reliable. The one thing in the cabin that felt like him.

He snatched it up, the familiar handle locking into his palm like it belonged there. The tremor in his hands disappeared, swallowed by something colder settling inside him. His rage was calmed with a sharp—precise predator's focus. As much as he didn't want to believe what was happening—or how—it was happening, he could feel it in his bones. Whoever was out there wasn't lost. They weren't wandering. They were here for *him*. Watching. Waiting. Closing in.

Fine. Let them.

He lifted his chin, shoulders squaring, the knife catching a thin slice of light. If they were going to hunt him, he'd make damn sure they felt him hunting them right back.

He stalked toward the door, shoulders squared, knife glinting in his hand. He cracked the door just enough for the cold to cut its way in—a narrow slit he could yell out without exposing himself. His voice ripped through his throat as he shouted toward the trees, "I see you out there!" His breath fogged in the freezing air, "I don't know who the hell you are—but you're trespassing! Get the hell off my property!"

A moment passed. Damon's own breath was the only sound—until a low, mechanical hum rolled through the trees, deeper and closer than anything he'd heard before. Not a drone. Not wind.

The moment the comms died, Hale hadn't stayed in the van. He'd grabbed a bullhorn, signaled two flankers, and pushed up the ridge on foot to get within shouting distance—cold, exposed, but close enough to control the scene and stay in visual contact with the snipers hidden in the trees.

Now his voice cut through the clearing, amplified and commanding. "Damon Roth," Hale called through the bullhorn. "Sheriff's office. Come out with your hands up."

Damon's pulse pounded. He laughed, harsh and unsteady. "No! Get the fuck off my property!" he barked, voice cracking at the edges. He backed away from the door, frantic, scanning the windows as if the trees themselves were closing in.

"This is a mistake!" he yelled, pacing hard enough to rattle the floorboards. "You don't know what you're doing!" His breath came fast, uneven. "You're looking for— for someone else!" He jabbed the knife toward the window, desperate, unhinged. "Maybe you're after Simon! He's the one mixed up in all kinds of shit! He's the one you want!" He slammed his hand against the wall. "I haven't done anything!"

"Simon is dead," Hale's voice thundered back, his tone hardening. "We know everything, Damon. R & J Ventures, Cryer's Edge, the women you buried in your past, what you've been doing to Andi—all of it. It's over, Damon. This ends now."

The words hit him like a brick to the chest. He stopped moving. The color draining from his face. For a moment, all that filled the air was the sound of his ragged breathing.

Then something inside him broke wide open.

He shook his head, muttering, "No. No, that's bullshit. Simon's not—" The denial came fast, but his thoughts tangled hard beneath it. *Simon is my safety net—the fall guy. I built this right. He takes the hit, and I walk away.* He blinked, shaking his head as if he could rattle the truth loose. *I'm the driver; he's the spare tire. That's how this fuck'n works.*

He continued pacing, pulling at his hair and muttering to himself. *No fucking way! He's not gone! He can't be; then there's no one left. No one to take the fall. It's not gonna be me.* His heart hammered now, hard enough to hurt. *No... No way he's dead. He's not. They're fucking lying!*

He pressed both hands to his head and screamed, "Fuck!" His voice cracked under the weight of it. Rage boiled over—he snatched a ceramic plate from the counter and hurled it, shattering it against the wall above Andi's head. She screamed, instinctively curling into herself, arms flying up to shield her head as shards rained down over her hair and blanket.

"If he's gone," he spat, chest heaving, "then that's it! That's fucking it!" He threw his hands up, pacing wildly. His gaze snapped to Andi, burning red. "You did this," he growled, voice enraged and lethal. "You and your goddamn lies."

He kicked a chair, sending it flying across the room. His chest heaved as he unraveled, his voice cracking with fury and fear. "You lying sons of bitches!" he roared toward the window. "You think you know who you're dealing with?! You think you win?! No—no, if I'm going down..." His voice dropped to a dark, shaking whisper. "...then this fucking bitch is coming with me." He turned to Andi, venom twisting his mouth. "You think you're getting out of this, sweetheart? You're wrong."

He lunged toward her and grabbed her arm, yanking her upright so violently her knees buckled. She cried out as he shoved the knife under her jaw, the cold steel biting into her skin. He was shaking now—breath coming in sharp bursts, a jagged, manic sound rising in his throat.

"This is how it ends, huh?" Damon roared toward the window, voice shredded with unhinged rage and panic. "They want a show? Let's go!"

Still gripping her, he hauled her from the bed in one brutal motion. The knife stayed fixed against her throat as he dragged her forward, her bare feet scraping across the rough wood floor, trying to keep up, trying not to fall. She gasped, stumbling as he jerked her along—no chance to catch herself, no time to find her footing.

"Damon—please—stop" she cried, her voice a thin tremor swallowed by his ragged breathing.

"Shut up!" he roared, slamming the door open with his shoulder. Cold wind and pine needles rushed in. He pulled her outside, half-carrying and half-dragging her through the dirt and snow toward the ridge. Her feet scraped the ground, as she winced but didn't fight—every ounce of her fear screamed that resistance would mean death.

Hale crouched behind a rock outcropping fifty yards away, his headset crackling with intermittent static. "We have movement—he's got her—he's heading for the cliff!" he shouted to the team, but the words fizzled into noise. The interference was still tearing their comms to pieces.

"Move! We need to move!" Hale yelled, signaling with his hand. The team broke from cover, flanking wide as Hale rose to his feet, stepping into the open.

"Damon!" he called, his voice cutting through the weather. "Don't do this! Let her go, and we can talk!"

Damon jerked to a stop near the edge—*Cryer's Edge*, a drop that fell hundreds of feet into the river gorge below. The wind howled up from the depths, snatching at their clothes. He yanked Andi tight against him, the knife pressed so close it nicked her skin, a line of red tracing her throat.

"Talk?" he spat, laughing wildly. "You think there's something left to talk about? You already decided I'm guilty. You already buried me!"

"Damon, listen to me," Hale said, his tone softening, steady but urgent. "It doesn't have to end like this. Step away from the edge. If you hurt her, this ends one way—right here, right now."

Damon's eyes darted toward the trees—shadows, movement, rifles glinting in the distance. "You've got snipers on me, don't you?" he shouted. "You think I'm stupid?" He pressed the knife harder against Andi's throat. She whimpered, tears mixing with blood as she struggled to breathe.

"No one fires unless I give the order," Hale shouted to his men, though the wind whipped his words away. He raised his hands slowly, palms out. "You've got one chance to stop this, Damon. Let her go. You can still walk away alive."

Damon's laugh came out broken and hollow. "Alive?" he sneered. "You think I'm going to rot in a cell while you parade my name through the dirt? You think I'm gonna let her sit in court and cry about what a monster I am?" His grip on Andi tightened. "No. I'm ending this my way."

"Damon, she's not your enemy!" Hale shouted, stepping closer. "She's your wife. She's your daughter's mother. She didn't do this to you. You're the one who can stop this right now. Save yourself, do the right thing."

Damon's voice cracked. "I gave her everything!" He jerked her toward the edge, her toes skidding on icy gravel. "I built her a life! And she ruined it! She ruined *me!*" His face twisted, a storm of hate and grief colliding. "You think you know what any of this means?! You don't know me. You don't know what it takes to survive!"

"Then tell me," Hale said. "End it without more blood."

Damon's hand trembled, uncertainty flashing across his face—just a breath of hesitation, just enough for Hale to think he might finally let go.

Then it vanished.

Something in Damon snapped into place. His features went still, eerily composed, as if a decision had been made somewhere deep and irreversible. A dangerous calm settled in his eyes.

"I'm not going to prison, but I am going somewhere..." he said, his voice flat with finality.

"...And where I go, she goes!"

"Damon—don't!" Hale shouted, lunging forward.

Damon spun toward the edge, dragging Andi with him.

She screamed. The knife slashed, and the world seemed to hold its breath.

Hale's hand went to his weapon, but before he could fire, the ground gave way beneath Damon's boots. The icy gravel slid, and he lost his footing.

Andi's hand shot out, clutching at a branch jutting from the rock face. A flanker appeared from the side, fast—Damon never saw him. She cried out, blood spilling hot against her skin. The flanker lunged, catching the fabric of her shirt just as the ground crumbled beneath her. Her hand slipped—a scream tearing through the air—but between the branch and the flanker's grip, she was yanked upward, away from the drop.

Damon's eyes widened as he fell, the knife tumbling from his grip. He dropped out of sight in a blur of limbs and earth.

Then—a sickening *crack* echoed through the gorge as his body slammed onto a narrow outcropping far below. From above, it sounded final, like a man hitting the bottom of the world.

For a heartbeat, the silence that followed felt like death itself.

"Andi!" Hale shouted, sprinting forward. She lay on her stomach near the edge, blood slick on her neck, shaking, her fingers still clawing at the dirt and ice as the flanker fought to pull her safely away from the drop.

Hale flew to his knees beside them, grabbing her under the arms to help pull them both back from the edge. "Hang on—we've got you!" he shouted, his voice breaking.

One look at the wound and the breath punched out of him. His hands flew to his vest, ripping open pockets, searching for anything—gauze, a clean cloth, anything—to get pressure on the bleeding. His fingers shook as he tore a strip from his own undershirt, folding it tight and pressing it hard against the gash in her neck, praying it would be enough until medics made it up the ridge.

"Get med here now!" he shouted, voice tearing through the wind. "I need a med kit—anything to pack this!" His hands were slick with her blood pulsing through his fingers, as he pressed down hard on the wound, fighting to stem the flow.

The flanker beside him ripped a strip from his own shirt and shoved it into Hale's free hand. They worked in frantic tandem, packing the wound, trading pressure in desperate, messy attempts to slow the bleeding.

Another officer sprinted up with a med kit and a blanket, breathless. "I got it!" he shouted, dropping to his knees. He traded places with Hale, hands diving into the kit as Hale shifted back to wrap her in the blanket, steadying her trembling body while the officer applied new gauze and pressure—anything to slow the blood loss.

Hale forced himself to his feet and looked over the edge—Damon lay motionless far below, broken, blood spreading beneath him like a dark halo. He hadn't fallen to the bottom; he'd slammed through branches onto a shelf of rock halfway down the cliff.

They were going to need specialized rescue to retrieve him—technical rope teams, mountain-rescue climbers with harnesses and rigging, maybe even a hoist-capable helicopter. Damon's lifeless body was stuck on a ledge no foot patrol could reach.

Hale exhaled, his jaw tight. "Get a retrieval team down there fast," he barked, "if there is any chance he's alive down there... I want to pull that bastard out now! He needs to face every goddamn thing he's done. Move your asses!"

As the wind roared through the trees, Andi clung to Hale's sleeve, whispering through shivering lips, "I'm sorry." Her voice fractured under the weight of it—guilt, fear, years of blame she'd been forced to carry. Even now, bleeding out on the edge of a cliff, she thought this was her fault.

Her eyes fluttered, rolled back, and her body went limp.

"Andi—hey—Andi!" Hale's stomach plummeted. As the officer beside her pressed harder against the wound, Hale tapped her cheek with his blood-slicked fingers, trying to pull her back. "Oh shit—no, no, no... hey, hey—look at me," he pleaded, panic breaking through the professional edge of his voice. Her head lolled.

"Andi! Stay with me," he begged, louder now, voice cracking in the wind. "Dammit—stay with me, Andi. Stay with me!"

Below, the wind tore through the gorge like it was alive—howling up the cliff face, dragging with it the echo of something shifting, sliding, then breaking against stone far below. And then—nothing.

No movement. No breath. No sound but the rise and fall of the storm.

The team froze where they stood, every rifle lowered, every chest heaving. The cliff seemed to vibrate beneath their boots, as if the land itself understood what had just happened and was holding its own breath.

Hale's pulse hammered in his ears. He pressed a bloody hand to his radio. "We've got two down," he said, the words raw, torn from somewhere deep. "What's the ETA on support units? I need rescue and med on this ridge—now!"

Only static answered.

A loose piece of shale skittered over the cliff's edge, bouncing down into the gorge with a distant, hollow clatter that faded into nothing.

It sounded like an ending.

For one long, breathless moment, it felt as though Cryer's Edge had claimed them both—Damon and Andi—devouring her story, her suffering, her final cries, and sealing them in the silence for which it was named.

Twenty-Four

Shattered and Whole

The hiss of oxygen was the first thing Damon heard as consciousness clawed its way back to him. The sound rose and fell like a slow mechanical tide, each breath reminding him that the world was still turning without his permission. His eyelids felt glued shut, his body a slab of weight he couldn't escape. He tried to move—nothing. Not a finger, not a breath under his own control. Panic surged, then vanished into the terrifying absence of sensation.

A voice cut through the fog—clinical and impersonal. "Mr. Roth? Can you hear me?"

The name dragged through the haze of his mind, distant and foreign. Beeping monitors pierced the silence, steady and cruel. A faint metallic clink, the hiss of oxygen again, the sterile burn of antiseptic—each detail slid into focus like pieces of a nightmare.

When his eyes finally opened, reality struck with the precision of a knife: gray walls, a single barred window, a guard by the door. The man's presence was unmistakable—armed and impassive. Not a hospital. A cage.

Damon's throat burned as he forced out sound around the capped tracheostomy tube, each breath scraping through his lungs. "What... happened?" The words were thin and ragged—more ghost than voice.

"You've been in a coma for quite some time," the nurse replied without looking at him, adjusting a line that disappeared into his arm. "Cervical spinal fracture. You're paralyzed from the neck down. You're in custody." Her tone was factual, final—like reading the verdict of a life already over.

The words hit one by one, cold and heavy. Coma. Paralyzed. Custody. They hovered, refusing to sink in. He was Damon Roth—money, control, influence. He wasn't the kind of man who stayed down.

But his body lay still. His hands refused him. His power was gone. And somewhere behind the hum of machines, a memory surfaced—the flash of blood, her scream, the cliff, the fall.

He clenched his jaw, forcing the image away. None of it mattered now. She was gone. A faint twitch of satisfaction pulled at his mouth—at least that part of his plan had worked. The thought almost comforted him. She didn't deserve to live, not if he was trapped here in the dark with nothing left but the sound of his own breath.

Andi's world returned in fragile pieces—a heartbeat, a light through her eyelids, the soft murmur of someone adjusting a blanket. Consciousness felt like swimming up from the bottom of a dark lake, every motion heavy, every sound distant. When she opened her eyes, the ceiling above her glowed white and merciful, a blank slate after everything that had bled her dry. Her throat ached; her neck wrapped tightly in gauze. When she tried to speak, the sound came out broken, foreign to her own ears.

"Welcome back," an angelic voice said. "You're safe now, Andria." The nurse's tone was soft but steady, like a light cutting through a heavy fog. "You're healing beautifully."

Andi blinked, the words didn't register at first. Everything felt distant, muffled, as if she were still surfacing from darkness. Safe? She couldn't grasp the meaning yet—her mind was still struggling to understand that she was awake at all, that the world hadn't ended on that cliff.

Then, a single question quickly rose through the fog. Her breath caught as she tried to speak, a fragile, emotional sound slipping out: "Was I pregnant...?" she asked weakly, her brows furrowing as confusion and sorrow flickered across her face. The question pushed its way out of her, hesitant and shaped by the fear of what the answer might be.

The nurse's smile softened. "He's perfect. A healthy little guy, growing strong."

The words didn't just hit her; they collided with every belief she had built to survive. For a moment, Andi forgot how to breathe. Her whole body went still, suspended in shock so complete it felt as if the world had stopped moving.

Pregnant? Still pregnant? And her baby was healthy?

The impossibility of it slammed into her. She had been so sure—so absolutely certain—that if she had been carrying life, it was gone. Damon, the stress, the terror, the drugs, the injuries... none of it left room for anything else. She had prepared herself for grief, for the hollow ache of another loss she'd never even been allowed to embrace.

But this—this was something she had never imagined she'd be granted.

A sound escaped her that wasn't quite a sob or a gasp, but something raw, fractured, and disbelieving. Her eyes welled up quickly, blurring the room. Her breath shook as she stared at the nurse, as if hearing a miracle that couldn't possibly be true.

Then everything inside her cracked.

Tears spilled, hot and relentless. Her hands shook as she pressed her palm to her bandaged throat, then lower—to her stomach—like she needed proof that her body wasn't lying to her. A thousand emotions tore through her all at once: terror, awe, grief, disbelief, hope so bright it hurt, and a joy so intense she almost couldn't bear it.

My baby... my baby... The words pulsed through her mind, uneven and desperate.

A boy. Her son was alive.

Her eyes closed, and a breath escaped her, followed by a prayer so instinctive, so primal, that it rose from the deepest part of her:

Thank you, thank you Lord. Please, please let him be okay. Please keep him safe. God I can't lose him. Not after everything. I'll do anything—just please don't take him from me.

Gratitude wrapped around her shaking frame—soft, overwhelming, holy. She didn't understand why she was being given this chance, but she clung to it with every fragile, trembling piece of her.

She thought she had been broken beyond repair.

But her baby was *alive*.

And somewhere in the middle of that impossible truth, she felt the first flutter of something she hadn't dared reach for in years: a tiny, trembling spark of hope.

Days folded into one another. Machines beeped, doors opened and closed, and life moved around her while she lay still, relearning how to exist again. Meryl came every morning, her presence a tether between worlds. She brushed her mother's hair with slow, careful strokes, whispering pieces of the life waiting outside—how the snow was stacked so high against the house it looked as if it were swallowed, how school kept getting delayed because the plows couldn't keep up, and how she was mostly staying with her friend Ellery now, but that Alex and Walker were helping her with everything. She told her how she stopped by the house a few times that week to shovel the snow herself, wanting to keep the place from looking abandoned.

And when she talked—hesitantly at first—about how excited she was to be a big sister to a little brother, Andi felt her heart swell until it ached.

But when the room grew quiet again, when Meryl had gone and the nurses stopped coming in and out, the silence pressed in around her. Andi would stare out the window and watch the pale winter light crawl across the wall, trying to gather the courage to face the people who knew the truth—people who had tried to protect her, tried to help her see what was happening, tried to pull her out of the fire long before Damon's flames burned her as badly as they did. The thought sent a fresh wave of shame rolling through her, heavy and familiar. She wasn't ready to see the faces of those who had witnessed her unraveling.

So she refused every visitor but Meryl—family, friends, even Alex. Word drifted through the nurses' station that Alex had come more than once, waiting in the hallway with flowers, but Andi still said no. It wasn't rejection; it was survival. She couldn't bear the look of pity, heartbreak, or fierce love in anyone's face. She wasn't ready for Alex's eyes—the ones that had seen her at her worst, the ones that had fought for her when she couldn't fight for herself.

Healing wasn't a straight line. It was jagged, unpredictable, cruel. She needed quiet. She needed space to sit with the hollow ache and let it settle instead of drowning beneath it. Damon's voice still curled around the edges of her thoughts, oily and insidious.

Alex isn't your friend.

She used you.

She laughs about you behind your back.

She lies about you.

You're nothing without me.

It's your fault this happened.

Even knowing the truth now, the echoes clung stubbornly.

Slowly, Andi began to understand that recovery didn't mean standing up all at once. It meant crawling out of the wreckage inch by inch, teaching herself she deserved to exist, to be seen, to be loved. It meant unlearning every twisted thing he'd made her believe, piece by painful piece—reclaiming herself in the quiet before she could open the door to anyone else.

One afternoon, after visiting with her mother for over an hour, Meryl pulled a sealed envelope from her bag. She hesitated for a moment, then offered it to Andi with a quiet, steady look that said everything she didn't know how to put into words. "Mom... you really need to read this."

She laid the envelope gently in Andi's hands.

Andi stared at it for a long moment, her thumb brushing against her daughter's fingers before she nodded. "I will." she whispered, clearly lost in thought. "Soon. I promise."

Meryl gave a small, hopeful smile, then leaned down and kissed her mother's forehead before leaving the room.

Later that evening, when the halls had fallen quiet and the room felt still in a way that made it easier to breathe, Andi let herself look at the envelope again. Her fingers traced the edges, memorizing the loops of Alex's handwriting as if courage could be found in the ink.

When she finally felt ready, she opened it.

Alex's words spilled into the quiet:

"My dearest friend,

You survived what was meant to destroy you. You are not broken—you never were. You were surviving. None of this was your fault. I know you need time and space right now, and that's okay. Healing is not something you owe anyone—it's something you deserve. But please know, even in the quiet, you are not alone. You never will be. I'm always here, praying for your peace, believing in your strength, and loving you from a distance.

There's one more thing I think you need to hear. It's a beautiful song that made me think of you—of your strength, even on the days that feel impossible. If and when you're ready, I hope you'll listen. And when you do, know that those words are from me to you.

Always your true north...

Your friend, Alex"

By the time Andi reached the end, she could barely see the words anymore. She held the letter against her chest and closed her eyes, letting its weight sink in. Alex's words weren't just reassurance—they were release—like a knot she'd carried for years finally loosening.

Her eyes dropped back to the letter, and that's when she noticed it—a simple code printed at the bottom of the page. She hesitated only a moment before lifting her phone and scanning it.

Stronger Than Your Worst Day appeared on her screen.

The words alone tightened her throat. She pressed play before she could talk herself out of it.

The music wrapped around her, steady and sure, and the dam broke. It wasn't comfort exactly. Not distraction. It was strength—the kind that reaches in deep and pulls you back to yourself. Andi closed her eyes as the emotion surged through her—raw, overwhelming, impossible to hold back.

Tears streamed down her face—silent, unrestrained. As the words of the song settled beside Alex's letter, something steady took root in her chest. It wasn't loud or dramatic, just real. For the first time in a very long while, she felt herself stand a little taller inside.

Andi rose slowly and walked to the window, resting her hand against the glass as she looked out at the pale horizon just beginning to fade. She stood there for a moment, breathing. Nothing outside was different. The parking lot, the snow, the sky—it was all the same.

But this—it felt like the first time she was really seeing it, taking it in without fear, without hurry. It was as if she were finally allowed to look at the world through the eyes of a woman who was no longer trapped.

The tight, guarded feeling in her chest was gone.

She felt steady.

She felt whole.

She felt free.

And she smiled.

When Damon opened his eyes again, each blink was a cruel reminder that he was still trapped inside himself. Almost six months of this life—this half-existence—had taught him that hell didn't need fire; it only needed time. The world had become a tomb made of beeping monitors and dim light. Every tick of the clock scraped against his sanity. His body was useless, a coffin of flesh, but his mind burned with fury. The only thing that soothed the fire was the belief that Andi was dead—that she had gone over the edge for good, taking his sins with her.

So when the guard said, "You have a visitor," he almost laughed. Who would bother visiting a ghost? Maybe, just maybe, it was Meryl. Yes, she was *her* daughter, but Meryl was the only thing he had left now. She'd do.

But it wasn't Meryl.

It was *her*.

Andi. Alive. She walked in looking like everything he could never touch again—light, breath, freedom. Her hair shone, her skin glowed, and the way she held herself sent a shock through him so sharp it felt like waking up paralyzed all over again. There was a confidence in her stance that hadn't been learned—it had been forged. She carried herself like a woman who had been dragged through hell and was still standing in it now—staring evil in the face without flinching. Every insult, every bruise, every lie was still there, but she wore them like armor, proof that he had not broken her and never would.

He was silent.

"Hi, Damon," she said, her tone calm, steady, almost tender. The kind of voice that could cut deeper than any scream.

His mouth twisted around air. "You... how... you should be dead."

Her lips curved almost into a smile—not cruelly, just knowingly. "You said that a lot."

She studied him, taking in every detail, and let out a soft, almost sympathetic sound.

"Oh, Damon," she said gently. "You don't look so good. Poor baby."

She stepped closer, her heels clicking softly, every sound measured, deliberate. Her voice dropped into something almost soothing. "Don't worry, honey. They're going to take very good care of you. The best of everything." A pause, perfectly timed. "Just like you always insisted on for me."

She cocked her head slightly, a small grin tugging at her mouth, then drew in a slow, satisfied breath.

"Anyway," she continued, light and almost cheerful, "I know you were always so concerned about me, so I thought I'd stop by and make you feel better by filling you in on how things are going." She smiled faintly. "They're going really well."

She let the silence stretch.

His face tightened, color draining from it as a wave of nausea rolled through him. For a moment, he looked like he might vomit—like his body was trying to reject the truth settling in.

"You know, it's funny," she went on, almost conversational. "You used to tell me I was nothing without you." A quiet laugh slipped out. "Turns out... It seems I'm everything without you."

She tilted her head just enough to make him understand this wasn't revenge. It was closure.

"I'm the sole owner now," she said calmly. "The truck. Both cars. The boat. The RV. Three houses." She counted them on her fingers without hurry. "The cabin too. And there's land—quite a bit of it, actually. I didn't even know most of it existed until recently."

Her eyes flicked back to his. "Oh—and for a little icing on the cake... Roth's Open Road Outpost."

She gave a mock shiver, her nose wrinkling just slightly. "But honestly, most of it just smells like you. Oozes you."

A pleasant shrug. "So I'm selling it. All of it."

She smiled then—slow, serene, devastating. "It's amazing how easy breathing is when you finally stop carrying someone else."

Then, softer. Almost kind.

"Freedom suits me."

His breath rasped through the ventilator tube, fury tightening what little control he had left. He tried to speak, to spit poison, but nothing came out.

She leaned close enough for him to see her eyes—clear, fearless, and entirely beyond his reach. "Oh, and thank you for the gift."

He blinked, confusion cutting through the rage. "What?"

"My son," she said with quiet resolve, placing her hand on her growing belly. Inside, she knew—because of Simon's admission—it could be either man's child, but it didn't matter. To Damon, it had to be his. That was part of his punishment.

"He'll never even know your name," she said, her voice calm and sure, each word deliberate. Her voice didn't waver—it was steady, controlled, and absolute.

He wanted to roar, to curse her, to rip back the only victory he thought he had. But the sound never made it past his throat. It stayed buried inside him, caged and useless, while she stood there—calm, composed, watching him with a measured, knowing smile.

Just then, a nurse stepped in with a chart in hand and gave Andi a small nod. Andi glanced toward the nurse and returned it.

"Looks like that's my cue," Andi said lightly.

She looked back at Damon. "They mentioned it was time for your catheter change and bowel program." She paused, just a beat. "Manual disimpaction, I think they said?"

Her lips curved faintly. "Well... I'm sure by now it's nothing new for you."

She stepped back. "Have fun with that."

Andi turned toward the door, a deep, satisfying sense of finality surging through her. She glanced back once, her voice cutting cleanly through the sterile air. "Enjoy your eternity in hell, Damon," she said. "You earned every second of it." Then she walked out, never looking back.

The sunlight broke through the blinds, tracing her figure as she walked out. For the briefest second, he saw what real freedom looked like—and knew it would never belong to him again.

In the months since the cliff, investigators had stripped Damon's life down to the bone. At the bottom of that drop, recovery teams didn't just find wreckage—they found bodies.

Seventeen. Women who had slipped through the cracks of the world. Women no one came looking for. Women authorities now believed were lured, broken down, and driven over the edge by Damon and Simon's quiet, calculated cruelty.

And detectives were convinced the number wasn't final. More cases were already being reopened with Damon Roth at the center.

He would never walk again, but the law had no trouble standing over him.

Though paralyzed from the neck down, Damon had so far been charged with:

- Seventeen counts of first-degree murder
- Multiple counts of felony assault, kidnapping, and torture
- Attempted murder of Andria Roth
- Conspiracy to commit murder
- Felony harassment, terroristic threats, and indecent verbal misconduct
- Aggravated domestic assault
- Drugging and poisoning with intent to cause bodily harm
- Fraud and insurance exploitation
- Obstruction of justice
- Concealment and intentional disposal of human remains

His paralysis didn't shield him. It only ensured he'd spend the rest of his life as a high-security medical inmate, locked into a prison hospital bed under constant guard.

No freedom. No unsupervised visitors. No room for sympathy.

For the first time in his life, Damon Roth was contained.

Twenty-Five

Clear Reflection

Spring arrived like a breath of grace, loosening winter's grip and softening the world around it. It felt like the first real inhale after months of holding her breath.

Alex stood in the backyard as laughter echoed through the cool evening air. Walker manned the grill, while Sheldon, Jason, and Theo stood nearby with drinks in hand, deeply engaged in a heated debate over the new generation Corvettes—whether the C8's mid-engine design was genius or if the C7 still had the better heart and soul. Melena and Rebecca were doubled over in laughter near the patio table, while Rebecca's three kids darted around the yard with Harper, their laughter mixing with the twins' clumsy toddling as they tried to keep up.

Charcoal smoke curled through the lilacs blooming near the fence—a scent Alex had always loved. It smelled like comfort, like calm, like a life gently stitching itself back together.

It had been months since the cliff and the wreckage Damon left behind—months since the lies he'd built his life on came crashing down. The truth about Alex spread through the dealership like a shockwave—but a healing one. After the cliff, once Rebecca knew Andi was going to be okay, she finally had permission to speak. She didn't have to carry Damon's secret anymore or pretend she didn't know the truth.

When she told the others, the guilt hit fast and hard. Deep down, none of them had ever fully believed Alex was who Damon painted her to be—they'd just been too afraid to push back.

Frank, Jason, Eddy, and even a few part-timers reached out within days, calling and texting with shaky voices and sincere apologies, each message carrying the weight of the trust they wished they'd given her sooner.

They told her they understood now. They knew she hadn't betrayed them—Damon had. They knew what she, Walker, Sheldon, and Melena had done to save Andi and exactly who the real threat had been.

Since then, those friendships had been finding their way back, steady and honest.

Now, tonight, with the dealership under new ownership—a process sped along by a few local professionals who helped Andi untangle the legal knots—she was able to decide its fate herself. With the sale finalized, the employees buzzed with relief and excitement, already talking about the new owners and their plans to fix the place up and breathe life back into it.

Then Alex's phone buzzed. A message from Frank:

Running a little late. Picking someone up.

She showed Walker. "Probably Meryl. She said she wanted to come tonight."

Walker grinned, spatula still in hand, his eyes brighter than his easy smile. "Hope so. It'll be nice to have her here."

The sun slipped lower, painting the yard gold. The fire crackled, conversations softened, and Alex relaxed deeper into her chair, feeling warmth seep into her shoulders. Her back was turned toward the narrow walkway from the front yard.

Frank always used that path. The thought made her smile. She hadn't seen him since everything came out.

She heard footsteps on gravel. Slow. Familiar.

Alex turned—and her chest tightened.

Frank stood there first.

Tiny. Her Tiny. In his faded flannel, sunglasses perched in their usual spot on his head, his eyes already glassy with emotion.

Beside him stood Meryl—beautiful and composed, her long dark blonde hair loose, her eyes bright. And next to them, soft and steady as always, stood Frank's wife Cora. Cora gave a quick wave, then a warm, teary smile.

Alex didn't move at first; she just grinned and let out a quiet breath of relief at the sight of him.

Then "Tiny!" she breathed, rushing to him.

He caught her in a hug so tight it lifted her a few inches off the ground. His breath shook against her shoulder.

"I'm so damn sorry," he mumbled, voice breaking. "It's good to see you."

"It's good to see you too," Alex said, holding him just as tightly. "It's over. You're here."

Cora stepped in next, hugging Alex and then Walker with a tender, almost apologetic warmth before giving Harper a kiss on the head. Meryl wrapped her arms around Alex, and Alex held her for an extra second—they hadn't seen each other in a bit, but they'd stayed connected through every scare, every update, every tear.

"I'm really glad you came," Alex told her softly.

"Me too," Meryl said. "I've missed you guys."

Frank clapped Walker on the back, and the group naturally shifted toward the fire pit, everyone welcoming them with genuine comfort.

Alex turned to head back to her chair—and froze.

Soft footsteps approached from behind her. Quieter. Hesitant. Almost cautious.

A hand brushed her shoulder.

Then a voice—fragile, familiar, hopeful.

"Alex."

She stilled.

Her breath caught in her chest.

Slowly, she turned.

And there she was.

Andi.

Standing in the glow of the string lights, wrapped in a simple sweater, her hair tucked behind one ear.

She looked different—softer, carrying the weight of everything she'd been through—but her eyes... Her eyes were clear. Clearer than Alex had ever seen them. She looked radiant.

"Hey," Andi whispered.

Alex broke.

A sob tore out of her, sharp and unguarded. Her knees went weak, her body folding in on itself as she covered her mouth, overcome by the sight of her friend standing there. For a heartbeat, she couldn't move—couldn't do anything but cry in stunned, silent relief.

Andi stepped forward quickly, reaching out and steadying her, guiding Alex into her arms. The moment their bodies met, Alex clung to her with a fierce, shaking grip, the kind of embrace that carried months of fear, hope, and every prayer Alex had whispered in the dark.

Andi clung back just as tightly, her face buried in Alex's hair. She whispered something—maybe an apology, maybe gratitude, maybe just Alex's name—but it didn't matter.

Everything they needed to say was in the way they held on.

Around them, the backyard fell still.

Rebecca swiped at her cheeks, overwhelmed. Melena pressed her hand to her mouth, eyes shining, the usual fire in her softened into something achingly tender. Sheldon stared into the fire, blinking hard as he fought the emotion swelling in his chest. Walker exhaled with relief, the tough exterior slipping as he looked away, trying—and failing—to hide how deeply it hit him. Meryl covered her smile with both hands, tears spilling over with the kind of joy that came from witnessing something she'd almost given up hope for. Frank stepped in beside her without a word, resting a steady arm around her shoulders, sharing the moment as she cried.

Every person there felt it—the weight, the relief, the beauty of a moment that shouldn't have been possible but somehow was. They all knew. They'd all planned it. They'd been waiting for Alex to be blindsided by joy.

And she was.

When they finally eased apart, Alex cupped Andi's face. "I can't believe you're here."

Andi smiled—a small, soft smile that held the strength of survival. "Took me long enough, huh?"

The moment lingered, warm and fragile, before slowly loosening its hold.

They sat by the fire, their chairs pulled close until their knees touched. The night wrapped around them—warm, gentle, forgiving. Andi talked quietly, sharing small pieces of her recovery. At one point, she rested a hand on her small belly, the fire reflecting in her eyes.

"You were right," she said, her voice steady with newfound strength. "I can't change what happened...but I get to choose what happens next."

Alex reached for her hand, their fingers finding each other effortlessly.

She let out a soft, emotional laugh. "Damn right you do," she said, squeezing Andi's hand. "This is your life now. Your choices. And I'm so excited for you."

This night had been a long time coming, a long exhale shared by all of them. The backyard was wrapped in a serene calm. The fire popped. Laughter drifted through the air. Stars spread across the sky like scattered diamonds.

And for the first time in a long time, the joy rising from the group felt whole. It wasn't forced or fragile—just real, the kind that settles into people and softens the edges of everything that hurt.

Andi leaned into Alex's shoulder, her eyes drifting closed, as if this small patch of warmth and family was the first place she'd felt safe in years.

Around them, conversation continued to hum, gentle and steady. Someone tossed another log on the fire. Harper shrieked with delighted laughter somewhere in the dark as she and the other kids chased Muttonhead around the yard. Walker leaned back in his chair, gaze lifted toward the stars.

Life, in its simplest form, moved on.

Alex looked at the faces around her—her people—and felt something she hadn't felt in a long time. Not just relief. Not just gratitude.

Peace.

Beside her, Andi exhaled, a soft, shaky breath. "Feels different," she murmured.

"It is," Alex said. "It finally is."

The fire crackled, warm and steady. They didn't need to say anything more.

Two women sat shoulder-to-shoulder in a backyard filled with the people who loved them—one who had fought her way back from the unthinkable, and one who had refused to let her face it alone.

The past would always be part of them, but it no longer defined the room, or the night, or the next morning waiting for them.

They were here. They were safe.

And they were moving forward.

From the Author

Thank you for stepping into this story.

If it stayed with you—
if it stirred something,
I would be deeply grateful if you'd consider leaving a review.
Reviews help stories like this travel farther—
reaching those who may need them most,
and allowing more to be written.

This story—and the music that walks alongside it—
exist for a reason.
They were written for the quiet battles people carry,
the truths that don't always have a place to land,
and the moments when someone needs to hear:
You're not alone.

If you feel moved to share this book or its music,
thank you for helping carry it forward.

With gratitude,
Nova Justice

Support & Resources

If you, or someone you love, needs help, please consider reaching out to the resources below. It may feel terrifying to take that first step, but there are people—truly good people—who will listen without judgment and guide you toward safety.

Immediate Support (United States)

- **National Domestic Violence Hotline**
  Call: 1-800-799-SAFE (7233) | **Text:** "START" to 88788 **Web:** thehotline.org

- **RAINN (National Sexual Assault Hotline)**
  Call: 1-800-656-HOPE (4673) | **Web:** rainn.org

- **NOVA (National Organization for Victim Assistance)** *A champion for victim rights and advocacy.* **Call:** 1-800-TRY-NOVA (879-6682) **Web:** trynova.org

- **VictimConnect Resource Center** (Confidential referrals for all crime victims) **Call or Text:** 1-855-4-VICTIM (1-855-484-2846) | **Web:** victimconnect.org

- **Crisis Text Line** Text: "HOME" to 741741

Support for Male Survivors

Abuse can happen to anyone, regardless of gender. These organizations offer specialized support for men:

- **1in6 (**Focuses on help for men who have had unwanted or abusive sexual experiences.) **Web:** 1in6.org (Includes 24/7 anonymous online chat)

- **MaleSurvivor (**Provides resources, therapist directories, and support for male survivors of sexual abuse.) **Web:** malesurvivor.org

Additional Specialized Support

- **Childhelp National Child Abuse Hotline Call/Text:** 1-800-4-A-CHILD (1-800-422-4453)

- **National Human Trafficking Hotline Call:** 1-888-373-7888 | **Text:** "HELP" to 233733

- **Hot Peach Pages (International Support)** A global directory for crisis centers in nearly every country. **Web:** hotpeachpages.net

Finding Local Support

Most communities have dedicated organizations ready to help. If you aren't sure where to start, search your local area for:

- **Shelters & Safety:** Domestic violence shelters, safe houses, or women's/family shelters.
- **Health & Advocacy:** Community crisis centers, counseling centers, or local health clinics.
- **Legal & Protection:** Victim assistance units within local law enforcement or nonprofit legal advocacy groups.

Digital Safety Warning

If you are using a shared computer or a device that may be monitored, please be aware that your browsing history can be tracked. If possible, use a safe device at a library or a friend's house, use "Incognito/Private" mode, and clear your search history after visiting these websites.

Thank you for reading this story and walking with
these characters. If your own journey reflects
any part of theirs, I hope you carry this truth with you:
You are worthy of love, safety, freedom,
and a life filled with peace.
You are stronger than you know.

Made in the USA
Coppell, TX
22 February 2026

71992878R00167